The Empty
Lot

Other books by Mary Gray Hughes:
The Calling
The Thousand Springs

The Empty Lot

a novel by

Mary Gray Hughes

~~~

another chicago press
another chicago press
another chicago press
another chicago press
another chicago press
another chicago press
another chicago press
another chicago press
another chicago press
another chicago press
another chicago press

Another Chicago Press
1992

Published by Another Chicago Press, Box
11223, Chicago IL 60611

Cover image © 1992 "Insight" by Joanna
Pinsky, represented by Perimeter Gallery,
Chicago. Used by permission

Library of Congress Cataloging in
Publication data:
Hughes, Mary Gray.
    The empty lot / Mary Gray Hughes.
        p.   cm.
    ISBN 0-929968-32-8 : $22.50. —
    ISBN 0-929968-29-8 (pbk.) : $10.95
    I. Title.
PS3558.U375E48   1992
813'.54—dc20
92-21458

                              CIP

ISBN: 0-929968-32-8 (cloth)
        0-929968-29-8 (paper)

Another Chicago Press books are
distributed exclusively by The Talman
Company, 131 Spring St., Suite 201E-N,
New York , NY 10012, 1-800-537-8894

John
always —

I

It began to seem to Haskell that every time he came to the house something else was being taken away. This time it was an outsized cardboard carton and his grandson, Larry, was bent over the box trying to shove it out the front door onto the porch.

The house was large. Huge. Painted dark blue-gray. A broad, white-columned porch, rising two full stories high, ran the entire width of the front, down one long side and halfway around the back. The house had been built by its first owner as a private hospital for general medical services and delivering babies. It was set seven steps above the ground to allow all the ventilation and accumulated coolness possible from breezes circulating underneath the wooden structure. The front stairs were steep and extra wide. Near the extreme left side someone had placed a plank against the steps, like a ramp, and braced it at the bottom.

From the foot of the stairs Haskell could see Larry's head and back as he struggled, and by the time Haskell climbed to the porch he could see that the cardboard carton had caught in the doorway. The box was heavy, jammed with old magazines packed until they bulged out against the soft sides.

"What are you doing with those?" Haskell asked. His voice was deep and gravelly. "In any case," he rumbled, "that box won't last."

"It's held so far," the boy said. "Pull the door wide."

"The door's not the trouble," Haskell said. But he opened the screen wider. "What are you going to do with them?"

"I'm going to sell them," Larry said. His voice was at the other end of the scale from his grandfather's. It was light and reedy with uneven shadings. His voice had sounded scratchy all summer, as if getting ready to change but so far had not broken.

"And if I can't sell them," the boy said, "I'll trade them for something I can, like I did with those old lawn chairs."

He stooped and leaned into the box so he could push with more force. One expanded side had lodged against a hinge of the inner door and would not give. Still hunched over, Larry scooted to that side, looking like a grasshopper, all thin legs and pointed knees, and tried again to edge the box around the hinge.

"Jeez, the thing's stuck," he said. For a minute he quit trying to move the carton and raised his head to look up into his grandfather's face. "If I can't do that," he told him, "if I can't sell or trade them, then I'll still have had a valuable learning experience."

"Where did you learn that imbecilic twaddle?" Haskell said.

Larry remained crouching beside the box with his head tipped back so he could study his grandfather. The boy watched him eagerly, but with a carefully restrained, blank face.

"That's an asinine thing to say," Haskell said. "Thinking like that ruined the schools. Did you learn that from one of your teachers?"

"Mom says it. She says it all the time," Larry said. He was beginning, irrepressibly, to grin. "She says it to her students, especially the failing ones. I've heard her. Lots of times."

Haskell jerked his head, snorting, as he might at a fly or a mosquito, then stopped himself. He had given enough of an indication that he had been caught out by the boy.

"What you ought to do," he said, "is eat more. You're too thin."

It was so. The boy was too thin for twelve. He was too thin for any age, and the thumbprints of lack of sleep were pressed deep beneath his eyes.

"You should eat more meat," Haskell added. "And potatoes. And go to bed early so you don't look like something the cat dragged in."

No man wanted something like this for a grandson. A man was supposed to love his grandchildren. He was supposed to feel closer to them than to his own children. A man was supposed to help his grandchildren in a time of trouble, like this divorce. Haskell felt that strongly. But what he could not understand was why he did not like his grandson this summer. Why the boy did not keep his face clean. It was streaked with dirt. From the attic, probably. Or that filthy storage space beneath the house where he was always scrounging for whatever he could find to carry away and sell.

"Here," Haskell said, reining in his rough-edged voice, "I'll help you."

He bent over and because his legs were short did not need to stretch far to reach the bottom of the box. His strong stomach, like another, more-rounded, carton, squeezed a grunt out of him as he and Larry lifted the box of magazines free of the hinge and slid it out onto the porch.

"That's heavy," Haskell said. "You must have put every magazine that ever came into the house in it." He pulled out his handkerchief to wipe his hands. They were smudged. So were Larry's, and a streak of dirt ran up one of Larry's arms where he had embraced the carton to free it.

The boy shoved the box across the porch until it was right in front of the plank. Then he stood erect and began unwinding a rope coiled around his waist in a way he no doubt learned from his climber father. He must have laid that plank over the steps, intending to maneuver the carton down with the rope.

His head was bent to the task of unwinding the rope; the back of his neck, flexing in small movements to follow the circling of his hands, was as thin as the rest of him. And the hollow depression in the back of his neck was sunk deep between the rigid tendons on each side.

"Aren't those your grandmother's magazines?" Haskell asked him. "Her gardening ones?" He poked them with his foot.

"She said I could have them," Larry said. "You don't have to believe me. You can phone her."

Haskell said nothing.

Larry squatted and wound the rope firmly around the box twice lengthwise and twice around the middle. With the excess rope he made a loop which he attached to the rope on each side of the box so he could guide the carton's descent. It was a skillful, deft piece of roping. When he finished, Larry glanced up at Haskell.

Haskell nodded to him. He did not say it would undoubtedly have been faster to unpack the box, carry the magazines down in separate batches and then follow with the box.

Larry inched the box cautiously toward the edge of the porch. Haskell came to help and together they eased the packed carton forward. Gradually the center of balance, a little back of the first half of the box, was pushed out beyond the porch's edge and inevitably the carton, controlled by Larry's loop of rope, slowly tipped over onto the plank. They coaxed and pushed the box again until all of it rested on the plank.

Haskell straightened and grunted. He was an agile man. He exercised regularly but his comfortable stomach made bending over difficult. He stayed upright to watch.

Because the carton was large and heavy with magazines, Larry had to crouch at each step and press himself fully against the box to budge it. Yet he needed to control the direction it moved lest it slide too far to either side. With each step he had more trouble. The box seemed determined to head away from him. By the time he was near the bottom the box had edged so far off center the plank began to tilt slightly, its near edge raised up off the steps like an eyelid opening. Larry jumped to the ground, reversed the loop and using it as a halter pulled the box down intact to the sidewalk. Done. He jerked the loop free with one expert flick.

"Neat, hey?" he said.

"True," Haskell said. "How are you going to move it now? I'm not going to drive you."

"I wasn't asking you to," Larry said. "I'll do it with the lawn cart. I asked Mother for the cart. She said I could use it."

"Does your mother know how heavy this box is?"

"I can push it. She won't have to help me."

"I mean does she know all that junk might break the cart? That's the only cart here for Ramón's lawn work."

"I use that cart all the time. I never broke it."

"You better see you don't," Haskell said.

The boy stared back at him.

"Come here," Haskell said.

Reluctantly Larry climbed the steep steps to the porch.

"Over here," Haskell said, his voice commanding. He took out his handkerchief, licked it and catching the boy by the back of his neck—

those separate tense ridges, those two taut wire tendons beneath his palm—cleaned the smudge of dust from the boy's cheek.

"There. You'll make a better salesman with a clean face," Haskell told him. "Only don't try to sell that cart. The cart belongs here."

Larry pulled away.

"Where's Ana?" Haskell asked him. "Isn't she supposed to be helping today? Aren't both of you?"

Larry vaulted the seven steps to the ground and ended squatting awkwardly, gnome-like, beside the cardboard carton. "I thought Ana was looking after Nessie for your mother," Haskell persisted. "Why isn't she?"

"I don't know. Ask Mom. She's inside." Larry hesitated and then added, "She isn't crying today."

"Certainly she's not crying," Haskell said. "Why would she be crying?"

"She jammed her thumb in your old stapler last night," Larry said. And again satisfaction poured from his eyes despite his effort to keep his face a pure mask. He rocked back and forth with excitement while he squatted near the box, there at the base of the porch, far too far away to be reached by his grandfather.

"She was loading new staples," he continued. "She couldn't get 'em in." Then, in a friendly way, a peace offering, he added, "That's Grammer's family name, Staples, isn't it?"

"I'm impressed you remember so much family history."

The boy laughed. He was suddenly carefree and younger. And he did not look so thin. He got up and turned to move away, presumably for the lawn cart.

"Don't forget to take that plank off the stairs," Haskell called after him. "You don't want an accident."

The boy waved his hand without turning. They always did that, Haskell thought. Walked off without answering you. Modern manners. And children never said good-bye anymore, either. More modern manners. Except for Nessie. Nessie adored saying good-bye. "'Bye 'bye, now. 'Bye 'bye, 'bye 'bye." Repeatedly. It was a game for her. Her newest game. He should get her another beginning words book. It was astonishing how fast she learned them. He could get a new one in town.

Haskell entered the house. The study was all the way in the back. It was a walk Haskell had made innumerable times in the years when he and Millie reigned here. Then the hall would have been immaculately tidy. It was not now actually in disarray. Not completely chaotic. But a shoe stood in the hall, upright, startling, facing in the direction of the front of the house and without its mate. A young person's shoe. Not Nessie's. Ana's? On the delicate hall table newspapers had scattered loose from a pile and drifted across the surface. Several had toppled on the chair and one to the floor next to a pair of yellow plastic roller skates. Near it a small sweater—in the summer?—definitely Nessie's, lay crumpled beside a young child's book. An uncapped felt pen leaned against the sweater.

"Life," Haskell had named the visibly lived-in condition of the house to Millie. "The friendly clutter of life. Three young Bosk grand-children free to play anywhere they choose in our old home. Exactly what the place needed."

That is what he said before there had been any talk of a divorce. Before his daughter and her husband chose to live apart.

Haskell picked up the raw pen. He did not see a cap. He set the pen on the table, clearing a space so it could not stain anything close to it.

He walked down the hall, which seemed narrower than it was be-cause the walls zoomed up to the twelve-foot-high ceiling. The study door was shut to protect the coolness. Haskell tapped but there was no response. He knocked, louder, and called Cora. Still nothing.

She was in there. He could hear the uneven sound of the air condi-tioner. She was pretending to be absorbed. Pretending to be working with such concentration she could say she did not hear his knock or voice. *His* voice.

Haskell turned the knob and opened the door. At first he did not see her. Then he realized she was behind and partly underneath his large desk, evidently searching for something.

"Can't find it," she said, her voice coming from under the desk. "Some poor student's essay and these kids never keep copies. I'll have to pass her if I've lost it. Damn. I've never lost a paper before."

All at once she rose, holding a paper in her hand. The window was in back of her because she preferred the desk turned facing into the room, and the light from the window lit up her hair. Neither Haskell nor his wife had ever had hair that color, nor did Cora's children, and Haskell was surprised, startled, as he often was on seeing her, by how pleasing the color was. By how attractive she looked.

"Found it," Cora said. She shook the pages. "I've already graded it, too. She did pass." She glanced at Haskell and noticed his strawberry-tinted cheeks. "You look hot," she said. "You look like you've been playing tennis."

"It is hot," Haskell said.

"I can't get used to seeing you free in the middle of the week. Doesn't it seem odd to take a vacation and stay here in the summer? You could carry your work with you and go somewhere else. To the beach."

"Your mother's too busy with her plants," Haskell said.

Cora smiled. She did not believe him. Her mother's gardening had never stopped them from traveling in the summer. Nor did she agree with Alan's theory that Haskell had taken time from his office to finish his article.

"You don't have to spend more time around us because Alan and I are separated," she said to Haskell. "It's nice of you, but we can handle what we're doing, including the children. Divorce is dirt common now."

"That is true," Haskell said. "And doesn't make it any better."

"I know you feel that way. I'm sorry. But it's our lives. We'll be fine, really. Tell me, what's it like coming to town and not having to show up in court or at your office?"

"I miss the secretaries. They laugh at my jokes."

Cora smiled. "Well, you haven't lost your sense of humor. Sit down. In fact, sit at your old desk. It's cooler here and you look like you need to be cooled off."

"I'm comfortable where I am," Haskell said.

Cora sat in her chair. The desk was cluttered with books and papers and folders containing other papers and near the front but to one side of her, clusters of boxes with paper clips and others with rubber bands crowded against mugs holding pencils.

"I want to transfer the title of the house back to your mother and me," Haskell said to her.

"You mentioned that the other day," Cora said. She slid the rescued essay in with the stack of other papers. "Why are you so convinced Alan and I can't deal with this divorce?"

Haskell did not say, deal with it like you do with this house? like you did with your marriage? He said, his deep voice emphatic, stressing each word, "I'm a lawyer. I've seen what happens. You and Alan have no idea what's ahead."

"We'll be fine," Cora said.

"You keep repeating that like a parrot," Haskell said. "Listen to what I'm saying. People pay me for this advice."

"I am listening."

Haskell moved past the desk and one of the bookcases built-in from the floor all the way to the high ceiling. He stopped at a window facing the enormous side yard and the many different gardens Millie had established there.

"What I'm willing to do," Haskell said, "is pay you and Alan cash for everything you put in toward the down payment. Plus enough to cover a reasonable increase in the value of the house. More important, I will invest that money for you, or hold it in escrow, with the understanding that the title could be acquired by you later if either of you wishes. I would take over the mortgage and maintenance costs. Freed of those, you and Alan should have no cash-flow problems. You would be better off in the present and would possess little visible property. If you and Alan are determined on a divorce, I guarantee you that you do not want divorce lawyers to know you own anything worth fighting over. You are innocents about what will happen."

He saw her annoyance increasing. "Don't be irritated, Cora," he said. "Hear me out. Almost all societies have some form of divorce, but we've turned it into a business for the benefit of the legal profession. We force divorcing couples who own any property to go through an adversarial process. Lawyers sniff out every hint of money and insist it be divided, down to the last family teaspoons. That way they work longer on the case and can charge higher fees. For lawyers the profit is in the squabbling over the assets and the children."

"Alan and I are not going to fight over the children. You don't understand us, Haskell. We aren't ignorant. We know about divorces and lawyers. We have friends who've divorced. We know what we're doing."

Haskell remained by the window, but turned towards her. His hands were clasped behind his back and his body tipped forward in her direction. Had the cast of his face not been so stern, so ready and determined to lecture, he would have seemed close to bowing to her.

"Are you unwilling to listen to anything I say because I'm your father or is this bull-headedness some part of the woman's movement?"

"You talk as if I don't know a thing. I'm not some uninformed twelve year old. I'm not Larry's age."

"You ought to pay some attention to Larry."

"Larry's fine. He's busy the whole day."

"Doing what? He's dismantling this place and selling it. Left alone, he'll bargain the entire house piece by piece. That's what keeps him busy all day, and you don't even notice it."

"I take good care of my children. No one can say I don't. This is not the nineteenth century, Haskell. Kids don't go around with chaperons. Kids wander around town with a friend or in groups. Or else alone. That's normal."

"No normal kid acts like Larry in any century. He looks like a freak. He's so thin anyone would think he's on drugs."

Cora jerked the telephone flat across the desk, scattering papers, and dialed.

"May I speak to Professor Belknap?" she said. "Alan? My father is here. He's convinced I'm not listening to him because I won't automatically agree with everything he says. That's what he means by not listening. He wants us to put the house in their name and he swears if we don't the lawyers will eat us alive. I know. He doesn't believe it. Yes. Yes, he is, right beside me."

She paused for something Alan said at length and then replied, "No, he's not joking. He's got a detailed plan. I know. I know that."

After a moment her face altered. She smiled. "Will you?" she said. "All right," and she handed the receiver to Haskell.

The very way Haskell reached for the phone, the way he moved around the desk and stood, his large head bent toward the side where he held the receiver, the tone he used to say, formally, "Yes," in his deep, rough-edged voice, solemn, important, were all characteristic of him. Every phone call he answered had significance. He fell completely silent with the receiver at his ear.

"Were you cut off?" Cora asked him.

Haskell made a face and shook his head to shush her. He covered the mouthpiece with his wide palm and whispered to her, but quickly, still listening at the receiver, "Alan's reading from his article in a journal," and went back, impatiently, to listening. As if she should have known. As if it should have been clear that her husband would want to read him something from an article of his.

Cora watched him. Alan was smarter than her father. Which was not totally true, not all the truth, but she could see it was true, in part, by the way her father listened. He did not listen to her, or to most people, that way—with his face looking much older, hard, showing its lines and the grooves of age without any cover, empty of all emotion as his mind strained to follow. When Haskell listened to her, there was always a coating on his face. At minimum, the desire to be polite or pleasant to her. Or else the blur and ugliness of annoyance. Studying him while he concentrated on Alan's words, Cora found an old phrase repeating in her head—"like calling to like." She thought that she was seeing the mind alone showing in her father's face, the mind coming out of the cocoon of feelings, sloughing off emotion so it could reach out for what it might grasp, for what was held out to it or above it, so it strived, strained, for this difficult new mental hardware.

She might engage him this way if she talked to him about some aspects of her own subject, she thought. Maybe she could tell him what sociologists had written about some aspects of bureaucracy. She had heard Haskell on the Manchu bureaucracy, on the Vatican. Heard him comment, with interest, on what must have been similarities between the Incan, Mayan and Egyptian civilizations since all were systems given over to prolonged and massive building projects.

"When did you say you published that?" Haskell asked. There was a quick reply and Haskell said, "And DuBost is the French linguist, correct? He called you from France? Nice, Alan, very nice to have him call. A call clear across the ocean."

("Call, Cora. Call and find out right now. There's no time difference. They'll answer you."

"It hasn't been long enough since I sent the manuscript. Six weeks is all. But if I could say they were publishing it, I feel sure I could get a job. What if I can't get a decent appointment down there? There's no question the offer you got couldn't be better, Alan. And it's true I'm not on tenure track here, not yet. I would be if I published more. But I don't know what position I can get if UT Austin doesn't come through with something. It's not like this area. There aren't universities or colleges every ten blocks. Houston would be better, but Houston is an impossible commute. The children are too little. If I could say I definitely had a second article coming out in a good journal, that might make all the difference. They might be willing to hire me."

"So call. Editors are only people. I know lots of them. Your paper is first-rate, Cora. You should have more confidence. You would have had this one and a half-dozen other papers in print if your supervisor weren't so lazy. Look how fast you wrote it when I showed you how. Call and tell them they're lucky to have a chance at it. Tell them you have to know. They'll think you've had a nibble from another journal. I've done that. It works. You mustn't let them push you around, Cora. Tell them you've got a degree from a top university. You've had two teaching awards. And you're married to a Ripkin Fellow, and the most prolific one in a decade. Don't let anyone make you wait. You want to know? Call them. They'll tell you. Call.")

Haskell was nodding in agreement with what he heard. The telephone receiver swung up and down with the grave movements of his head.

"Send me a copy," Haskell said, the words deep, significant. He cleared his throat, an underground rumble. "About the house, Alan, Cora felt I should discuss my offer with you. Cora is confident, as always," and he bent his head in her direction, his eyes flicking to her, acknowledging her, then away. "I realize neither of you is willing to consider that your divorce could possibly entail problems. But I am alarmed, dismayed, because the two of you may find yourselves at the mercy of the worst sharks in the legal profession. Are you aware this is a community property state? No matter what you've heard, that means any house or real estate a divorcing couple owns excites a divorce lawyer's appetite. Assessing and dividing up assets are the ways lawyers pay for their homes. Or, if they're lucky enough to catch a pair of innocents, pay for their second homes and their boats out on Lake Travis. Neither you nor Cora needs that. Nor do the children, if you want them to come out of this with anything. My plan would protect your holdings by putting them in my name until this is settled. If I take over the house expenses, that should solve the main cash-flow problems you have."

Haskell was obliged to listen in return. This time the effort required for him to understand was not demanding and a jungle of emotions flowed across his face. He glanced again at Cora and began to speak into the phone.

"You and Cora both say you don't regard yourselves as adversaries," he said. "If that's true, why divorce? But if you do divorce, the law will turn you into adversaries. You will find you cannot have one lawyer as you suggest. They will insist you each have one. Once you're both enmeshed with your own lawyers, you have adversarial law. You and Cora may feel yourselves to be at the bottom end of the middle class financially. In fact, I rarely meet a client who does not consider himself in the center or the bottom of the middle class. Believe me, once two divorce firms look at you and discover your big home, with its extra lot, the fancy apartment you just rented in Austin, your two professional incomes, your two retirement funds and your two insurance policies...yes, that's what I said. Retirement funds and insurance policies. You hadn't considered those, right? I thought not. Add to that the expected earnings of each of you over the next twenty-five or thirty years and the total makes you and Cora a pair of very fat pigeons. Ready for plucking."

Haskell fell silent. His expression became contained, uncommunicative. With the years Haskell had taken on weight. His face had grown heavier, the jowls almost pendulous and his prominent cheeks flushed. He had a short mouth but a full one, well-formed lips and an unexpectedly sweet smile. The smile broke out suddenly, lightening his face.

"You're right," he said, traces of his short smile lingering. "I am someone with day-to-day experience and I think no one can learn what I know any other way. But I do know what I am talking about. I have seen it happen over and over again."

Another pause and again he listened. A briefer pause and a more exasperating one. His eyes went repeatedly to Cora, caught her eye and moved away.

"Then I have nothing else to add," Haskell announced into the receiver. "Clearly, what I'm saying has no meaning to you, at least not yet. I hope for both your sakes that continues to be so, though I doubt it. It won't happen the way you think, Alan. As for all your assurances, what you keep telling me is that you and Cora are doing what you think best. But that's what everyone always says, isn't it? No one sets out to have a disaster."

II

"We must be unique—divorcing without anger."

"Don't be so smug."

"Not smug. Accurate," Alan said.

Cora laughed. "You are in high spirits. Still, we have been doing well. We've even managed, so far, not to feel like failures."

"Too much divorce everywhere for that."

"Maybe it's because we get on better."

"We have to. We have all these worldly goods we must come together to divide."

They had been more involved with one another. There was so much they had to do—to make arrangements, to sort and separate—all of which they needed to do together. And, there were the children.

Naturally, they were concerned about the children, but they pointed out to one another that nothing devastating would happen to the children if the two of them used good sense. It was true that Ana, at fourteen, was extremely young to be going out with an older boy. Young man, really. But they could deal with that. It was what you would expect of Ana, they agreed, being so flamboyantly romantic. Yet they both liked Norris. He was kind to Larry. And if Larry was unquestionably too absorbed in selling and trading odds and ends all day and would not do his share around the house, Alan maintained this was only a phase for him. At least Larry was keeping himself busy. You might even call him an entrepreneur. And he was not hanging out with kids they did not know. Anyway, Alan intended to take the boy climbing, but that would have to be later on, after Alan's project at the Institute was finished and his University classes over for the term.

As for Nessie, Nessie was never a problem. Considering how much everyone adored her and how pretty she was, with those soft waves of fine beige hair and her little pointed chin, it was amazing she was so unspoiled. They had done well with Nessie. They could congratulate themselves on her. Basically, they could congratulate themselves on all three children. They had only to make sure the children understood the divorce had nothing to do with them and would not in any crucial way affect them.

They admitted, Cora and Alan did, there were bound to be difficulties. Some they could not anticipate. This was understandable and did not mean there would be anything they could not handle. Not with their intelligence.

Take the question of the house. When they had decided to divorce, they had not considered the house would be an issue. They had thought, without actually saying so to one another, that Cora's father would help them with the mortgage payments. He understood their position. He knew Alan had to rent an apartment for himself near the University and in January, when he moved, Cora had told Haskell exactly how high the rent was. And what he had to pay extra for garage space. It had been Haskell Bosk, after all, who urged them to buy his rambling old house in Riles because he knew they could not afford anything that spacious in the city. And because a small town was a better place to raise children. Haskell had arranged for them to take over the home from him, persuaded a local bank to give them a mortgage with a low interest rate and, in the end, had himself provided much of the down payment.

"To tell the truth," Cora said, "some of these worldly goods of ours we barely own."

"But we own the title to the house. And when land values skyrocket, that's all that matters."

"Land values skyrocket!" she repeated. "You must've been listening to rumors about speculators."

They were standing between the massive desk, which had been her father's, and the filing cabinet set beside the bookcase. Cora had thought Alan was driving out from the city to separate their old files and before he arrived she had begun removing the ones he might need and putting them on the desk. She was tall, as tall, almost, as he, and with no difficulty had started with the folders high on the bookshelves and worked down to those in the top drawers of the large filing cabinet when Alan arrived. Now she put one stack of folders sideways on top of another to clear enough space so she could sit on the corner of the desk.

"There's always talk of land speculators in Riles," she said. "Even when I was a kid. It comes in cycles."

"Not just talk this time," Alan said. "That's why I came out to see you. We've been approached by someone supposedly representing a real estate agency. They want an option to buy this place but they won't say why." Carefully, causing almost no sound, Alan slid the file drawer shut. "You and I don't need an intermediary negotiating for us. The way for us to make a real profit is hang on to the title ourselves and wait to see what happens. We don't have to sell at the first hint of an offer."

"I don't want to wait," Cora said. Her manner had changed. She had become serious, her eyes alarmed. She brushed back and away from her face part of her mass of hair. Her hair was an extraordinary color, a mixture of shining, silken-looking warm browns and the deepest russet red, the colors of an old highly polished cedar chest. "I can't manage this place by myself," she persisted. "What's more, I don't want to. It's too big. I can't do what I plan to do if I stay here. The idea was to sell this house so we could *both* have apartments."

"We didn't think the house might be worth a fortune," Alan answered. He walked around the desk to the big window air conditioner and faced it, then turned around so the cold air blew against his back. Even this early in the summer the heat was sweltering and the ancient unit cooled best only what was directly before it. "We can't sell now," he said. He pulled the sides of his shirt free from his skin and flapped them against his body. "We can't sell until we find out what the house might be worth if we wait."

"Who talked to you about this?" Cora asked.

"B.K. Quint. Your old high school pal."

"Bunky? Bunky's with the bank."

"That's how I know the offer is genuine. And must be developers or there wouldn't be all this secrecy. No one buys a single house through a bank. It's too expensive."

"Did you tell Bunky you and I are divorcing?"

"No."

"Why not? We've told others."

"I kept thinking about what your father said. I'm not going to be an 'innocent' and lose a fortune because of it."

"Haskell was talking about the costs of getting a divorce, not selling the house. He said the lawyers will end up with everything we have. That's why he asked us to put the house back in his name. Now that I've had time to think about it, I believe he was trying to help us."

"I wonder what Haskell found out about land values?" Alan asked. His eyes, a light mingled hazel, like clear butterscotch with specks of gold, were alive, were shining at her from behind his contact lenses. "We're lucky we didn't agree to his suggestion. We'll have to watch what we do from now on. We mustn't let word get out that this house might be tied up in a divorce. Or even that there's going to be a divorce. That could scare off a buyer, or make him lower the price because he thinks we're desperate. I'm not going to be tricked, Cora. You and I aren't absent-minded professors."

"Maybe not, but I don't like becoming secretive professors. Suddenly we start being crafty and won't tell anyone about our divorce. That's not like us."

"We're not yelling our plans to the whole world, that's all. We have every right to keep quiet. It's our business. Didn't you wonder why Haskell suddenly wanted the title? You didn't think there might be some other reason?"

"I believe what he told me. He's trying to help us."

Alan ran a forefinger lightly back and forth across his lips. "You would think that. He's your father. I don't share all your convictions about him. I think he's a little less than perfectly selfless, or virtuous. Like I think there's something comic in the way he can't finish that super article he's trying to write."

"He'll finish his article this summer."

"If he does it will only be because he gave himself part of the summer away from his office to do it. I bet he's sorry he started. I should offer to supervise it for him."

"Come on, Alan."

"OK, OK. I'll be good. But your father never spoke to me, or you, about the house before. Not a word. And suppose his motives are as pure as you say, why should we transfer the title back to him? You and I aren't going to get caught in any court battle. We're too smart for that."

He moved from the window and crossed behind the heavy swivel chair toward the other side of the desk, closer to her.

"All right, suppose we do keep the title," Cora said. "Then we can sell whenever we decide. So why pretend we're not divorcing?"

"Developers aren't dummies. They investigate the whole area they're interested in. They don't start buying until they're sure they can get clear titles to everything they want. If they can't, they develop somewhere else, or in another town."

Cora stood up from the corner of the desk so he was not looking down on her. "They'll go to some other town anyway," she said. "They'll go to Layton. Or north of Austin. Nothing ever happens in Riles."

"How do you know? Don't say that just because you grew up here. Do you actually know anything about this development?"

"I would have heard at Dawson if this was really happening in Riles. They'd know in the Dawson development office."

Alan shrugged. "Be serious, Cora. It's too early for that. Which is why we weren't asked about the house openly. And now's the time for us to act extra carefully. I tell you, if we don't, we'll lose a fortune. Simply by being naive. Being criminally naive."

"Being naive seems to bother you more than losing money."

"I care about money, like everyone. I'm not one of those 'innocents' your father makes fun of. And I'm not going to miss this chance because someone thinks I've got my head stuck in an ivory tower. I am not going to be outwitted. By anyone."

"What a swell macho statement. More ego in whether you'll look street smart than whether you're doing the right thing. That's typically male."

"Women aren't so clearheaded. They confuse pity and sympathy with love," Alan countered. "The warm cozy feelings overwhelm them. They can't tell which is which."

"Men confuse fear with respect. They terrify their children, their employees, their students and each other and say it's respect. If the terror gets directed towards them, they call it admiration."

The tense planes of Alan's face broke into laughter.

"True enough," he said. "Touché."

"There's something in what you said, too."

"We're not a bad team."

"When we're not living together," Cora said. And almost idly, not seeming to be compelled, she asked, "So tell me, how much money is this 'fortune' you keep talking about? What are we dealing with, in round figures?"

She might have asked something shockingly intimate, so charged was the air between them. Yet Alan did not step back. He was a beautifully proportioned man, trim, with fine regular features. He was so close to her she could sense the pause in his breathing while she waited for his answer. Sense the texture of his skin as the time stretched out between them, see the mole on the side of his neck, dangerously near where he shaved every morning.

"Three quarters of a million," he said. His eyes were brilliant, gleaming. "Or more. It could be almost a million."

Cora sat down slowly in one of the two straight chairs. Once down, she remained still, immobile, as if that single slow act of sitting had been so complex she could not make the first effort, could not take the necessary deep breath, to make another move.

Alan explained that the value was in the land, not the house. The old house would be torn down. What was valuable was the large plot of two wide lots, one empty, both running from the street behind them all the way through to the street in front. And the location. Once Austin started to develop again, and with the slow but definite growth of high-tech around the city and University, Austin was bound to grow, the surrounding towns would grow, too. Zoning laws would be changed. Bound to. And Riles was a choice area. Everyone realized that. The developers were planning a new center for Riles. And a shopping mall. Kincaid might be involved. Kincaid, as she probably knew, specialized in urban reconstruction and building malls. Kincaid was one of the best financed companies in the business. It had survived all the downturns. No one developed more successfully than Kincaid. She must have heard of it.

"Three quarters of a million," Cora said.

"Or more," Alan said.

"There's never been talk of that kind of money," Cora said.

"You see why we have to be careful. We have to think out everything. Calculate every move."

"Haskell's going to be right," Cora said. She gazed up at Alan, studying him, as if she were trying to fit his words, like misplaced pieces of a puzzle, into the clean features of his face. "We will end up fighting over the house," she said. "Maybe Haskell has plans like you think. It would be hard to say he doesn't have a right, especially if there's going to be a huge profit. And suppose Kincaid tries to develop here and can't get the zoning laws changed? I've seen plans fail before. Suppose you and I do all this conniving and put off our divorce so we can hang on to this museum and it turns out to be worth no more than it is now? How are we going to look? We laugh about Haskell polishing the wood panelling he put in himself, when he thinks we aren't watching, or being pleased we moved here and filled the house with his grandchildren, but those are good human motives. We don't have good motives."

"So we'll have normal greedy ones, like most people. And we'll take intelligent care of our money."

Cora got up and moved to the opposite side of the desk. Alan watched her. He watched her while she put one pile of folders crosswise on another, tidying them to be put back in the file. She was disturbed and she would not look at him. But Alan knew her. He knew how to argue with her.

Casually, he said, "You wouldn't object if we were talking about someone's gift to Dawson College. You'd be as hard-headed as anyone. That's why you've done so well there. You'd say exactly what I did—hang on to the property to see if there is going to be a jump in value. If there isn't, fine. We'll lose nothing compared to what we might gain. That's what you should do—act like we're Dawson College."

Cora was also used to arguing with him. She said she had to go get

Ana. Ana was at her ballet class. If no one met her, she would call Norris for a ride. Ana was still spending far too much time with Norris. At least they had been smart to put her in the summer program at the high school. Otherwise she'd be with Norris all day long.

Alan could do nothing but follow her as Cora collected her handbag and went to the rear of the house. He followed her outside and down the porch steps and toward the garage where they kept the car she used. Their old car which was big enough for all of them.

"Doesn't her Don Juan work?" Alan asked, as they walked through the deep backyard. "How can he hang around with her whenever she asks him?"

"You know Norris has a job. Which doesn't help. Anyone his age should be in college instead of having all that money to spend on her. And he takes her everywhere in his car. You should have heard my mother when I told her why we were worried."

"Millie would say it's nature's way to have men chasing avidly after members of the opposite sex. Keeps the species going."

"Worse. She says there's a natural attraction to much younger girls because they breed better."

"I bet she didn't say that to you when you were fourteen."

"You know she didn't. And she wouldn't say that to Ana."

"She may be right about the physical side. Millie's usually up on her biology, almost as much as her botany."

"Except we're not plants. She's so...." Cora paused.

"Detached?"

"Yes. No. Not detached. She's interested enough. She's passionately interested, but as if we're kernels on an ear of corn. Like what that geneticist worked with. The woman."

"Barbara McClintock."

"Right. Like she's studying people, collecting data for charts on them. Do you realize Millie's never been involved in a single good works cause? Not even in Riles and no matter how prominent Haskell's been. A waste of resources, she says. If people must hunt out ways to keep themselves busy, they should do something really useful. They should concentrate on bringing up a better new generation. She makes it sound like it's producing improved crops. Sometimes my mother appalls me."

"I love your mother," Alan said. "I can hear her arguing for a new crop of better humans, probably while weeding culls from her flower pots. And never wasting a word. She's terrific. In one sentence she can expand plant techniques into a universal Darwinian scheme. She gives me a sense of close kinship to our amphibian stages. I feel gills and taste ocean salt in my mouth." He smacked his lips, as if he did.

"Good thing for us she does feel strong ties to her grandchildren. I took Larry there today. She's trying to get him interested in working in her gardens. Or shipping plants, or keeping records. Anything."

"You took Larry out there this morning? Did she say anything about the title?"

Cora shook her head. "She wouldn't. She'd leave all that to Haskell. She never cared for the house anyway, not the way he did. She's been planning for years to build in the country. She's yearned for those greenhouses. And a little modern house to look after. No woman would want to be stuck with this place."

"Depends on why you're stuck with it," Alan said.

"Don't explain it to me all over again," Cora said. "I have to get Ana." Yet before she got into the car, before she opened the door, she said, "That kind of money, the amount you mentioned," not stating the actual figures, speaking in a slower, almost dreamy way, one hand on the handle of the car door, "that's a huge amount of money. You and I have never been near that kind of money. Not for ourselves."

"It's not just the money. I don't want to be…"

"I know. I know. You told me before," Cora said.

She climbed into the car and Alan lifted the heavy garage door for her and the sunlight sliced instantly through the grayness of the garage. Cora backed the car out toward the street but stopped when Alan leaned forward to speak to her.

"Did I tell you my latest article is causing a furor? I'm being asked for reprints before it's out. DuBost asked me for one."

"I think this is the fourth time you told me," Cora said. Alan laughed as if she had pointed out some new example of a well-known, silly, yet endearing trait of his. Cora found herself smiling with him.

They had left the coolness of the study minutes ago and were both beginning to show the effects of the heat outdoors. Alan stood beyond the shade of the garage and his straight brown hair was glazed by the sunlight. His face glowed in it. The first beginnings of perspiration glistened on his forehead and across his upper lip. His eyes had narrowed, turned into tiny gleaming slits, the way Nessie's did, because of squinting against the light and because of smiling. Cora felt a jab of admiration, a kind of envy, for his satisfaction with even the foolish things he did. Things someone else—she—would cringe to have revealed. He was so unquestionably pleased with himself.

"You put up with a lot," he told her, fondly.

"I used to," she said.

~~~

Late that night, in his new apartment, Alan wrote a letter to his brother:

Dear Mike,

Here's the check towards my part of Dad's bills this month. Why can't the medics bring his blood pressure down? Tell them to make sure he's on a totally salt-free diet. There's no point stuffing him with pills without cutting salt.

I'll get the rest of the month's money to you in two weeks. We've had unexpected bills for Ana's teeth. And Cora's car, our old one, had to be towed. Vapor-lock trouble again. Also, Cora insists Ana go to a special enrichment program given at the high school since she—Cora—can't be home much. She'll be working long hours at the college. Some of these goofy little private colleges make absurd demands on their faculty.

The high school program is going to be just what Ana needs. We both think she should be with kids her own age more and get on top of some basic school work. She's doing French and two math classes. Gives her something serious to think about. Once she's been in it longer, she'll love it.

Is Dad more alert? Last time I spoke to him he was confused. I hate hearing him that way. He must loathe it. He's been such a tough old bird all his life.

I'm trying to keep myself in good shape. I can't fit in much climbing but I play a lot of tennis. I used to play with my father-in-law. Or former father-in-law. Or soon to be former father-in-law. Our language is poor in words surrounding divorce but we are rich in divorces. We linguists call this language lag.

I miss playing tennis with him. His conversation's swell and he's quite a player for a man in his sixties, with his sturdy pot belly. On second thought, and out of proper respect, I'll call it a profound belly. His profound pot belly. He was good for doubles. Turned an intriguing mix of colors whenever he lost. This will interest you—he is worried the divorce lawyers will gouge Cora and me. He declares they fatten on the likes of us. He's more suspicious than you about your mutual profession. He's wrong about one thing—I won't have trouble. I'm not as naive about the 'real' world as he thinks.

By the way, Cora and I are holding off a while on the divorce. No change in plans, just a matter of what is best for all of us. We'll go on being separated but we've decided not to rush. Better for the kids this way.

Did you get the Xerox of my last article? It's short, but a first-rate paper. There's a sure way to tell—I'm getting requests for reprints before it's been published! I got one from René DuBost. Not bad, hey, to be asked for a copy of your paper by the top French linguist? Everyone in the profession is going to have to read this article.

Give the old man an extra tight hug for me.

Love,

Alan

PS. I liked your last lawyer story. Here's a new Texas tale for you. The parents of one of my students came by. Classic west Texans, from somewhere beyond Midland. They had come back from a long round-trip drive to Vermont for a nephew's wedding. With her blue-bonnet eyes wide with surprise, the mother tells me, "We drove all the way up there and back and, do you know, up there you can drive through more than one state in a single day?"

Have you been reading about the furor over protolanguages? Some of the Russian linguists like the idea and claim they can concoct languages back to our primal grunts. The heat of this controversy reminds me of the turmoil in the late '60s and early '70s over whether apes had language capacity. One faction decided to prove they did, despite their lack of the physiological equipment necessary for speech. They planned to show how well apes could communicate after being taught ASL—American Sign Language. If the primates did communicate, that was supposed to upend the claims of Chomsky *et al.* that language was species specific. The guys who advocated this idea got absolute fortunes in research grants. Fortunes. There was a sad little limerick during those days posted on our department bulletin board, and also mailed to the deans:

The Linguistics TA's Lament

There now is an ape named Nim Chimpsky
Who signs ASL for big grantskies.
Since Washoe can too,
While we TA's get few,
We'd best brachiate off our asskies.

We've got at least one TA with us now who'd probably pull off a stunt like that—Wendell Meyers. He's the irrepressible NYC wit I recruited and one of our top students. If only we can stop him making jokes at the wrong times. So far nothing deters him. Ah, the bliss of carefree youth.

A

Double-spaced and in capitals so it would be easier to read, Alan wrote the second of his two letters a week to his father:

DEAR DAD,

DON'T WORRY ABOUT MONEY. MONEY IS NOT IMPORTANT.

DON'T WORRY ABOUT MY DIVORCE. WE WON'T GET IT FOR A WHILE ANYWAY. WE DECIDED TO WAIT SO WE CAN MAKE THE BEST PLANS FOR THE KIDS. THE KIDS ARE TERRIFIC. VANESSA, OUR OWN LITTLE LOCH NESS MONSTER, IS A JOY. SHE'LL STAY WITH ME FOR THE COMING WEEKEND. LARRY IS MOSTLY WORKING FOR HIMSELF THIS SUMMER. AND ANA IS IN A TERRIFIC SUMMER SCHOOL PRO-GRAM. SHE'S LUCKY TO GET IN IT.

I STAY HERE IN AUSTIN, DAD, BECAUSE I HAVE SMART STUDENTS WHO MAKE EXCELLENT TEACH-ING ASSISTANTS. AND I HAVE SUPERB COLLEAGUES AND THE BEST ARRANGEMENTS FOR MY CAREER. REMEMBER THE INSTITUTE WAS SET UP IN PART FOR ME AND BY ME. I CAN WORK WELL HERE. I HAVE A SHORT ARTICLE COMING OUT I WILL SEND YOU. AND I AM WORKING HARD ON A VERY IMPORTANT

LONG PAPER. THAT'S WHY I CAN'T FLY OUT THERE
AT THE END OF TERM. I WILL GIVE MY PAPER IN
PARIS. I AM GOING TO BE ONE OF THE MAJOR SPEAK-
ERS AT A BIG INTERNATIONAL CONFERENCE THERE.
NOT BAD FOR 43!

PLEASE DO WHAT THE DOCTORS SAY. THEY
AREN'T UNEDUCATED AND UNTRAINED YOUNG IDI-
OTS EVEN THOUGH THEY MAY LOOK THAT WAY TO
YOU. THEY ARE SMART DOCTORS AND THEY ARE
ON YOUR SIDE. SO AM I. ALWAYS.

LOVE,

ALAN

III

Friday was going to be a busy day. Haskell had to meet a visiting lawyer for an early lunch in town and later in the afternoon drive in again with Millie so she could supervise the children for the evening. Cora would be at a planning meeting for Dawson and then afterwards at a dinner and reception. Usually the children managed by themselves for brief periods, but Cora felt they had been left alone too often lately and her erratic household helper was down again with summer flu, so she had asked Millie to come. Millie wanted to make sure the gardens were getting enough water in the summer heat anyway, she said, and while she was there she could easily fix the older children a decent meal. Nessie was no problem. Alan had again taken Nessie with him for the weekend.

Haskell had arranged to meet Alonzo Aikens at the restaurant in Riles where lawyers liked to meet, near the courthouse. The menu was limited, but the rib-eye steak was good, there was a lavish salad bar, and the drinks were generous.

"Everyone tells me you're missed, Haskell," Alonzo Aikens said. Aikens would have talked to everyone. It was what he did. Frequently, it was what he was used for. He was a man of nearly Haskell's age, heavy-boned and long-faced, with eyebrows bushy as worn black shoe polish applicators and under them deep-set, anxious eyes. He had not done well in the law. He could not win his bigger cases.

"Don't stay away on this vacation of yours too long," he added. "Even if you've got associates holding the fort for you, think how much time it'll take to get back into the cases."

"I'll remember all I need," Haskell said.

His companion laughed. "Modest fellow. That's your ole' Virginny heritage. Always confident you'll beat the local talent."

"I've lost some cases," Haskell said. He was drinking iced coffee and not a cocktail or any kind of alcohol. Aikens had scotch. "Thanks for these, Alonzo," Haskell said. He patted two aging red volumes Aikens had set down on the table.

"Nothing to it. I had to come back anyway, as you well know. All I get in this court is continuances. Are those the right volumes?"

"Oh yes," Haskell said. And he went on, his deep voice satisfied, and congratulatory. "I knew you could convince even the stuffy Historical Society to let you take them."

Aikens nodded, gratified. "You're keen on local history, aren't you? Because of that old Virginia background?"

"Riles interests me," Haskell said. "It's older than you'd believe. Remnants of Indian camps run all through these hills. My grandson and I found three unbroken arrowheads in a stream once, when he was a little boy. And that was in a spot only five miles north of the old Spanish mission. Ever had a chance to get out to the mission's foundations? Or those early ranch houses along the river? You should. Anyway, the old town buildings are easy enough to see. They're right in the heart of the place."

"Yeah, with modern glitz crowding in around them. Twinkie shops and micro-chips. The whole area is going to look like Los Angeles. Get in more of this high-tech and it'll be Silicon Valley east."

"That is true," Haskell said, "maybe."

"Unless it all goes flat bust again," Aikens said. "Still, I've heard talk condos are coming to Riles and Austin may grow out this direction."

"There's always talk," Haskell said.

"With all you know about land deals and land titles," Aikens said, "you'd be a natural to do some speculating in real estate. A natural. And make yourself a pile of money." His busy hopeful eyes searched Haskell's face.

Haskell gave his sweet quick smile.

The waitress brought their lunches and Haskell began cutting into his steak.

"OK," Aikens said, "fair enough. Your business plans are your business plans. I have respect for confidentiality and all that, as one of

our presidents called it. But I know deals are being made. I can feel it."
When again Haskell kept his silence, Aikens said, "OK. I'm not pressing. But I do want a favor in return for the books, Haskell. Two
favors. One for each volume."

Haskell nodded.

"This case I've got here is never-ending. Is there a way I can get
Judge Hoffrey to stop granting those damn continuances? You know
him. Have I missed something obvious? Is there a fix in on the case?
I'm sick of hopping over every three or four months. Not to mention
my client."

"I'll see what I can find out," Haskell said.

"Thanks. I mean it, Haskell, thanks. I seriously don't want to blow
it. I damn near have to win this one. The second favor is a snap. I need
exercise like hell. Work off steam and so on. Do you still play tennis?"

"Delighted to," Haskell said in a rumble of pleasure.

"How about a game around four?"

Haskell frowned. "I'm committed to something for my wife," he
said.

With some other lawyer, with many men he knew, Aikens would
have come back with bantering about wives. Not with Haskell. Never
with Haskell. Nor did Aikens ever make casual and possibly pin-prick-
ing comments about Mrs. Bosk to anyone. In his view, she was not the
sort of person for that. Not one of those high-toned social ladies, the
fashion-plates. Snobs. He would not be comfortable saying anything
about her that might be misunderstood.

So Aikens simply said, "Maybe tomorrow then?"

Haskell shook his head. "I might be able to manage today, if I can
arrange for someone else to do these things for Mrs. Bosk. You still
play doubles?"

"Not as much as you and I once did. When I travel I play singles
more. Too hard to get the right combination of players free for doubles. How about you?"

"I used to play doubles with some men from the firm and my son-
in-law."

"Lucky for you. I can't stand the sight of my son-in-law. I wouldn't
mind beating the son-of-a-bitch, but naturally he doesn't play. If he

did, he'd cheat. He'd figure out a way to cheat the Pope at bingo. You like your son-in-law?"

"He's very intelligent," Haskell said.

"Bell...something, isn't it?"

"Belknap. Alan Belknap. He's a professor at the University."

"Sure, sure. I remember the story in the paper when he came here. About three years ago, wasn't it? A fancy appointment between an institute and the University. There was a big picture of him. And your daughter was with him."

Haskell partially folded his napkin and placed it by his plate.

"She teach at the University, too?" Aikens asked.

There was no change in Haskell's face yet Aikens knew she did not. The news excited him but he was careful. He remembered the talk, over many years, of Cora's success at a college in the east, of her two fellowships, of her Ph.D. She was bound to have tried to teach at the University. He would not ask. He offered Haskell sugar instead, though he knew Haskell did not take sugar, and he gestured broadly for the waitress to give him the check. Haskell was an old friend, one of his oldest friends. Haskell had stood by him. He did not want to, and he would not, not for the world, hurt Haskell. He would not, for the world, want to lose this contact.

"She teaches at Dawson College," Haskell said.

"That's great," Aikens said. "Here in Riles, too, near her kids. No wonder. She would do that. That's swell, Haskell. Swell." But continuing to be anxious, gauging Haskell warily, he went on, "Tell me, Haskell, what does your son-in-law teach at this special institute?"

"Linguistics."

"No kidding. Linguistics." Aikens waved to their waitress to fill their cups again. "Linguistics. That's all kinds of languages, hey?"

"Partly," Haskell said. "Part of it is discovering the laws which underlie all languages. Sort of a science of the way we talk to one another."

"No kidding. If my son-in-law taught, he'd teach the science of four-flushing. The laws underlying double-crossing. He isn't even good at it. He gets caught. Know what I mean? Every damn time. He doesn't even make any money at it. But Louella won't leave him. Got one kid by the bastard now and another on the way." His eyes peered worriedly out at Haskell.

"Hmmm," Haskell said. His voice stretched the sympathetic murmur out in a low rumbling, like an airplane engine being tested before it took off.

Both men fell quiet. Aikens tore open another packet of sugar for his coffee and said, "Back to the subject of tennis, will it be easier if we go for singles?"

"You bet, always," Haskell said. "I'll see what I can do. Call me around two."

~ ~ ~

Millie arrived at the old house in the late afternoon. Ramón drove her and she climbed down from his battered pickup truck and began to inspect the gardens. They were imaginatively designed but by now only moderately cared for. Ramón worked on them once or twice a week before going out to their new place in the country. Millie looked after them every time she came to town. This Friday she began by snipping off the overblown flowers. She cut the occasional better blossoms and carefully put them in a jug of water to keep fresh. Then she wove the canvas hoses through the beds and set herself to clearing out and weeding in the vegetables. She worked late for she had planned a quick meal for the children's supper.

But the children did not come.

Ana ate with Norris. She had tried to call, she told her grandmother, when she finally did get home a quarter past seven. She had tried to call from the high school but there were too many kids ganged up to use the phone and she didn't want to stand there all the rest of the day and probably half the night, too. And Norris was waiting for her outside in his car. She couldn't keep him waiting. Anyway, she had come home before her mother usually did, hadn't she? She didn't know where Larry was. They weren't supposed to be together. Larry had been told to stay around the house to help Grammer. She had heard him being told that. In fact, he was probably on his way home right now and just forgot how late it was. How could anyone tell what time it was in the summer?

"Here," Millie said. She handed Ana a basket filled with red and green tomatoes and green peppers from the vegetable garden. She herself carried two jugs filled with cut flowers, including roses. She led the way up the steep flight of stairs, across the wide columned porch, which she called "the gallery," and into the house. She was favoring one foot. Ana followed with the basket.

In the hall Millie set the jugs down, took the newspapers from the chair and put them in a neat pile on the antique hall table. She sat on the chair and took off one shoe, shook out a small globe of dirt, and popped it in Ana's lined basket. She put her shoe back on.

When she rose Ana still waited for her. The girl was pretty. She had creamy skin, luminous and fresh with the soft look, the seeming texture, of rose petals. Her face was going to be prettier as she grew older but was tremulous at this stage, emerging, and overlaid with hints of sulkiness. Physically much like her mother, she was already tall.

Millie mopped her forehead and chin with a tissue and patted the base of her roll of salt and pepper gray hair. Ana waited impatiently, with a sigh but a carefully inaudible one, still standing by the table and holding the basket and almost willing, finally, to be obedient. Ana was not unafraid of her grandmother.

Millie took the jugs and carrying them both headed for the kitchen. Ana followed her. In the kitchen Millie began searching through the cabinets for the right vases for the flowers, and for bowls and a platter for the vegetables. While she did, Ana picked up a sponge and made quick furtive swipes at the counters and the table. But she was pushed aside repeatedly, from one place to another, by her grandmother—from in front of a cabinet, from in front of the doors beneath the sink—so Millie could keep on looking, all the while not saying a word about what she was doing since, to her, that was obvious and Millie never felt the need to explain. She simply did what had to be done.

"They're beautiful flowers, Grammer," Ana said. "You know, Norris loves flowers like anything. He comes over a lot just to look at the gardens. I bet he'd think your gardens in the country are awesome. He could drive out, you know. Norris has a new car."

Millie had taken two half-empty bowls out of the refrigerator and was gazing at them. Ana suspected she and Millie were not going to be in that kitchen another five minutes before they would get caught up in cleaning the place, defrosting the refrigerator, scrubbing out the oven. She felt resentment mounting at being trapped. She would be the only one who had to help because she had been the one who had come home more or less when she was expected. She perfectly well could have stayed out longer. Yet she was not angry enough, or brave enough facing her grandmother, to walk off openly to her own room. Nor could she bring herself to say she had to study. That would work. Not that there was anything yet from the summer classes to study. They'd only started. But her grandmother had this thing about books and learning. Her grandmother would have believed her.

"I could go look for Larry," Ana said. "I'm sure he's OK, but if you're worried, I could do that for you. I could call Norris and he and I could drive around looking for him." Millie motioned for her to put water in the flowers.

"Larry stays out this late lots of times now. It's summer'n all. You don't need to worry about him. But we could go see where he is." She shut off the water. She had filled the vase and turned to hand it to Millie. "Oh," and she stopped, "oh, I like that a lot. That looks fabulous, Grammer."

Millie had been setting red and green tomatoes and several peppers and a lemon from the refrigerator on a large brass platter.

Ana began to help, handing her tomatoes. "We used to do this in art class," Ana said. "Here, let's use a Spanish onion, too. The red purple color and the skin look different. I know, Grammer, there are dried flowers on the back porch. The ones from last year. I'll get them."

When she came back Ana said, "Don't you like these? I love these. They're so delicate. I told you, I saw pictures of dried flowers like these in a book about Japanese flower arranging. It's all in the direction you have them move. Seem to move, I mean. The way you're doing it. That's beautiful, Grammer."

She looked directly at Millie, at the round sturdy face, the glinting rimless glasses before eyes so pale a blue you had to stare at them to be sure of their color.

"Are you going to keep shipping plants, Grammer? Mother says your vines sell great. Daddy told us you were 'creeping' ahead. He's funny that way, isn't he? You could sell flower or vegetable arrangements, too. You do them as good as in the books at school."

She moved closer to her grandmother, putting the dried stems one by one into Millie's thickened, root-like hands. "Grammer, I'm sorry I didn't phone," she said. "If I could drive, I'd take you home whenever you want. Did Haskell bring you?"

"Ramón did," Millie said.

"In that old truck?"

Millie's head nodded and she went on arranging roses in a smaller vase.

Ana wanted to say that it did not look right for her grandmother to drive around town in an old pickup truck which had wood slats attached to raise its sides and paint knocked off the body and one headlight so battered clearing brush it gaped like the bared eye of a huge insect. She had asked Millie once, hinting, irked, all set to protest, why Millie came into town that way. To get there, Millie said, stopping her cold, so Ana had not dared ask why she didn't come in the car Haskell bought for her to be driven in. She was sure Millie would only give her a thin-mouthed look and say why take the time to get the car out of the garage when the truck was there, handy, and Ramón used to driving it. As far as Ana could tell, except when Haskell drove her, Millie got no use at all from the second car.

"How come you never learned to drive?" Ana asked.

The question made Millie pause. She had been breaking a dried stem and her strong fingers held it suspended, snapped in two.

"I used to wonder why, but I had too many reasons. They couldn't all be right. I decided I don't know why." She discarded the lower part of the stem and eased the dried flower in among the roses.

"You don't, Grammer?" Ana said. "Not at all? Sometimes I don't know why I don't do things, either. Even important things I'm supposed to do. Here, could we put these on a different platter? We could make another arrangement? And leave them all in the kitchen. No one goes in the dining room anymore. Not for anything. All my friends come in the kitchen."

"Do your girlfriends say a date with any boy is better than no date at all?"

"We don't say it out loud," Ana said, "but it's true. Only lots of times it's not like that. Nanette 'goes out' with Ellery McCloud. You might 'go out' with someone, but mostly a gang of kids go somewhere together. That's not exactly a date."

"Is it hard for the ones who don't 'go out'? Something you keep secret it's so awful?"

"Really," Ana said. But she did not explain further. She was uneasy about where the conversation might lead. Millie might begin to talk about Norris, who was not approved. Or how it was better if girls her age did not go out at all with one boy, especially on dates. And absolutely not if he was older. Grammer, Ana knew, had not had dates when she was young. Only a few with a second cousin. Grammer had never been pretty. The pictures showed that. Ana and Larry, when they were little, had speculated on how it could happen that Haskell had married Grammer, what with Haskell being so important, which is what everyone said, and his fancy clothes and vest and gold watch chain. And in the same photograph his marble-like, solemn good looks and polished, obviously golden, hair. Carried away against almost insuperable odds, lifted by passion right up over the roof, Haskell had told Ana, here in this house, when she and Larry were small. Felled like the tallest of the trees, totally smitten the very first time he had taken her driving and right there lost his heart and never never never got it back. Sounding silly, Haskell had been. Sounding like their father did when he was clowning with them. But Ana, who did not even like Haskell and was surprised that he, who usually was mostly indifferent to her, was standing by the doorway and taking the time to reply to her, Ana believed him. Completely.

That was the summer she and Larry had been visiting alone. After Haskell answered her question, she would sneak up mornings into her grandparents' bedroom, filled as it was with all kinds of strange smells and always dark and immaculately tidy. And once she was in that room, all by herself, she would stare and stare at the picture in the ornate silver frame, right there in the front on grandfather's bureau where he must see it every day—Grammer, younger, young, not a bit beautiful, not pretty, round plain face and pale blue eyes. So pale you could not see any limit in them, just as you could see no limits in a pale sky. Grammer, to whom Haskell had lost his heart for ever and ever.

~~~

Larry did not go back to the house to help Millie or have supper because he was in the Deemers' backyard. His friend, Kyle, was not there. Even so, very carefully, saving all the parts, the screws and bolts, Larry was dismantling the bicycle he and Kyle had agreed they would use to make a large wagon once they got another bicycle for the other wheels. They did not yet have another bicycle. The one coming apart belonged to Kyle. Larry was sure that he wouldn't mind because he would get the second bike soon, or the necessary wheels and parts. If Kyle turned out to be really mad, he would let Kyle borrow the computer game Alan had given him. And if they couldn't get hold of a second bike or enough money to buy one, he would give up his own ten-speed, for he had decided riding a bicycle was not going to be nearly as useful to him, this summer, as having a truly large wagon for carting things.

~~~

"May I get you a drink?" A tall man, unusually tall, who had moved steadily through the crowded room toward her, asked Cora.

"I think I had enough to drink before and during dinner," Cora said.

The man smiled and nodded affably, not indicating that he agreed with her that probably she should not have anything more, but accepting her decision, not putting pressure on her. "I met your husband, Professor Belknap, yesterday," he told her.

"Oh?"

"After the public lecture he gave at the University. Did you drive over for it?"

"No, I didn't."

"The University's lucky to have him. He must get offers all the time, from all sorts of places?"

"How is it you're so interested?" Cora asked him.

He was one of the UT regents, he confessed, somewhat embarrassed. Cable Poinsett. His family had their home place not far from Riles and old ties to Dawson. In fact one of his daughters was going to the college. He involved himself as much as he could, which is why he was here tonight. He had long ago realized the importance to the state of education. That was why he was a regent. And truly, he had not been trying to pry information out of her about her husband. He was sure she knew the Institute and the University did their own recruiting. Regents were not allowed to meddle. He should have introduced himself to her immediately. He apologized for that. But still, he did worry about being raided by other universities. He certainly hoped Professor Belknap was happy at the University.

"Don't apologize," Cora said. "You were doing your job as regent."

"Thank you," Poinsett said and smiled at her again. This time more broadly, relieved. "You're very understanding. Must be why you're in administration."

"Maybe I understand because I'm a sociologist. I do some administrative work, even fund-raising," she nodded towards the crowd surrounding them, "but I was hired in the sociology department because of my published work." She ended without giving the actual number or the date of that one paper published from her unpublished dissertation.

"You make quite a pair, you and Professor Belknap," Poinsett told her. "Dawson's lucky, too. Beauty *and* academic success." He looked at her with approval, impressed, no hint of sarcasm.

"I'm enjoying the college," Cora answered. She was surprised that what she said was true. "I'll tell you a secret," she went on, cheered, and happy to be pleasing him, "a great secret—I quite like the time I spend in administration. I'd be careful admitting that to another academic."

"Your secret's safe with me. I'm as far from an academic as you can get. I was lucky they let me out of college with any degree. Not like you and your husband. But I have learned a little about what professors do. I know your husband's rare. He has an astonishing list of achievements for his age. I hear he's a rock climber, too. How does he get time for it all?"

"Mr. Poinsett, I'll be as open with you as you've been with me. I can't really answer that. My husband and I are separated at present."

Poinsett was so dismayed Cora felt compelled to keep on talking to help ease the shock. She chatted about Dawson, about Poinsett's daughter going there and about Dawson's growth, until Poinsett regained his balance and told her how easy it was to say the wrong thing in this age of changing marital ties, told her Lord knows he had not meant to make anything awkward for her, he certainly wouldn't, he was himself divorced and went on to tell her of his other two daughters besides the one at Dawson. And during all the time that she had spoken and while Poinsett talked to her, Cora kept rehearing, like something shocking, like something exposing her, her voice saying "separated" and "at present." She had not said "divorcing."

How had the words altered so easily? Did a hint, merely a hint, of money—but real money, a huge amount of money—do that to her? She thought she had been resisting. She thought she had argued against Alan and listened out of courtesy solely, a courtesy only, politeness. Yet she had changed so thoroughly—had she?—that even a response coming reflex-fast was converted to a safe deception.

Poinsett was continuing to tell her how impressed he was with the personal attention his middle daughter received at Dawson. Twice as much as the older girl got at UT Austin. Perhaps, he finished, perhaps he should develop closer ties to Dawson.

"Mr. Poinsett," Cora said, "I believe I will take you up on that drink after all. Would you get me one? Gin and tonic, please. And very light on the gin. I don't need much."

~~~

Late the same night Alan wrote his brother.

Dear Mike,

Money, brother, money. I said I'd mail a check in two weeks. I finally got paid. I wish the government paid interest when they're late the way they make us do on our taxes. But at least they do pay—even linguists. You'd be surprised at the

kinds of work the government wants us to do, besides talking
to dolphins.

Back to money, it turns out Cora and I may get hold of a
considerable amount. Real estate prices may shoot up here.
Developers are coming in and we may sell the hulking manse
for an impressive profit. Funny thing, the real profit won't
come from the old house itself but from the empty lot. Seems
the sizeable amount of land we own, plus the location, makes
this a prize for developers.

If we do make a deal with them, I agree with what you
said, a year ago, you and I should set up an emergency fund
for Dad. And if Cora and I make a big profit, I'd have no
more worries about the kids' college educations. Or the IRS.
That means I could spend my time on my own research. I'm
doing first-rate work, Mike. You don't know what it would
mean to me to be able to do this the way it should be done—
full time and flat out, with no other commitments.

I was surprised you asked me if Cora and I are back together. We're still separated. We're going slow with divorce
papers and talk of divorce because of the kids, and also,
frankly, because of negotiations on the house. We aren't going to take any risks. But our basic plans haven't changed. We
know what we're doing.

Matter of fact, I've begun seeing someone else. An intriguing young woman. Very attractive. Very. One of my TAs,
Wendell Meyers, the fool, made a crack about her in front of
Nessie. Fortunately, Nessie's too young to grasp his meaning
and I was able to cover it. I made doubly sure about this after
Nessie and I left. I never want her, or any of the kids, worried
about anything.

Nessie's staying with me all weekend. I forgot her security
blanket, but an old couch cover substituted and she's sleeping
away. I took her to a puppet show. She sat on my briefcase
with her jaw hanging open the whole time. I'll have to get her
a puppet and teach her how to use it when I get some free
time. She's a super kid, Mike. I bet I could teach her anything.
She's fast as lightning.

Give my love to Gail and the boys. I think I'll send little Alan a computer game for beginners on his birthday.

Hug Dad for me. Tell him I'll write extra soon.

Love,

Alan

PS. Joke department. I've got a good one for you, but I'm too rushed to do it justice tonight. Tell you next time we talk on the phone.

A

~~~

Much later that night, in the still dark hours of Saturday morning, Cora was also writing. She sat at the desk in the study with the windows open, for the air had cooled after a brief shower. The incessant high shrieks of cicadas and the smells of Millie's gardens after rain came in through the windows. Cora's expression was tranquil and attentive.

$750,000, she wrote.

Alan had said that was the lowest, absolutely the lowest, figure mentioned. It might go higher. Deduct $50,000, which was ample, on the high side even, for mortgage repayment and the legal fees. And that was truly being high; it could not cost more. So $700,000, at minimum, was left. She wrote the figure down.

Half of that was $350,000.

The calculator blinked quick clear numbers back to her. It was satisfying to use the calculator. 350,000. Satisfying also to write the numbers down on paper. And put a dollar sign in front of them. $350,000.

Would there be something in taxes? Maybe. That might be built into the price. Demand they pay the taxes? Why not? Kincaid was a big company. They could pay it.

Subtract $75,000 or even $100,000 to buy a condo for herself and the children. And probably Alan would help since it was for the children, too. Then $5,000 straight off to put Nessie in a good all-day private nursery school until she went to public school next year. Alan would pay half, for nursery school, so that would be $2,500. $250,000 less $2,500 was $247,500, at the least, to invest. Suppose she did. Suppose she invested cleverly and could get 9% or 10%, yet fairly secure. That meant $24,750 extra, totally extra, above and beyond her salary and what Alan would certainly provide for the children. $24,750 simply gravy. And the security of the $247,500 invested.

She could buy a car.

She stopped writing numbers or pressing the little keys on the calculator and stared into the softer, slightly lightening dark beyond the range of the lamp.

She could. She would get a car with automatic transmission. No more vapor-lock trouble. Ever. She could travel, if she wanted. Take the children along or leave them with someone she could pay and not always just her mother. With extra money, she could pay for more help.

She wrote the figure down again and deeply underlined it. $24,750. She looked at the numbers. Every year. Extra.

That was a lot of money, especially down here. She could live the way she wanted. Until the children went to college. There would be college fees. There would have to be college for all three of them.

They might get more money for the house. The price could go higher, Alan said. There could be more than $24,750 every year. And Alan would help with college.

She knew why Alan wanted money. He wanted it to do his own research. No more consulting. No more summer teaching. No more government work. He had an important reason to want money. She wanted money for a car and a smaller place to live that would take less of her time. She wanted money for more domestic help. For grubby things mostly. All the same, she wanted them. And good schools for the children weren't grubby. Why shouldn't they have good schools? Why shouldn't she have what she wanted?

IV

"Do you think I don't know where I fit? That because I have this funny combination job at Dawson and have to do some administrative work, which I do well, and because I don't make a big effort to stop them calling me 'Dr.' all the time, I don't know what that means, or what Dawson is? Do you think I've forgotten what you used to say, and I did, too, about little rinky-dink private colleges where everyone goes around calling each other 'Dr.' or about incompetent academics who hide out in administration because they can't do any real work? You act like I no longer understand the difference between a whole loaf and a crumb because I take the crumbs. Not only take them, I'm grateful for them. They beat nothing. They help pay the bills, too, you might notice. Only what makes you think all I ever wanted was to be at a second-rate school, Alan? Or an 'nth'- rate one, as you and I both used to call them? You've been rattling on the whole weekend, ever since Jamie Rayker phoned, about the ambitions you and he had when you started. What about my ambitions?"

All this was said way over half a year ago, in the very beginning of winter, such winter as there was in this hot section of the country. Yet even so, some days were cold. The sky could turn gray, as it had this Sunday, and a haze of rain slip to the ground all day long. They were in the kitchen and the house was chilly because old houses here were not built with central heating, nor were they insulated. The large, makeshift central gas heater beneath the floor in the main hall left the rooms outside its reach with little heat, and the kitchen was so far away it was especially cool, unless someone was baking.

"I don't get everything I want," Alan answered her. "I have plenty of trouble. I didn't get my NSF grant. I told you. Lehrman must have blocked it. He's the only one's got that much influence. I have no idea how I'm going to finance extra computer time. Or support four grad students. That's four lives, Cora. You're wrong if you think everything is a snap for me. And you've done fine here. You've done hundreds of things since we moved. You...."

He had to quit. Cora had risen from the table and crossed the room. The floor of the kitchen sagged in a familiar, almost cozy way, about one-third of the distance from the table to the sink and Cora lengthened her step to allow for the unevenness. She began running water over the dishes which needed to be loaded in the mobile dishwasher. The kitchen was too old to have a built-in dishwasher. The kitchen would have to be ripped up and redesigned for a built-in machine.

Over the noise of splashing water, she said, "That's what I mean. You take away even my disappointments. Only yours matter."

She shut off the water.

"It's like being ugly," she said, which seemed to him an absurd beginning, for half-turned towards him, leaning against the sink with one arm resting so its pale underside was visible as were the few light, reddish freckles on her skin, she looked like a full and sumptuous Titian, her extraordinary hair a warm glow in the day's cold gray.

"Ugly people," she said, "don't want to be ugly. You act like they do. You blame them the way ignorant peasants did in the Middle Ages. Like the Nazis blamed the Jews for being Jews. I'd like to be a 'super achiever,' as the stupid counselor at Dawson calls all our students who get A's. I'd like to have—wait a minute, Alan, let me finish, for once— I'd like to have a job at the University, or at one of the better colleges. You don't think my sole ambition was to end up at Dawson? Back in my own hometown? Maybe it would make you feel better if I pretended what I am doing *is* some great achievement and I never hoped for anything more. Well, I can't pretend. I know you tried to help, but just because you couldn't doesn't mean I never wanted something more."

Alan got up, too, and crossed the room to stand next to her.

"Careers don't follow pre-ordained sequences," he said. "Sometimes you don't get what you want at a certain time. I didn't come up the easy way. It wasn't Trinity, Andover and Harvard or European schools, MIT and Harvard for me the way it was for Crimmins or Bob Lehrman. You've got years ahead. Years. You want to do research, do it. I'm not stopping you. The kids don't take up much of your time now, except Nessie. Anyway, you said you wanted children."

"It has nothing to do with the children. You don't listen to me."

Alan braced his hand against the sink, close to her, close to her arm which was almost totally upturned. Yet not touching her.

"Are you trying to tell me you're interested in someone else?" he asked.

"Christ, Alan."

"Nothing else makes any sense," he said. "I'm home all the time unless I'm teaching or working at the Institute. I help with everything. This is what we planned—living in a small town because of the children and so we wouldn't have to earn so much money. It's perfect for us. There must be another reason. There is someone else."

"Yes," Cora said. "Me."

"Christ yourself, Cora," he said, angrily, "that is so trite."

"Wasn't 'We're the perfect couple' trite? You used to say we were the perfect couple all the time."

"Don't start being sarcastic," Alan said. "I hate it when you start being sarcastic." He walked past her, still not touching her, and circled the uneven kitchen floor. "No one gets everything. I don't either. And nothing you've said is worth putting us through this kind of turmoil. You make me feel like a criminal."

"There you go again," Cora said. "You exaggerate your concerns until nothing else is important. I'm not trying to blame you. I'm trying to talk to you. About me. Not the children. Not the University or your NSF grant. But me. I may not have done what I expected in my career. My job may be 'nth' rate, but it's what I do. And I work hard at it. Only don't pretend it's some amazing achievement. That's patronizing. It insults me."

"I never insulted you in my life. That can't be what's bothering you. First you don't get attention, then you get too much wrong attention. You've met someone. Where? At the college? A new member of the faculty? Some businessman?"

He was a man who was super smart, a phrase he often used. Intelligence shone in his face. His eyes were brilliant, electric, with intensity. The most alive eyes she had ever seen. At the least change in the ordinary use of a word, at a new joke or idea, at the sight of an unusual hill or an unfamiliar rock face in some gorge, his eyes lit in response. It had seemed to her, before, that he could never miss a thing.

She turned on the faucet and began to finish rinsing the remaining dishes and fitting each one in the dishwasher.

~~~

"I could adopt a religious pose and claim all work has equal merit in the eyes of some deity or other," Cora said to Alan in another conversation, a month later in that so-called winter. They were in bed but not ready yet to sleep. Entirely on his own Alan had told her she was more cheerful, perhaps because she was far busier. She was meeting regularly with the President, spending hours on college problems. She must be getting satisfaction from it.

She could take the religious pose, she had answered. "Many people here in Bible-belt country do," she continued, "especially women. They use that to comfort themselves for all they don't have. You know, the worse your life, the more Jesus loves you." Their arms rested outside the covers, for the night was not actually cold. Cora held his wrist loosely in her hand. It gave her an inner smiling pleasure that he was not, in fact, much larger boned than she. She could stretch her hand almost as wide as he could his. She could reach her fingers around his wrist, however much he exercised to build up his arms.

"Many Dawson parents are like that," she said. She lifted his wrist and held their forearms, their wrists and hands, upright in the air, their elbows resting side by side on the bed. "You wouldn't believe how angry those people are in their conviction. They come to conferences with a polite air, but underneath is a torrent of rage saying—who are you to say my kid isn't a genius in some way you aren't smart enough to test? Who are you to decide who has value in the eyes of God?"

She pulled their arms back down on the bed. "That covers the deeply religious ones. It's always 'deeply' religious. And 'deeply' concerned with traditional American values. 'Deeply' compassionate, if they're humanitarians. The deeply humanitarian parents want a totally accepting, totally understanding and totally non-discriminating attitude from teachers. Plus all A's for their kids. And we're supposed to consider every student brilliant, or at least highly creative, no matter how badly the poor kid fails. In fact, we don't have many humanitarian parents. Practically none. Humanitarians live in cities, I've decided. Or send their kids to state universities, like yours."

She tightened her hold on his wrist and again raised their forearms from the bed.

"We've had repeat conferences this week for parents whose kids are failing," she said. "A last effort to keep students from being thrown out. 'Crashing,' the students call it. I hate these conferences. But Dawson is good about rescuing students. Private colleges are. You'd say it's because Dawson needs every paying kid, which is right. Listening to those parents talk about their youngsters, it occurred to me the parents' standards for their kids are as rigid as ours, but they measure other things. The church-going families give A's for volunteering to be a church camp counselor all summer. That's a big plus with them. B's for regular church singing or weekly youth work. C's for occasional attendance at Bible school. If it's one of our rare humanitarians, A's for being friendly to Mexicans, especially the poor Mexicans. The Garzas don't count. In fact the kids don't call the Garzas Mexicans. B's for reading the *New York Times*. C's, I suppose, for at least saying to their parents that money doesn't matter. The parents aren't any more flexible than the Dawson faculty."

"I like your hidden grading systems," Alan said. His voice was entertained, content.

"The saddest thing," Cora said, "is you can tell what the parents really want though none of them will say it. It doesn't matter how confident they seem, underneath it what they really want is to have their kids get good grades."

"You bet. That's the only real game. Failing never does anyone any good," Alan said.

She made a companionable, an inarticulate sound that could be agreement. Like those parents, she could not say aloud what she wanted.

"Now if we *did* have your all-seeing omnipotent and just deity up there," Alan said, jerking the thumb of his free hand ceilingward, "I'd have Bob Lehrman's job at Harvard. I'm not only better than he is, I work harder, I'm younger, and I have more productive years ahead. Also, I'm a nicer guy."

She laughed aloud, burbles of pleasure that left him also smiling.

"Laugh some more," he said, nuzzling his face into her hair. "You don't laugh enough anymore."

She tugged their arms so both fell back on the bed. She loved it, almost every time, when he revealed his arrogance so blatantly to her in private. As if he let her share something secret about him, something unbelievably vulnerable.

~ ~ ~

Other talks between them were not so pleasant.

In the spring they drove to see Larry play soccer, at a small town to the north which was holding a sports fair with other junior high schools. When they arrived they found the school grounds swarming with sports outfitted youngsters from different schools, playing different games. They found the soccer field and were both excited, Alan more than she, until gradually they realized Larry might not be allowed to play. He had said nothing to them of this. He might not know, Alan said. Look at him, he did not dare turn his head toward them.

Cora had already stopped looking openly in their son's direction. He stood not far away from them. There were no stands, only the flat school grounds, and he stood on a worn strip of grass with several other boys on his team. Every one of them had already played. He was standing partly turned away from Cora and Alan and not that close to the other boys and he held his body stiffly, drawn into itself, narrowed, the way he did when he was cold. Cora glanced briefly, surreptitiously, at Alan. She could feel his anger rising as Larry was not sent on the field, even at the end, with the score so lopsided it would have made no difference.

When the game was finally over, Cora was relieved Larry could not drive back with them. He had to go in the Riles bus. She and Alan left the school in silence, crossed silently to Alan's small sports car, and in silence began the drive back through the gentle widely spaced hills.

Obviously, she had not made Larry practice, Alan began telling her. Larry was as good a soccer player as the others. He was probably better. He was fast. More important, he had balance. Superb balance. She probably did not realize how importance balance was, but he, Alan, did. Larry was the only boy dressed to play who did not get into the game. It could only be a punishment for missing practice. He, Alan, knew how coaches acted. She must have let Larry skip practice. Regularly. He wasn't doing well in his classes either. Was she making sure he did his homework? Did she let him blow off classes as well as team practice since she had become so involved at Dawson? Larry had better start learning to do what was required of him and she should see he did or he was never going to amount to anything.

"You talk like life is nothing but one big successalator," Cora said. "One misstep and Larry's doomed forever." She was as angry as Alan, yet the word, which leapt out, delighted her. Struck her as a marvelous word. She could not resist using it again.

"I don't want to be any part of your successalator," she said.

"You want success," Alan said, his voice sharp. "You just won't admit it."

In the customary rhythm of conversations between them it would have been her turn. She would have denied what he said or argued or perhaps, part-way, agreed, for she saw there might be much in what he said.

But Alan went on, without waiting for her. "Don't kid yourself that you're superior because you don't get down in the mud and compete like others. Believe me, you want the results competition brings. Everything you complain about not having you get from competition. If," he added, his tone thick, clogged with anger, "if what you're always complaining about really is what's bothering you."

Cora's head jerked forward. She stared through the windshield and did not start an answer. Her lips pressed tight shut and she took a deep breath, and another, then turned her face further from him and toward her own window.

The countryside through which they were driving and the hills beyond were unfairly lovely. Some distance from the highway green broadly-spread live oaks gave thick shade. Occasional mesquite trees, with tough twisted branches and thin flimsy leaves, pocked the landscape. Scattered in small groups stood Spanish daggers. They were beginning, just beginning, to bloom. Crazy barricades designed to guard the treasure of their heavy blossoms, Alan had said of them, the first spring he had seen them. Imagine having three whole feet of thick white petals around a solid upright core. Flower gigantism. They were southwest flora's match for African fauna's goofy ostrich. The next season they came into bloom, he said, if he could get the time, he wanted them to cut the pointed, sharp-edged daggers from one side of a plant and extract the whole core of waxy flowers. That would beat chopping a Christmas tree. Or tapping maples for syrup. They would all do it together, the whole family, he had said, the next time the Spanish daggers bloomed.

("Why did you keep it secret?" Alan kept asking her in the first months after they moved to Riles. "This country is fabulous. Let's go swimming. Sure, absolutely, on Thanksgiving Day. I'll tell Mike while he's freezing we've been paddling around in what's practically our own lake. He doesn't have to know it's unusually warm this year. Even if it weren't, we'd swim. We've swum in colder weather in the middle of summers in New England. Let's pack up the old car and go."

She had not thought the country beautiful until he told her. He pointed out the constant greenness of the oaks, which did not shed their tiny leaves in fall. He made her see, as her gardening mother never had, the cozy nesting shapes of many of the hills. The deep mixed cream and light cream and sometimes white of the limestone bared in places where the hills were split apart.

"Here you go, Nessie, you'll like sitting on this," Alan said, later that Thanksgiving afternoon. "Vanessa's throne," he named it for her the first time, and he set her on the flat rock with a soft blanket beneath her. "Up north it's snowing," he told her, "piling up all around everyone's house. But we get to be outside with no coats. You'll get too cold in the water, sweetheart, so you stay here with the blanket and I'll bring you something. That's my girl." It was their family's first non-freezing winter and Alan had them all, except Nessie, in bathing suits under the clothes they took off. He and Larry took out an inflated inner tube and Ana carried it to the edge of the water.

"Daddy, the water's so clear it's like you can't see it," Ana said to him. "It's like there isn't any water at all except where it's moving. Watch me, Daddy, here I go."

She tossed the tube onto the surface and yelling, exuberant, flung herself after it. From the bank above her, Larry was wildly trying to pull the tube out of her reach with the cord tied to it. There was too much slack in the cord and Ana reached the inner tube, grasping it, just as Larry pulled the cord tight and spun the tube, and Ana, to one side.

"Stop it," Ana yelled, and pulled against him. "Let go, I had it first." She got her footing and stood up. The water was no deeper than her waist on this side. Her skin was pebbled with cold because the water was chilly, but the sun was already warming her face and arms as she pulled back hard on the cord.

"Larry fish Ana," Nessie said and getting up on her feet, steadying herself, started down the slope toward the bank.

Cora had been unloading the picnic from the car. She saw Nessie's progress, caught up with her and engulfed her.

"No, sweetie, you can't go in. Much too cold for little sweeties. Mommie'll let you splash." Aloud, to Alan, Cora called out, "Nessie'll be all right, Alan. I've got her."

Nessie stretched out from beneath Cora's arm, edged her feet down the last lip of the incline, and with a grunt stepped in the water, shoes and all. She beamed up at her mother, her pointed face sun-lit and her eyes squinting, converted into tiny brilliant triangles by her smile.

"Fish me," she demanded.

Cora scooped her out and sat down with her to take off her wet shoes and socks and roll up the bottoms of her overalls.

Alan was swimming across at the widest part of the bend, a broad curve where the stream expanded into a deep pool. At the far side he dipped down, head diving beneath his feet, and shot back in a smooth uncoiling motion.

When he reached the bank on their side he stood up and called out to Nessie, "I brought you a pink rock from the bottom, Ness. Cora, you let her get wet."

"She's warmer than any of us. She's dying to go back in. It's like you said, she's too New England to mind cold."

Alan grabbed up Nessie and a towel. "Rub-a-dub dub, ten toes in a tub, and how dry do you think they'll be; we'll dry one, we'll dry two, we'll dry fat number three..." until he rhymed and rubbed each toe dry, kissed the squiggling soles of her feet and wrapped her in the blanket from the flat rock. But he let her down when she kept twisting to be loosed and once on the ground she padded determinedly back to the edge of the water where Larry and Ana had beached the inner tube and were piling fine gravel and sand around it.

"Look after her, Ana," Alan called. "Now pay attention. Don't let her go in the water again."

"Did you see the way she walked barefoot over those rocks to get to the water?" Cora said. "And she's barely two. She's going to be even more of an outdoor enthusiast than you are."

"Meanwhile you haven't even got wet," Alan said and smacked her on the bottom of her dry bathing suit. His hand lingered, circling fondly, caressing, assessing. "Hmm," he murmured, appreciatively, and then, "eating a little too much of your own good home cooking nowadays, I see. Or too many lunches with Nancy Lou. You better work out in the gym if you get the job at Dawson College. Burn up the old calories on the machines."

"Dawson doesn't have that kind of gym, remember?"

But Alan had put his head in his sweat shirt. His head popped out of it, wet hair stuck against his scalp and forehead. He reached into her picnic basket for his glasses. Contact lenses were impossible for swimming.

"Look at that stream," he said, settling the frames on his face. "Incredible. Why did you keep it secret?" He bent down for Nessie's towel to take to her at the water's edge and called out to Larry to stop playing in the sand and come join him.

"I'll teach you how to skip stones," he said. "It'll be good practice for your pitching arm. You're bound to be on a team next year. I'm sure of it.")

Then there were days, in that year, when Alan would not take time to talk to her at any length, even if she tried to argue. He did not have the time. He had to work.

She had married him, in part, for that concentration. It was as much an aspect of him as the fact that he was smart, as his size, as his zest for whatever interested him, and as the sudden unexpected signs he showed, startling her, that he had been thinking of her—as when he asked if she were not happier since she was often being consulted by Dawson's President.

Alan had been envied by other graduate students for his concentration. No one else had been able to study so unremittingly over so long a stretch of time and remain so enthusiastic about linguistics. No one else published a note, in a logic journal, not even a linguistics one, while finishing a dissertation.

He would not take time from his teaching schedule and the hours he had blocked out for research. She had to understand that if he could get his model to work the way he wanted, the NSF rejection would not matter. He could reapply. He'd show Lehrman he was right, if Lehrman had been the reader on his grant. If he brought this paper off, if he were given another NSF, he would get outside offers. He would use them to raise his salary. They needed more money. She must have noticed they needed more money than they were making, even with all his outside work. They were spending like millionaires. They were throwing it away. He ought to be using all his time on his research but he'd have to do more consulting to get money for them. Not to mention his father's bills. She knew how much those were. And now they were going to need more money if they had to send Larry to a private school and he clearly couldn't go on where he was.

"And I have to buy a better car for you," Alan said to her. "You have too much trouble with our old one. I'll get any car you like so long as it's a stick shift. With a sound car you won't waste time on repairs. Then you can do whatever you want."

"A sound car will solve all my problems?"

"Don't be sarcastic. I hate that. If you don't want a car, fine. Just say so. But I meant what I said about doing more consulting to buy a car for you. I'm still willing, if a car's what you need."

By the end of that year they did not live together anymore.

V

On Tuesday Haskell drove to town unusually early. He had organized a quiet meeting at the city library with four other men. The five of them would be enough to make a quorum of the Commission, enough to validate a set of records and old bills in order to approve a claim. They met in the upstairs windowless conference room, next to the children's library. The documents and two volumes of county history and the thick black-bound folder of city records, opened and tabbed at the significant places, were solemnly passed around, going counterclockwise from one man to the next.

"Everything seems in order," the man at the head of the table stated.

"You'd be flabbergasted if anything Haskell presented wasn't," another said.

The men muttered agreement and Haskell nodded, acknowledging the compliment.

The one who had stretched back in his chair, arms locked behind his head, said, "You near vacationed out, Haskell?"

"Just about," Haskell said.

"Good. You can do a lot better for lunch company than Alonzo Aikens."

A soft chuckle from the others, amiable but lightly disparaging.

"Our itinerant gossip," another said, "the would-be big-time real estate dealer."

Another chuckle from all four, more open this time, with an edge of excitement, potentially malicious.

"Aikens is all right," Haskell answered them. "Aikens manages well enough. And he plays good tennis."

The man who was town clerk, and also a notary, prepared the official forms for them to sign. "Shall we, gentlemen?" he asked, ready to witness their signatures and attach his own.

When they all finished, the town clerk collected the official forms and the black folder of city records. Haskell took the original bills and the two red volumes of county history and put them in his briefcase. They cleared the table and left the room, which was cold, as empty rooms in libraries often become in the summer. They filed downstairs to the copying machine to make all the copies Haskell and the town clerk and any other of the Commission felt necessary. In all they made twenty copies.

Outside the library they told Haskell again it was a good job, a well-substantiated claim. He shook hands elaborately with each one, shaking their hands longer and holding more firmly than usual. Especially with the last one, the town clerk.

"A good job, Haskell," the clerk repeated, "obviously right. High time it was done."

"That is true."

"How's Mrs. Bosk? Still enjoying all that space way out in the country? And the greenhouses?"

"Oh, yes. Yes, she does."

The town clerk shook his head, indicating amazement. "I hear she's already shipping out plants. Selling them as fast as she can pack them. She's going to guarantee your financial base, Haskell."

Haskell smiled.

"Marvelous woman. Marvelous. Right in the forefront of her time, too. Imagine setting up a business like that."

"She has ways of getting things done," Haskell said.

"A marvelous woman. Absolutely." The town clerk tapped his bulky leather case with the official forms. "And she'll be pleased about this," he said, "it being her home, too."

"Hmm," Haskell said.

After he had separated from the town clerk, Haskell walked north along the street. His heavy high-colored face brightened frequently by his short sweet smile. Gradually, he grew more thoughtful. He passed a candy store, retraced his steps and entered to buy Millie a present.

He picked out a large apothecary-style jar to fill with hard candies.

He chose the largest sized jar and had the woman behind the counter pack it with Millie's favorites and a small number of those he liked best. He would not take a box of chocolates, he explained. This kind of weather chocolates got too sticky, especially since he and Mrs. Bosk were averse to incessant air conditioning. But he wanted the candy to look like a gift, even though it was only hard candies. He wanted the biggest jar and several different colored layers, ending with a red layer of cherry-flavored candies on top. And he wanted the jar decorated with a big ribbon.

When the jar was filled and had its ribbon, even with a bow, Haskell decided it was not enough. He needed something else. Something more lasting. More personal. He would go to a women's clothing store and buy a nice blouse. Or a delicate light summer robe. Or both.

~~~

There was a message for Alan to call Cora when he got back to his office. It was early in the afternoon and Alan had been playing tennis, as he usually did at noon on Wednesdays. He was still invigorated, and the hair on the back of his neck was not quite dry from his shower. He opened the latest issue of a journal he had picked up when he got his mail, dialed Cora's number and, while he waited for her to answer, glanced through the table of contents.

"Cora?" he said, flipping journal pages to an article by an Icelandic linguist, a few years younger than he, who worked at Harvard with Lehrman. "You call?" he said, "children OK? Nessie? Yeah, I know. I was in a meeting with my grad students all morning. I just walked in." He was scanning the first paragraphs as he spoke.

The article was ingenious. The opening paragraphs were excellent. Original.

Alan quit reading. "That can't be," he blurted out, his head raised. "That isn't possible. Even in Riles your father couldn't do that in secret."

He listened to her, his eyes not focused, fixed far above the journal in linguistics.

"Have you talked to Figaller?" he asked. "What do you mean he's at a golf tournament? So what did his partner say?"

Again he listened and this time slapped the journal shut and put it to one side.

"Read me the letter," he said. "Don't paraphrase it. You may be familiar with letters like it because of dealing with Dawson's property, but I'm not. I don't know about this sort of thing. How in hell can our house be turned into an historic landmark overnight?"

Alan pressed the receiver against his ear, to be closer. "That's enough," he said, after a time. "What it means is the house can't have alterations or repairs without some crazy preservation committee's approval. All right, some preservation *commission's* approval. And it can't be sold except to someone who accepts the conditions. Right? Which means it could only be sold to some historical nut. Certainly not Kincaid. Kincaid wants to tear it down. We'll get our own lawyer. A real one, from Austin."

Something else was said to him, something urgent. Alan waited, shook his head and broke in, "Don't start that. This was *not* inevitable. And it's not settled. No restriction done that fast, and behind our backs, can be legal. It's some bluff of Haskell's. I don't care what Figaller's partner said. We own the house and that partner is an imbecile. He's like all the lawyers in Riles, he's scared to death of your father. I tell you your father's not that powerful. We'll get a first-rate lawyer from here, or from Dallas. Someone who knows what he's doing."

He paused again as Cora tried to respond but he cut in impatiently. "Be realistic. How could anyone pass some rule turning our house into a site that requires all this protection without our knowing? And in Riles? Come on, Riles isn't full of historic landmarks. It isn't Plymouth Rock or a subdivision of the Alamo. Sam Houston never slept there. What's anyone going to preserve? I never heard of the Riles Preservation Commission."

He was silent again until he finally stood up from the desk.

"Haskell is not God, Cora. Look at what you found out in just one morning. You've already seen the records in the court house and you know who was involved. We can use that when we get a lawyer who's not a half-wit. You mustn't let Haskell shake you. And believe me, Haskell's not doing this to get at you. He's doing it because of me. He found out how valuable the house is and he can't stand me getting the money. That's what this is all about—me. You mustn't feel bad, Cora. Don't take it so personally. It has nothing to do with you."

~~~

Once the children were all home, late in the afternoon, and after Ana had been told to look after Nessie, Cora drove out into the country to confront her mother. It was typical of Millie that Cora found her in the packing shed so late in the day. Millie was making double-layered containers from a stack of gray perforated sheets of cardboard. The latest in her series of efforts to ship her plants most safely and profitably to colder climates that paid more.

It was also typical that Millie made no effort to deny it was Haskell who had caused the house to be designated an historic landmark. Nor did she say she regretted what he had done. She went on folding the cushiony sheets into individual boxes, fitting each second container into the first.

"But you didn't know anything about this ahead of time?" Cora asked.

Millie shook her head.

"Stop that a minute." Cora put a hand on the stack of cardboard sheets in front of Millie. "I want you to tell me what's possessed him?" She searched her mother's face, now turned toward her. "Haskell's known since January, since before January, that Alan and I planned to live apart." As she said the words, she felt herself grow warm. Even while angry, even while trying to bully her mother, she had not used the word "divorcing." She had said, instead, that they planned to live apart. "Did Haskell tell you why he did it?" she went on.

Millie made no reply. She tugged lightly at the cardboard. Cora removed her hand and Millie folded another pair of boxes and gently eased the second into the first, tapping each side lightly until the inner one settled to the bottom with a soft sigh.

"Do you realize what this is going to mean?" Cora pressed her. "You may not have thought it out, but Haskell has. I know he has. I've talked to him, as much as he'll talk. What he's trying to do is run our lives, the way you and he do Ramón's?"

"Ramón runs his own life," Millie said.

"You know what I'm saying," Cora said. "What about a nursery school for Ness? You and I spent hours, days, talking about one. And a private school for Larry? Haskell himself made suggestions about schools for Larry. We won't be able to afford anything like that. None of it."

Millie's light clear eyes moved up and down between the next containers she was making and her daughter.

"I wanted to move to an apartment," Cora said. "You know that. So does Haskell. I don't want to stay in that house. I'll never have enough time there to do these assignments for the President."

"They didn't hire you for that."

"More and more it's what I do. It could be a big chance for me, Mother. I want to do it right. Couldn't you tell Haskell? Tell him what he's doing isn't fair. Look at all we'll lose, the children, and I..." she paused, began again, "I wanted...I thought if I could get somewhere else...I...."

There were tears in Cora's eyes. She had thought she had been acting, trying to persuade her mother, in the same way she had so deftly avoided the word "divorcing." But the tears were real, unplanned, edging down her cheeks. She shook her head angrily, her mass of reddish hair brushing against the hand she had to use to cover her face.

Millie ripped off a paper towel and handed it to her. Cora took it and, partly groping, pulled another from the roll fastened to the end of the worktable. She blew her nose.

"You're not the person I should do this to, I know," she said, wiping her eyes. "I can't understand Haskell's purpose."

"To keep the house from being sold to developers."

"God, that is so like you, Mother. So basic. Obviously it can't be sold to developers now. You can say that calmly, like you fold up boxes, but you don't have to live there anymore."

Cora moved nearer to throw the used paper towels into the bin. She stood next to Millie, right beside her. Her mother's short solid body, standing so resolutely before the work table in the packing shed, stirred her with irritation and at the same time a familiar feeling of protectiveness. A feeling she was sure she shared with her father. How odd that despite her mother's independence and sturdiness, her persistence in sticking to her own sometimes outlandish interests, despite her business and its growth, she could seem, even so, heartbreakingly vulnerable. All the lost children, the babies who did not live, Cora used to think. Later she was not so sure that was the answer.

"Forget about the house," Cora said, "there's something else going on in Haskell's mind. You and Haskell don't have some crazy idea that Alan and I will get back together if you stop us selling the house, do you? You're not contriving a great reconciliation, are you? Mother?" And when Millie would not answer, "That isn't going to happen. Not a chance. Alan has a girlfriend."

Millie stepped away from her.

"Don't be startled," Cora said. "Good Lord, Mother, you of all people should be the first to agree it's only natural. Male and female, instinct, nature, hormones and so on. Not only that, she's younger."

"Alan told you?" Millie asked.

"Nessie did. It's not what you think. Nessie doesn't know anything about it. She didn't understand what she overheard. Alan told her 'popsy' was a word for 'popsicle.'"

Millie looked so incredulous Cora stumbled on, explaining, "Some idiot teaching assistant of Alan's made a crack about Alan's 'popsy'—you know how they use it—and Nessie overheard. She thought it meant popsicle. Alan let her think she was right. He told me in case Nessie mentioned it to me. You can see he had to tell me."

"You think Nessie believes what Alan told her?"

"Nessie's not five years old. She adores Alan. She'll believe anything he says. And he took her out and bought her a popsicle immediately afterward, so she'd be convinced."

"Bought her a 'popsy.' What's he going to buy Ana and Larry?"

"We aren't going to hurt the children, Mother. We agreed ahead of time we'd talk over problems like this and settle them." Millie continued staring at her.

"I just didn't think Alan would go out with someone else so soon," Cora added. Her voice became uneven, uprooted on the last few words.

"You had no idea about this woman?" Millie asked.

Cora shook her head.

"You never thought there might be someone else?"

"There wasn't. You asked me that when Alan moved."

"Was sex good between you?" Millie asked. "So good you wanted it?"

It was the sort of question her mother would ask. Once get her attention and she plunged straight to the core. The usual approach tossed aside; the proprieties ignored or, more likely, not strongly felt in the first place.

"Sure," Cora answered.

("Oh, that was lovely. That was so good. That was perfect," she tried saying to him once after they had made love in a way particularly glorious for her, that left no part of her at all unsatisfied. "I feel so close to you," she said. "I can't get close enough." She was lolling diagonally across their bed, half droning out her words, almost chanting them, and trailing a finger up his fascinatingly hard thigh. He was like wood beneath the skin. All muscle. He sat beside her on the side of the bed. "Sometimes," she went on, pleased he had not stirred but sat near her on the bed, "sometimes you know what I'd like to do? I'd like to cut you open and crawl inside."

She ran her finger back down his thigh.

"I aim to please," he said, cheerfully, and patted her, patted her lightly, on the shoulder. Then, sitting on the edge of the bed, he turned back to studying his hands.

"I'll need to strengthen these," he said, flexing them, "especially the fingers, before I try climbing Enchanted Rock.")

"It *was* good," Cora said. "Sometimes."

Millie caught the word tagged on, the hesitation. "You did understand each other in that way? You understood about each other's bodies?"

"Obviously we did." Then coloring, her movements and her body clumsy, "Maybe not all the time, but enough. We did."

"Did Alan get a bigger apartment because of this woman?"

"You know Alan better than that. The new apartment is so he can work. He gets interrupted at the University. And his first apartment was too small. And the children couldn't all visit him together."

"Did he plan to move some time ago?"

"Alan was not involved with this woman. He wasn't involved with any woman, before we separated. I know. Don't start blaming him. I was the one who wanted to live apart."

She was aware, she could not help but be aware, that she once again did not use the word "divorce." How deep that yearning for money lay, she thought. At some mesmerizing level. For wherever else she might make her slips, she never did there. "Alan and I *are* being careful about the children. Ana and Larry are doing well. They are not being hurt. You can see for yourself that Nessie isn't."

"And you?" her mother asked. And unexpectedly, for one who rarely touched others, Millie reached across the table and clasped Cora's forearm, half-way between the wrist and elbow, with a grip so firm and unyielding it would set bone. "What about you?"

~~~

Dear Mike,

Of the two lawyers you recommended, I'm going with Gus Morand, of Morand and Albright. A lawyer who plays tennis with me—the guy I first met wall climbing in Utah— and a dean in the business school both told me the same thing you did, that Morand's one of the best for this case. He operates on a contingency basis. Takes a nice hefty one-third of what we get. Plus costs. Ugh. Still, no need for a loan from you. Thanks for the offer.

We will keep Figaller for routine legal work in Riles and as a kind of cover, a shield, as long as it works. We'll move as fast as we can. Obviously the more time without Haskell knowing what we're up to, the less mischief he can cause.

I'll phone you again Sunday. I'm writing Dad to say I can't come up there but I won't say why. I agree with you. Dad can't help us now, so we shouldn't lay our woes on him.

I hate what's happened to him. So must he. He was the toughest warhorse ever. The proverbial rock, once.

Talk to you.

Love,

Alan

PS. No jokes this time.

~~~

DEAR DAD,

I CAN'T FLY OUT THERE TO SEE YOU THIS MONTH. SORRY. WE GOT STUCK WITH A COMPUTER PROBLEM AND I HAVE TO STAY UNTIL WE GET IT SETTLED. NOTHING SERIOUS. IN A WAY LIKE YOUR PROBLEMS OVERHAULING CARS.

THE KIDS ARE SWELL. LARRY IS RECOVERING. HE DID NOT, REPEAT *NOT*, BREAK THAT SHOULDER. YOU AND I HAD A BAD PHONE CONNECTION AND I COULDN'T MAKE MYSELF CLEAR. HE JUST PULLED A MUSCLE. HE WAS LIFTING A PIECE OF OLD MACHINERY IN THE GARAGE. HE'S QUITE A LITTLE BUSINESSMAN. WANTS TO SELL EVERYTHING. YOU'D BE PROUD OF HIM. CORA AND I ARE TAKING GOOD CARE OF HIM AT CORA'S.

KEEP FIT AND WORK ON YOUR EXERCISES.
LARRY WILL HAVE TO DO THAT, SO SET HIM A
GOOD EXAMPLE. WHEN I GET TO SEE YOU I EXPECT
YOU TO GIVE ME A TOUGH GAME AT ARM-WRES-
TLING.

LOVE,

ALAN

VI

"To handle your father," Alan said to her, "we need to hire a whole law firm. Morand tells me it will take a clerk two days to check Haskell's citations."

"You've always said what Haskell secretly wanted was to do what you do—be a scholar and write articles. You should have helped him. Shown him how. Written an outline for him the way you do for some of your slower graduate students and assigned one of your top research assistants to keep him busy. Get him working on something else so he wouldn't be free to devote himself to us."

"You didn't think this was funny before," Alan said.

"I told you my father is considered unbeatable. Now you see why."

Alan laid a sheaf of papers on the desk which had once been Haskell's. He took a chair and swung it around. The study was cooled by the loud uneven efforts of the air conditioner and the perspiration Alan brought in from outside was turning cold on his skin and evaporating. He sat down in front of the desk.

"Don't you want to go on chatting about Haskell's legal abilities?" Cora asked him.

She was slouched in the swivel chair behind the desk, her legs stretched out underneath and crossed idly at the ankles. She was being irritating and knew it.

"I have the estimates of what Figaller is going to charge us for openers," Alan said. "Not to mention Morand's third. Your father's famous abilities are going to cost us a mint."

"So you said on the phone."

"You want to look at the figures?"

"I'll take your word."

Alan opened the folded papers and sheets with rows of figures lay before him. Cora did not bother to sit up in the chair to see them. Her chin was pressed down above the soft space between her collar bones. Her expression was sulky, like Ana's could be.

"What's wrong?" Alan asked her. "I take it from the way you're acting you've been talking to Haskell?"

"Yes."

"And?"

She remained stretched out in the chair, her ankles crossed underneath the desk.

"You didn't call him, did you?" Alan asked. "You better be careful. You're not supposed to say a word to Haskell about this."

"Don't be absurd. Haskell's my father. Anyway, he called me. Millie asked him to call me."

"You didn't tell him about Morand?"

"No, Alan, I didn't tell him about Morand."

"Did he say anything? Has anything changed?"

"He isn't going to change. Ever." She recrossed her ankles. "And you're wrong about his interest being money. He doesn't want us to break up our family."

"Bullshit," Alan said.

She leaned farther back and without getting out of the chair switched down the air conditioner. It gave a startled whir, softened, then wobbled on irregularly at a slower pace.

"He thinks we're bored," Cora said. Her voice was strained, each sentence ending with a guillotine's finality. "He said this was simply a mood. A stage we're passing through. Standard at our age. He said if we were not allowed to rush straight into disaster, that soon enough we'd change our minds. We'd be glad we'd been stopped. Grateful. He said it would be criminal for him not to delay us if he could. Absolutely criminal." Again the chopped-off ending to the final word.

"He wasn't exactly being consoling," Alan said.

"He said he couldn't change what had been done now if he wanted to. It's too late."

"You don't believe that?"

"He believes it."

"Come on, Cora. Haskell was never moved to make statements

about our family and the importance of us staying together until you and I started to sell this house for real money."

"I said that to him," she said. "He told me he had no way to make us listen before. He tried but we, I, wouldn't pay attention."

"Too bad you didn't offer him a share of the profits. That would have got his attention. If you had offered him Morand's third, he would have found a way to change the Commission's decision."

"You're wrong. Haskell would never try to change a ruling to make money."

"You can't stop believing him, can you?"

"I believe him when I know what he is saying is true," Cora said.

By now she had slouched lower in the chair. Alan contemplated her. "I realize he's your father," he said, saying it not provokingly but thoughtfully. "This can't be easy for you. You mentioned he phoned because Millie made him. I take it she's against what he did?"

"She's like all mothers. She wants peace in the family. She never said she disagreed with him. So far as I know, she may feel he did right."

"You mustn't let Haskell get to you this much. He'll immobilize you. All right, so he wasn't enthusiastic when we separated. We never expected him to be. In fact, we were surprised that he was less disturbed than your mother. He said almost nothing. Now he suddenly presents you with this fancy story. And you believe him. I'll tell you what really upset Haskell. He found out the amount of money we were going to make. News about Kincaid must be known to someone like Haskell. He might have made some profit when he sold us the house, but nothing in the same league with what we're going to get."

"Haskell sold us the house at less' than the market rate, Alan. You shouldn't forget that."

"That's what I'm saying. That's what makes him so bitter."

Cora stared at him. Her face showed growing irritation. "Maybe he would mind that. But Haskell would never do anything to hurt us because of petty envy about money."

"It's not a petty sum of money."

She would not answer him.

"I know this was Haskell's house and his lots for decades," Alan said. "How could he not feel that in some way they're still his?"

Cora still would not answer.

Alan continued, "Anyway, we're foolish worrying about motives. Motives don't change what's been done. It doesn't matter whether Haskell acted for good, bad or indifferent reasons. It could have been greed or envy or a conviction that he's helping us, but you and I have to cope with the results. And I promise you one thing, you'll be impressed by Morand. We have an appointment with him early next week."

"I know. You've told me."

Alan folded the sheaf of papers. He made small adjustments in their position on the desk. Cora watched how deftly his fingers, merely with their tips, flicked the slim packet out of alignment and back into alignment again.

"There's something else I have to tell you," he said. "This appeal about the house could take quite a while. Especially to build a strong case against your father."

"How much time?" Cora asked. She sensed significance from Alan's manner and from his steady flicking of the papers.

"Morand brought this up. I didn't ask him. He said to construct a persuasive case might take six months. Or possibly until next spring."

Cora sat up instantly. "I will not stay here until next spring," she said.

"I know you don't want to, Cora. I don't want that, either." He tapped his finger tips firmly on the papers on the desk, emphasizing his words. "But the whole point is to be able to sell the house to Kincaid. It won't be an unnecessary delay. At all. It may be the only way we can get the price we want. That's what Morand said to me. And very earnestly."

"You're like Haskell. You both say I should stay on here for some excellent reason you give me. Only Haskell and my mother didn't stay. And you don't, either. I get stuck with the place."

"All right, then you tell me how we can unload this museum. *You* think of something else we can do with the house."

Cora said, "It's not that. You want to go to France. Instead of staying and taking care of what's happening here, you want to go to France for a term. That's why you drove out here." She knew she was right. She saw it in his face. "You've already talked to DuBost about it, haven't you?"

"Yes. But Morand brought this up first, on his own. He told me we would need time because of your father's claims. Cora, you've told me for years your father's a legal wizard. It shouldn't surprise you it takes time to build a case against his. Or would you rather give up? We could do that. We could quit."

He got out of the chair and walked over to a bookcase and took out a volume, looked at it, slid it back in the case.

"I'd have a chance to work with DuBost on the ideas I started this fall," he said. "I know he's excited about them. He phoned me. I already told you that. There's a chance I could get leave at the Institute."

"You'll get leave," Cora said. "You wouldn't have brought up the possibility if you didn't know you could get leave."

Alan sat down again in the chair across from her. He rested both hands on the desk.

"I can't miss this chance," Alan said. "I'll borrow again. I'll take out another loan. I'd even ask Mike, if I have to, so I can be sure we have enough money to put Larry in St. Andrew's. Larry needs that. We aren't going to miss out on anything, Cora. I promise you. What we'll do is presume we are going to sell the house at Kincaid's price and make use of their money ahead of time. We'll act as if Haskell hadn't pulled his stunt. I guarantee you money for Nessie for a decent nursery school, too. We'll have everything, as if we'd already won."

"How long would you be gone?" she asked, and to herself, inside, yelled out—mistake, mistake, mistake, you idiot. She should not have given an inch. He would absolutely go to France now. Not only that, she would end up urging him to. Watch her, just watch her. She would be saying he must not miss an opportunity to have the great DuBost help him with his work. He must not harm his career. She understood how important it was. That is what she would be telling him. She never learned. Never.

"Six months," Alan was saying. "Absolutely no more than six months. And maybe not that long."

Cora leaned back in the swivel chair, but not tipping the chair from its almost upright position.

"I've been asked to travel for Dawson this summer," she said. "They're trying to raise the endowment."

"This summer?"

"This August," she said. "A tour with the President and a dean and one or two of the senior faculty. We'd meet with alumnae and business people around the state."

"Because of your administrative work?" Alan asked.

"Yes. The President asked me himself."

"I have to be in Paris in August," he said. "I'm reading a paper at the international conference there. The first results of last winter's work. What DuBost called me about."

"We'd have to make arrangements if we're both going away at the same time," Cora said.

He was quiet. The air conditioner growled and hummed lopsidedly.

"That's going to be tricky," he said.

"I suppose it will."

"Your mother'll help out."

"Maybe."

"Didn't she say she would?"

"I haven't asked her."

The air conditioner shifted, caught again, blew in cooler air.

"I've already made my reservations. I'm listed on the program."

She sat in the swivel chair, rocking very slightly back and forth, a striking, full sized, impressive looking woman.

"You're sure then that you're going to go?" Alan asked.

"Yes," Cora said. "Yes, I am."

~~~

The trellis on the back porch of the house ran up two stories as if an earlier owner, who had been a lumberman, in his access to cheap wood and his love of elaboration, could not resist adding on the finely wrought frame structure. There was enough to brace two flights of trumpet creeper or honeysuckle or some other vine which could withstand the heat and sun and give back shade. Nothing had ever grown all the way to the top of the trellis, but the vines did reach almost three feet above the second story porch floor and provided a pleasant hiding place for children.

Nessie kept toys in its shade and often retreated there in the summer when she did not want to play with Ana or Larry any longer. Larry knew to look for her on the second story back porch when he was in charge of her and she had slipped off again. For the porch was a half-obscured place where the three of them all liked to rest.

Ana sat cross-legged on an old cot on that porch, late Sunday afternoon, drinking a coke and badgering Larry because he had not started to paint the downstairs sections of the trellis.

"You're getting away with murder," Ana said. "Mother's already paid you by ordering a new bike wheel for you. You were supposed to do the trellis to pay for the wheel but you haven't. Your arm's not that sore. You fake it, Larry. What would Dad say?"

"He doesn't care if the trellis is painted. They're going to sell this old house. I heard them."

"Not if you keep dismantling it they won't. Maybe it's good you hurt your arm. Now you can't take everything away."

"Where's Norris? You're nicer when Norris is here. You're nicer when Norris hasn't forgotten about you."

She spewed a mouthful of coke on him and he rolled rapidly away from her.

"Jeez, don't throw coke at me. That stuff's sticky. If you spill it all over you, you won't look so great if Norris remembers to come. If he does, if he does, if he does."

"You should go live with Dad. You're becoming impossible at home. You get away with double murder since your arm is supposed to be hurt. You're a mess with that fake arm."

"It is hurt," Larry said, "but there's nothing bad wrong with it. The doctor said I could pitch next summer."

"We won't be here next summer," Ana said. She pulled on the frayed wires of a square wire patch fitted by Haskell or Alan over an old worn slit in the screen. "I'll bet Dad's going to be staying in Paris before next summer," she said.

"How do you know?"

"The same way you found out they're going to sell the house."

It was not the first time they had mentioned selling the house but the words came out louder, and they both turned their heads and looked toward the corner where Nessie lolled on the floor. With her were a small plastic yellow shovel and a worn stuffed rag duck. She was propped against the rounded corner post, breathing slowly, with her eyes half shut and the duck held so loosely in limp grubby fingers it rested for support on her thigh. Probably they should have put her to bed for her nap, as their mother had told them.

"Nessie," Ana said, "you sleeping?"

"Course she is," Larry said. "What do you think, that she's pretending to be asleep so she can listen? She isn't. She's sleeping." But he lowered his voice. "Anyway, she'll find out. Dad will have to tell her. And I bet she gets to go with him to Paris. He likes having her. She's no trouble. She's small and everything. Dad says she can learn anything super fast. She'll probably learn French over there."

They swiveled their heads again to look at her. She was as limp and malleable as before. Earlier they had fixed her lunch. They had a deal. Ana remembered to put the cream cheese out ahead of time to get soft and Larry cut the salad olives in round slices, the way Nessie liked, but kept her from trying to use the knife. Then Nessie got to mush the olives and cream cheese together in a bowl and plop it on her bread. Ana or Larry smoothed it out and cut the sandwich in half but it was usually Larry who cut the halves into smaller triangles. Nessie liked smaller triangles.

Afterwards she had claimed she would not nap and had promptly got up off the bed and followed them downstairs every time they put her on it. They had let her do what she wanted and she followed them around while they argued over what to have for lunch and who would make it and ended with each making something separate to eat. She had followed them all the way back up the stairs and out onto the porch and neither one had picked her up and taken her to bed.

Even being stared at by them, even the break in the sound of their speaking, did not stir her from apparent sleep.

She had scraped her knee immediately after their mother left. Ana had begun to bandage it with band-aids, ignoring Larry's assurance that it would rot, would get infected and rot, go bad and turn into gangrene if Ana did not use gauze and tape and lots more antibiotic salve than that little bit. First aid, like their father would have done, was what was needed, Larry insisted. And their mother would have washed it with something that burned.

"That's great. That's just like you, Larry. Make her cry more. Scare her to death."

"I am not. I'm trying to help." But he had been abashed and offered to fetch the other size band-aids.

Applying an array of band-aids had slowed Nessie's crying because Ana let her peel back the covers of each one and use as many as she liked. By the time the bandaging was finished, Nessie had quit crying entirely but she would not let any of the excess band-aids be removed.

"I guess she didn't scrape herself that deep," Larry said. "It's not bleeding anymore. She's going to yell her head off when the band-aids get taken off. Honest. When Mom gets home, she'll have to rip them off to clean it. She's going to think her whole leg got scraped."

"I'll tell Mother what happened when she comes home, dumbbell," Ana said. "And she'll soak it first, so it won't hurt. Mother knows how to do that."

"It's going to get worse if Mom doesn't come home pretty soon," Larry said. "It'll get all solid and yucky. Mom won't like you leaving it that way. She won't like it you didn't take good care of her."

Larry did not have to move away from his sister. He knew she had finished the coke in her glass.

"You know she won't like it," he continued. "She never likes it if something goes wrong with Nessie. She'll tell Dad on you. Dad'll be mad as anything."

With a blaze of fury Ana said, "I don't care. When they ask me, I'm not going to go with either of them. Not either one."

"Where'll you go?" Larry asked. He was awed. She was all at once immensely older than he. She was grown up.

"I'll know. And it won't be with either of them."

She got up, tall and full-bodied, with marvelous heavy hair, though it was not the color of her mother's. She crossed the porch to Nessie.

"Time for bed," Ana said, reaching for her.

Nessie was damp with sweat and soft, as if she had commenced to melt from sleeping in the heat, for the vines held in the afternoon heat the same way they blocked the sun. They held in also the fragrance of the clambering jasmine Millie had planted below so there was about Nessie a mixture of the odor of sleep and sweat and of being young and of the faint pleasing perfume-like tint of jasmine.

Ana lifted the seemingly boneless body. "Up you go, old Nesso." She held her small sister against her and Nessie's head sank into her neck. "I've got Puddles for you, too. At least Larry can't sell Puddles while we hold onto him. Time for a real nap in your bed. Your blanket's in there waiting. Poor old blankie, mustn't make blankie wait any longer."

She carried Nessie into the house and to her own room.

VII

They met in one of the University's gyms. Haskell had driven into Austin on business and to bring Millie to a horticultural show. Because he and Alan could not time their meeting at a better place, they had agreed to see one another in this enormous building not far from a thruway Haskell would take on his way to pick up Millie.

"You could be sued," Alan said, which instantly produced Haskell's quick sweet smile. "We could sue you," Alan went on.

The sound of many balls being bounced echoed back to them from the large indoor space.

"You sold the house knowing there could be limits on resale rights and you didn't tell us," Alan persisted.

"Sue me after a sale four years ago? Did your lawyer suggest that?" Haskell asked. His smile jumped out again, as if he could not hold it in.

"You knew there would be legal restrictions. Figaller told us you were one of the drafters of the preservation laws."

"I suppose Figaller told you that could constitute misrepresentation, or possibly even fraud on my part? Tell me, what else did Counselor Figaller say?"

Alan stood beside a cold-drink machine. He slid coins in its handy slot, shoving each one into the thin unblinking eye, and waited for the can to come rolling out at the bottom. He wanted Haskell to believe that Figaller was their sole legal advisor and all their attention was centered on this single feeble lawsuit within the family. Nothing else. What Haskell did not know, Alan fervently hoped, could only hurt him.

Alan extended the first can to his father-in-law. Haskell took it in his strangely shaped hand. He had stubby, squared-off fingers, not long enough, they looked, to grasp the can, or ever hold a tennis racquet. But his palm was wide and under a covering of soft, deceptive flesh his hands and forearms were unexpectedly powerful.

In the corner of the gym where they were standing, next to the vending machines, there was a dead spot from the low ceiling overhead. The noise from the higher, open gym room and partitioned sections vibrated around them but did not drown out their voices. They did not need to raise them.

"Not telling a buyer about the possible limits to his ownership, which you knew, *is* misrepresentation," Alan said.

He collected a second can for himself. He popped it open and while he sipped it gazed over the rim at the intelligent indecipherable face of his father-in-law. Without doubt the old boy must have known what use he could make of the house's age. He had stored up that knowledge and used it to prevent the sale. He might believe, he just might believe, this was all they were going to do in response. After all, it was what Haskell would expect of Figaller. He might believe they had thought of nothing else. Certainly not considered an outright charge that the house was not authentic throughout and should not be preserved.

A ball caromed off a board beyond them. There was an instant's silence then a shout followed by bursts of laughter. Without thinking what had brought them together, Haskell and Alan grinned at one another.

"Must be a wild shot," Alan said.

"Sounds like quite a game. Listen to them," Haskell said. "I assume, by the way, Cora agrees with these plans? I admit that startles me. I did not think Cora would bring a suit against her father."

"She's extremely distressed," Alan said. "She hates the whole idea. That's why she asked me to talk to you."

"I see." Haskell paused briefly. When he continued, his deep voice was constrained, as if he were with effort keeping it within bounds while he explained the obvious. "Alan, you and Cora must understand I don't have secret powers. I cannot undo the Commission's action. It's been done. Finished. I tried explaining this to Cora but she won't listen."

"Try me," Alan said. If crafty old Haskell Bosk with his sun-reddened solemn face was ready to believe this was the only way they expected to outwit him, let him explain away.

"No one can change a decision once it has been agreed on by the Commission," Haskell told him. "It's not a matter of some old boys' network, as Cora keeps calling it. Obviously, influence helps. And connections help. But neither is of any use beyond a certain stage. It's the same in your kind of work. A professor can't be unprofessored. Or take your Institute. No one can take control of an Institute like yours once you've been given it."

Bastard, Alan thought. He's found out somehow—how? *how?*—about the problems at the Institute.

"It is hard to bounce a professor today," Alan said. He did not mention his Institute. "Though a professor can bounce around himself. I may take off myself and work in France for a while." That should distract Haskell.

"Not a bad profession you're in," Haskell said. "But back to why we're here, I hope you and Cora will begin to realize that the Preservation Commission made its ruling according to strict city laws. Cora ought to know this. I'm surprised she's being so naive. Think of the experience she's had negotiating between the city and Dawson."

"Cora has great faith in you personally," Alan said. He spoke earnestly, without smiling. "She has complete trust in your good will, especially toward her." Don't overdo this, he thought. "And she hopes to reach some agreement with you privately and not drag the family into a lawsuit. Especially in public."

"I'd be happy to settle in private, any time, but what Cora wants isn't possible. I can't use influence I don't have. As for a lawsuit and all the publicity, that's up to you and Cora. You must use your judgement, as you've both told me repeatedly. I'll be sorry if you insist on suing. I don't invite it. All the same," and he spread his free hand wide, palm up, strong short fingers open and his quick bright smile simply dying to come out, "all the same, you and Cora mustn't expect me to be alarmed by the possibility. Where would I be, if I were frightened by the hint of litigation? What do you think I do for a living?"

His confidence, his light-hearted warning convinced Alan Haskell had no idea what they were planning. In some way he had found out about the trouble at the Institute, but he did not know that he and Cora were consulting Morand. Alan became more certain as Haskell continued talking.

"I'm sorry Cora is upset," his father-in-law was saying, "but that won't last. She'll get over it. The damage you and she were starting would have been permanent. Cora should give me credit for being truly concerned about her. I always am. Her welfare and the children's. Yours, too, Alan. You and Cora have both told me you're getting on marvelously together, coping with everything. Then why break up your home? It's absurd. There is nothing you would gain worth the harm you will do yourselves and your family.

"And I care about Riles. It's a pretty little town and it should be kept that way. With no developers. That's why you and Cora settled there. I've heard you call Riles idyllic. The perfect place to raise children. You didn't even mind the long drive to the University because you got so much in return."

"Are you trying to needle me, Haskell?"

Haskell shrugged, but amiably. He was in better spirits than when they first met. He had that satisfied smooth look, like icing on a cake, of having virtue on his side. Of having prevented himself from being cheated yet having at the same time made it clear that what he was doing was for the benefit of others.

The sounds of balls bouncing around them diminished until there was only the heavy thudding of a basketball being dribbled on the wooden floor. A single voice called out and someone blew a whistle.

"The game must be starting," Alan said and glanced at his watch.

He crushed the empty can in his hand and pushed it through the lid of the missile-shaped trash can. Haskell did the same with his.

"It's always a pleasure to see you, Alan," Haskell said, "although I would rather it not be about lawsuits. Why don't we play tennis again one day? On a court, I mean."

~~~

DEAR DAD,

MIKE TOLD ME YOU FELL. FOR GOD'S SAKES, DO WHAT THE ATTENDANTS SAY EVEN IF YOU DON'T LIKE THEM. USE THAT WALKER. THERE'S NO RISK WITH A WALKER SO LEARN HOW. LISTEN TO THE PHYSICAL THERAPISTS AND LET THEM TEACH YOU. SOME THINGS YOU HAVE TO BE TAUGHT. THIS IS ONE.

NEXT MONTH CORA WILL TRAVEL TO RAISE MONEY FOR DAWSON. SHE WILL BE ONE OF A SMALL GROUP GOING WITH THE PRESIDENT. THIS IS A BIG STEP FORWARD FOR HER. SHE IS GOOD AT MEETING WITH BUSINESS AND FANCY SOCIETY PEO-PLE. FAR BETTER THAN I AM.

I'M UP TO MY EARS IN WORK FOR THE INTERNA-TIONAL CONFERENCE IN FRANCE, BUT I WILL COME SEE YOU BEFORE I GO.

WHAT MIKE SAYS ABOUT YOU WORRIES ME. DON'T GET DEPRESSED. THERE'S NO REASON FOR YOU TO BE DEPRESSED.

THERE ARE NO MONEY PROBLEMS. NONE. FOR-GET MONEY.

I EXPECT TO SEE YOU USING THAT WALKER
WHEN I COME. THAT WILL RAISE YOUR SPIRITS.
WHEN YOUR SPIRITS ARE RAISED, MY SPIRITS ARE
RAISED, TOO. I MEAN IT, DAD.

I WILL BRING YOU AN EXTRA COPY OF MY NEW
ARTICLE. THIS IS THE BIG ONE I AM GOING TO GIVE
IN FRANCE. SOMEONE AROUND YOU MAY KNOW
FRENCH. ANYWAY, IT'S A LONG ARTICLE AND YOU
CAN SHOW IT TO EVERYBODY. *SO CHEER UP.*

LOVE,

ALAN

~~~

For two days that week Cora did not go to Dawson. Larry had flu. Both mornings Cora arranged for someone else to teach her classes. The second day she made up a bed for Larry downstairs on the living room couch. She put her papers on the table next door in the dining room, so she could hear if he needed her.

The papers were not about the courses she was teaching nor connected to Dawson nor were they any of the many revisions she had written of that still unpublished second paper from her dissertation. Scattered on the dining room table were copies of the town's zoning laws and names of companies and individuals who very likely would cooperate in an effort to diversify the zoning laws. And a copy, too, of the regulations governing Riles' historical landmark sites.

She had explained to Alan yesterday, when he came to see how Larry was, that getting a zoning change was not going to be easy. He had chided her for doing Kincaid's work for them. Too many requests for similar changes failed, she had told him. She had seen them fail. She had begun to realize what was important watching real estate settlements between Dawson and Riles. To persuade the city council and important people in the community, Kincaid was going to need all the local and personal information they could get. She had started accumulating some.

"Show me," Alan had said, moving to her side of the desk in her study.

He had looked at her list of people and companies in Riles and turned the pages of her notes on their backgrounds.

You can't always convince them just by talking about profits, Cora explained. She had learned that when Dawson failed to get a variance to convert the old Cater home to a dormitory. The opposition always knows you are doing it for profit and expects you to claim that everyone else will benefit, too. You need something stronger. Options they can't resist. Kincaid and Co. should offer inexpensive room for public art or a library or a community theater in their plans for the shopping mall. But most of all, offer something for children. Good things for children were impossible to vote against. Like New York City giving up an invaluable area of Central Park for a children's zoo. Nothing was better than children. Kincaid should propose special low cost space for a day care center for the community's children.

"That's brilliant," Alan had said. "Damn, you're good."

The words, the hard concentrated stare—she might have been DuBost, she might have been Lehrman—had formed a solid memory Cora took out at will, held, turned over and over in her mind.

Don't get too smug, she cautioned herself, and forced her attention to her papers. She organized them in piles on the long table. Remember, nothing's been won yet. The look on her face did not reflect her wary thoughts.

There was a noise from the living room. Just a cough, she thought. She waited. At least his fever had broken. Not all gone, but lowered. When she had settled him on the couch, he still had that dark earth smell of flu and fever, but his temperature was lower. No longer roasting. And he was fretful, always a sign of getting better. He had been ill too much this summer. No, not really. The shoulder didn't count. The shoulder was an accident. There had been too many accidents. Nonsense, all young boys had accidents, especially in the summer.

Larry called out more loudly. Cora went into the living room.

He had pulled himself up against the arm of the couch and was tangled in the sheet and wide awake. His eyes were shimmering, mirage-like, from the remaining touch of fever.

He needed something to drink, he told her. He twisted restlessly, his legs wrapping more tightly in the sheet. He was dying of thirst, he said. She hadn't left enough apple juice. And why couldn't he have a fan? He wouldn't get in front of any dumb draft if she got him a fan. He knew better than that.

His fretfulness and the fact that he looked so much younger than his age touched her. She bent to feel his forehead and he held his head solemnly still under her touch.

"Not nearly as bad as yesterday," she said with the firm cheerfulness that seems obligatory when caring for sick children. "I'll get you something to drink and sponge you off. You'll feel better, without a fan."

She brought another glass of apple juice and a pan of lukewarm water with a washcloth. A large light towel was tucked under her arm.

Larry moved to make room for her and she settled on the couch beside him. She squeezed the washcloth half dry and dampened his face and neck and then an arm and hand. She let the water evaporate on his skin to cool him, covering his arm with the lightweight towel so he would not get chilled. He shivered once but said immediately he felt better, he liked it. She should not stop. And he held out his other arm to her, telling her to be careful. This was his hurt shoulder.

"I know, honey," Cora said. "Did you hurt it more pulling Nessie and her friend in your cart?"

"That didn't hurt. Kyle was pulling, too. Anyway, they aren't heavy."

"They had a marvelous time. Now Nessie says she wants a cart to pull her duck."

Larry lay more quietly on the couch as she sponged him off. She wiped his arm and hand and each finger, one by one. His fingers were slack and unresisting. The middle one had a jagged nail. The knuckles were thick ridges, bony bulges blooming on each thin finger.

His eyes had slid half shut, lizard-like above lightly flushed cheeks. His face was beginning, just beginning, to look older and showed hints of Alan's lovely raised cheekbones. He lay very still.

("Be still," Alan whispered above Larry's ear, his face against Larry's, both profiles turned toward her. "Be very still."

They were camping. It had rained the night before and the early morning sunlight, caught in the minute drops of water glistening on each pine needle, glinted back at them like endless fragments of the sun. "That's a nut-hatch," Alan was saying softly. "Don't move. See?"

"It has almost no tail," Alan whispered, "and a tiny shallow brain-pan. They're the low IQs, with long beaks to make up for no brains. Watch. They run right straight down trees headfirst. Lickety-split. There he goes, straight down. See him?"

He was holding Larry on his lap so they would have the same view but he raised his eyes and looked over his son to Cora. This early, in the fresh fall light, her skin gleamed against her red-brown hair. She sensed the pause in his monologue, felt his gaze and turned her eyes. Like him she kept her head still so she would not startle the birds. She did not smile yet he smiled back at her. Very carefully, without notice-able movement, he turned his head just slightly more toward her and shaped a kiss to her with his lips. "Fun?" he asked Larry softly, while over his son's head he looked at Cora deliberately, at her stomach, fuller, as they both well knew, than showed beneath her coat and soon to grow even fuller, looked lower yet, then back up, lingering at her stomach, and to her eyes again.

"I love it," Larry whispered, his light child's voice made thicker, muffled with whispering, not seeing his father's face or the direction of his father's gaze, only hearing his voice. "I'll tell Ana I loved all of it."

Still with no marked movement, his eyes fastened on Cora while he held his son, Alan said, "Mmm, me too, love all of it. All of it."

"Yeah," his son murmured fervently, "and watching birds is great."

"Oh yes," Alan said, softly, softly, his eyes shining at Cora. "Watching's sometimes best."

Without a real movement, with only a suggestion of movement, Cora shook her head at him. Not fair, she meant. Don't tease. Not here, now. Not fair. But her lips trembled like those seemingly endless beads of rain holding slivers of the sun, and she broke, irresistibly, into a grin.

Alan jerked his head back in triumph, and the nut-hatch and four juncos, wearing their executioners' hoods, so Alan had described them to Larry, burst into the air and out of sight.

"You moved," Larry accused. "Daddy, why'd you move?")

"You'll feel better, honey," Cora said. "When Ana comes home I'll ask her to make something special for you while I get Nessie. Ana's an expert at concocting cool drinks."

"Ana's mad at you," Larry said, opening his eyes. "She's mad at you and Dad both." He tried to alter his position but he was caught by the sheet on which Cora was sitting. She raised up enough so he could shift towards her.

"She's really mad. Honest, Mom."

Cora slipped the cloth into the water.

"Don't you want to know why?"

"Not particularly," Cora said. "People get mad sometimes. I'm mad at Haskell."

"Are you?" Larry pulled himself higher. His eyes shimmered with interest as well as fever. "How come? How come you're mad at Haskell?"

Cora wiped his face with the cloth and, since he was more erect, wiped the back of his neck and then began on the arm and hand nearest to her.

"You're not mad for real?"

"Yes. For real."

This time she wrung the cloth dry, folded it over the edge of the pan and covered Larry's dampened arm with the towel.

"Don't go yet," Larry said. "Tell me why you're mad. It's because of the house, isn't it?"

He was too restless to wait for her to answer. He answered himself,

"It is the house. You and Dad are going to sell it. We all know you're going to sell it."

"Who's 'we all'?"

"Ana and I."

"You both know, do you?"

"We don't care. We don't like it here, either. We don't like the house any more than you like it."

"You liked it when you were little," Cora said, knowing perfectly well she was not being fair, knowing she would not defend the house herself, the opposite in fact, attack it, no doubt. "You loved it," she told him.

Larry jabbed one leg uneasily until the knee poked sharply against the sheet. "Well you and Dad sell it anyway so you'll get a ton of money. Then Dad can go to France and everything."

Cora pulled the sheet out for him and he inched up higher.

"Anyway the house is too big," he said. "And it's old. It leaks all over."

"You're still running a little fever, Larry. It's time you had more aspirin."

She left to get it and when she returned Larry was sitting upright with his back braced against the arm of the couch.

"Don't feel bad, Mom. You don't feel bad, do you?" He waited. "Is it because you're mad at Haskell you're going to sell his house? Is that why you and Dad didn't tell us?"

"Don't be silly. Grown-ups don't act like that. We don't need a big house anymore. And we didn't need to tell you, did we? You found out by yourselves. Here." She gave him the two tablets and water. "Take these. Then lie back down and quit talking so much. You're only making yourself worse."

She watched while he took the aspirin, one by one. He took pills the way Alan did, tossing his head way back to gulp them down. He tipped the glass higher at the end to finish the water. Watching his thin neck swallowing, the muscles working up and down along each long side, her heart slid loose.

She put her hand on his knee, noticing automatically, not planning to notice, but noticing all the same, that he was cooler than yesterday.

"Honey, please try to rest. You'll be practically well tomorrow." She took the glass. "Maybe you could have Kyle over then."

"Why don't you stay in here, Mom? I won't bother you."

"I have to work at the dining room table. I need to spread out all my papers."

"You could set up a bridge table here."

"Not big enough. Play your tapes, honey."

"I still ache, Mom. I ache everywhere."

"Quit talking then and give the aspirin a chance. It'll help you sleep. Sleep's the best thing for you. I know it's rotten having flu in the summer. You have to help yourself get well. Lie back down." She pressed her hand on his unhurt shoulder and slid him down on the couch.

Almost prone except for his head, which rested on the pillows, his eyes did not shut. They were fixed on her.

"Come on, play a tape, Larry."

"Are you mad because Grammer and Haskell will get money when you sell the house?"

"Why should they get money? They sold the house to us. You know that."

"But they owned it for years and years and they took care of it all the time. Haskell put up new panels last year and he's fixing the roof'n all. And what about Grammer's gardens? You'll be selling Grammer's gardens."

She knew what he was doing. He was trying to keep her. He did not feel well. He was miserable in those tiresome aggravating last days of flu, not really ill but not well, either, only miserable. She did not care. She could not let him go uncorrected. She could not let him continue believing what he had said.

"When you sell something you sell all your rights in it. Your father and I own this house. It doesn't matter how long anyone else owned it or what they did about it or how much they liked it. We can do anything we want with it. That's what owning means, Larry."

He did not nod an acceptance of her statements. He was not convinced. He turned uneasily on the couch—which admittedly was Grammer's and Haskell's and had been bought, well, transferred, to be accurate, with the house along with about half or more of the furniture in it, and which the children had grown up knowing, and were familiar with, and had always been told belonged to their grandmother and grandfather, only now it belonged to their parents.

"It's not as if Grammer and Haskell need money," Cora went on. "If they did, we would help. You know we would. We'd help whether or not we ever sold the house. But they don't need money. And we have to take care of ourselves and manage all our obligations."

"I know. I know, I know. They don't have kids anymore. Kids cost a fortune, every time you turn around." He jerked at the sheet until he freed one foot. "I hope you get tons of money from the house. Tons. And there's lots of things in here you could get money for, too. You could get a hundred dollars for the big air conditioner. The one in your study. You know, what used to be Haskell's study. It would take two men to ease it out the window but you could maybe get more, maybe even get two hundred for it. The guy at Messeldene's told me."

"Larry, you're talking nonsense, just to talk. I'm not going to argue with you anymore, you're getting too wound up. Lie back and listen to a tape, like I told you. I have to work."

She tucked the sheet in around him, making sure both feet were covered. Then she bent to take away the pan of water and the towel.

"You know that friend of Dad's?" Larry said. "The lady who plays the French horn?"

Cora straightened.

"I know her name," Larry said.

"Good," Cora said. She had stood straight up leaving the pan on the floor but holding the lightweight towel in her hand. "At your age you should learn the names of adults you meet. That shows you've learned some manners."

"Her name's Meredith," Larry said.

"Meredith," Cora said. "Meredith is a lovely name. She must be a lovely person if your father likes her. The next thing you need to learn, Larry, since you're becoming so grown up, is what you shouldn't talk about. You shouldn't talk about things that hurt people."

He flushed, more than earlier, more than all the time he had a high fever.

Overkill, she thought. God, overkill. Still clasping the towel fruitlessly for there was nothing she could do with it. She placed her free hand on his arm. Cooler, his arm was cooler from being sponged off.

"Honey, if your father ever wants to tell me something about his life, he'll tell me. You don't have to."

"But he always asks about you," Larry said. "He doesn't ask flat out or anything, but he wants to know. Every time. So I tell him."

"Tell him what?"

"That you aren't going out with anyone," Larry said.

VIII

Cora shot out of the comfortable chair, she who was usually languid physically, who with her large-boned frame and swelling curve of hips could sit still as a sculpture. Who had never been one to stir instantly if a child called or a car turned in their driveway. Alan did that. Now she moved impulsively in the lawyer's office, striding past an oil painting and windows facing toward the University tower and back to the wide leather chair which she tapped sharply along its back before she sat down in the seat.

"I can't believe what I'm hearing," she said. "You should understand right now that even if we were impressed by what we heard about you and have followed your advice this far, we wouldn't consider inventing some story against my father. We're not going to lie."

"I would not dream of asking you to, Dr. Belknap," Morand said. Cora was always exactly "Dr. Belknap" in his limpid tones. He had a distinct voice, smooth, pleasing, a musical silver sound like a lighter echo of the tower bells. "Nor would I expect any such act from the Professor." He inclined his head toward Alan.

Alan sat at the other side of the lawyer's desk.

"I am speaking solely of a matter of emphasis, Dr. Belknap. That's all. Emphasis." He glanced quickly at Alan and continued. "A matter of emphasis which you may recall if you allow yourselves, without advance prejudice, to remember what you think you have forgotten."

Cora waited, her position in the chair unrelaxed.

The lawyer proceeded, speaking carefully, his voice bathing the words in exquisite tones. "Members of commissions which control historical preservation operate much as members serving on local zoning boards do. When a zoning variance or an appeal from a current restriction is sought, the boards or commissions take into account the background of the case. Now, these groups are almost always made up of sensible men and women, like yourself, Dr. Belknap. They know change is inevitable. Their prime function is to guide change in directions that comply with the wishes and the laws of the community. Yet still allow progress. Even your father, Dr. Belknap, has spoken out for progress. I have heard him."

"So," Morand took a pencil from his desk to bolster his point, "when a formal request for any change is made, the total validity of the argument is considered. Also, and this is what I have been trying to say, the case against a change is reviewed. When we petition the zoning board, I believe we will do well. Not only because development in Riles is wanted and the developers will join with us, but because of the imagination and effort you put into planning the appeal, Dr. Belknap. Your idea of incorporating a community center for children in any development would give us a powerful case. In my opinion, overwhelming."

"That's not what you just said," Cora said.

Like a pianist, the lawyer raised his hands, the pencil, too, almost level with his face, then let his hands descend gently to the desk. "Indeed," he said. "Indeed. But I am trying to make clear to you that your case has two distinct parts. Combined into one in your mind, perhaps, but separate in law. The appeal for a zoning variance is one part and there we should do well. The other part, the other factor, I must now persuade you and Professor Belknap to consider."

"Does the other factor involve making up stories about my father?" Cora asked.

"As I was saying," Morand began, neither rattled nor rushed, his voice as pleasing as it was before Cora interrupted him, "in addition to zoning restrictions, there are constraints on the sale of your house and lots because the house has been designated a historic landmark. I am obliged to tell you, Dr. Belknap, that a variance in the over-all zoning laws could be granted for blocks around while your and Professor Belknap's house is not freed because of the claim of historic significance."

"So we're supposed to counter this by saying not all of the house is old, that my father convinced them by a fraud and we know this because he told us privately?"

"No, no, Dr. Belknap."

"That would be lying," Cora said. "Neither of us is going to lie."

"I sympathize. I sympathize completely," Morand said. He once again looked at Alan who had pressed himself back in his chair, one hand braced against the arm, staring at Cora.

"I respect your feelings," Morand said, "but I am not suggesting what you think. Let me explain the legal background more fully. Naturally historical commissions want to preserve older structures. That is what they exist to do. At the same time, when the owner of a building seeks a release, as you and Professor Belknap will be doing, all the arguments opposing release must be examined. The reason for this is because in some cases the original assignment to historic status was not justified. Lifting the classification corrects an unwarranted decision."

"Please, wait," he broke in to constrain Cora's growing impatience, "let me continue. Remember status as a historic landmark entails special benefits. First, there are enormous tax advantages. Even no property tax. Second, access to low, or possibly no interest money for care, maintenance, and extensive repairs and improvements so long as they are done in the approved style. These benefits cost money and that money comes out of state and local taxes. For that reason, Dr. Belknap, it is in the public interest to reevaluate these claims."

Cora sighed but the lawyer, with unaltered patience, with the same ease, continued, "Bear with me just a trifle longer, Dr. Belknap, please. Only a trifle longer. The point I am making is that some designations as historic landmarks should, in plain justice, be lifted. For example, you said finding out the house had been established as such a landmark shocked you. Why? You lived in the house all your life. I suggest that with reflection you, or the Professor, or both of you will recall conversations which indicate the house is not, in fact, a historic one. Take the improvements which have been made during the years your father owned it. Was there ever any discussion about how well those changes fit with the original style of the house? Did Mr. Bosk take care that all changes conformed to the town's requirements for its historic buildings? Did he talk to you about that?"

"I hate what we're doing," Cora said. "This is contemptible."

Morand took out a handkerchief and touched it to his nose. He had a long narrow face, somewhat equine, and pale blond hair. With the white handkerchief held against his nose, he had the look of one of those old silent movie characters seen in frames of shivering, shaky whiteness. He had a courteous way, too, of waiting for a disagreeable comment to settle while he showed no signs of irritation, merely a polite pause, his cool eyes uninvolved until he felt it time to speak again.

"Perhaps," he began, as pleasantly as before, "when your father sold the property he did say, at one time or another, joking perhaps in the way one might in the bosom of one's family, that you were making a sound economic move because the house was such a good investment?"

"He did," Alan said. "He said exactly that."

"Not because he expected us to sell the house to any developers," Cora answered.

"The fact is Haskell told us we were making a wise investment," Alan said.

"No," Cora said to him, "he meant we would not have to buy an expensive house in the city. You know what Austin prices are. You know how much money we had. Or didn't have. Besides, we wanted to raise the children in a small town. Believe it or not, at one time that was what we wanted."

"Are you sure your father meant nothing other than that, Dr. Belknap?" the lawyer asked, pulling her back to the subject of the house. "And let me point out that this conversation is what I refer to as freeing your minds so you can be more accurate in what you recall. That is exactly what I want you to do. To remember if your father said anything further to you, or your husband, about the profit you might make from the house? A profit not just by saving money because you did not buy in Austin, but from the rising value of property in Riles? Was there happy speculation, at times, about the price the home might fetch for you and Professor Belknap in the future?"

"I see what you're getting at," Cora said. "You want us to say my father conspired against us only after we thought of selling the house on our own. That he never thought it was a historic site before. So when he arranged to have these restrictions slapped on, he did it on fraudulent grounds."

"Insufficient grounds," Morand said, "merely insufficient grounds. That is entirely different. It is not fraud."

"Haskell did tell us our money would grow when we bought the house," Alan said to her, "and he meant it. Why else did he have us sign a repurchase agreement with him and the bank in case we couldn't meet the mortgage payments?"

"Did he do that?" Morand asked, and made a note with his pencil.

"He did it for the children's protection," Cora protested. "So the children would always have a home."

"You're unbelievable," Alan said. He spoke directly to her. "There are times you see your father clearly and others when you can't understand the first thing about him. I hope to hell you're going to like it when we can't sell this house."

"Dr. Belknap," the lawyer interrupted, his voice still calm and unhurried, as silvery sounding as when they began, "perhaps if I may, if you'll let me. Repurchase agreements are common. They can be done for security for children of the next generation, certainly. Especially in cases where property has great potential value. I wonder if you can recall your father ever talking about the inevitable growth in value of your home because this entire area was bound to develop?"

"No," Cora said.

"Yes," Alan said, at the same time.

They both stopped.

"Often. Many times," Alan said. "And he never mentioned any constraints on selling the house. That's why we were shocked. So far as we knew there would be no problem."

"This *is* contemptible," Cora said. "It's despicable. Because Haskell never mentioned something in the quiet bosom of the family, as Mr. Morand calls it, now we'll report that as proof there were no real grounds and he committed fraud."

"Not fraud," Morand said, in his lovely voice, "insufficient evidence."

"Why do you think he kept all those records on the house?" Alan asked her, raising his voice to her. "He did it to keep track of the appreciation."

"Haskell keeps records of everything. He always has. And how do you know the developers will come to Riles, anyway?"

"How do you know they won't?" Alan asked. "You believed it enough to put in all that effort. You bring this up now as a diversion, because you don't want us to say openly what Haskell's done."

"Dr. Belknap," rang the soothing silver tones of the lawyer, "we can't give you guarantees about the developers, obviously. Obviously. But Professor Belknap is correct, there have been strong indications. Close to guarantees. And since, if I may put it bluntly, I work on a contingency basis, I would not myself be involved if I were not confident Kincaid intended to develop in Riles."

But Alan was on his feet. He had pushed back his chair.

"We might as well stop," he said. "We're not going to get a rational agreement now. I better go on back to the Institute." Openly he examined his watch. "I can't waste any more time."

He and Cora went out of the office building together. Together they walked toward their old car, parked in front of the building, although they had arrived separately.

"I wasn't just creating a diversion," Cora said.

"Have you heard something definite at Dawson, then? Or from that hot-shot Poinsett?"

"No...it's not...I didn't. But I'm just not sure."

The sun was blazing on them. Alan squinted against the hard glare to see her. "I can understand that," he said. "You don't feel sure because you have to confront Haskell so strongly."

"Haskell told me in the beginning that fighting over the house would change us," Cora said.

"You bet it will," Alan said, "it will make us rich."

"While we tear each other apart? Like pigs at the trough? And that lawyer gleefully egging us on because that's how he gets his cut?"

"You can look at it that way if you insist, Cora. But the only reason we're talking to Morand is because of your father. Haskell can advise you to be holy and avoid lawyers and meanwhile he acts as his own lawyer. We didn't start using legal tactics. Haskell did. You should have seen him telling me why he had a right to block us. He was no doting father then."

"We aren't so full of virtue either. We sneak around hiding the fact we plan to divorce. We're afraid we might lose that precious money. Neither of us said a word to our fancy new lawyer about divorcing. That's how honest and aboveboard we are."

Alan turned from her.

"Shit," he exclaimed, because of her and because he had grabbed hold of the blistering door handle. He yanked his hand back and flipped it in the air. More carefully he unlocked the old car and pulled the door wide. The baked air burst out at them.

"What's evidently impossible for you to do," he said, rubbing his palm, "what's utterly impossible is to take that one simple step to get what is yours. Honest to God, I don't understand you. Your reasons are specious. It's perfectly all right to bring an honest lawsuit. It's all right to defend your property against your father if your father is wrong. And you don't have to be some kind of saint to do it, either. I don't know how long this mess will drag on with the house bound up in restrictions like a mummy, but Kincaid isn't going to wait forever. They will go to someone else, like you say. We're going to lose and it won't be because of Haskell's legal genius you're so proud of or because we did something stupid. We'll lose because for some unknown reason which you can't even explain you find it too hard, you find it plain impossible, to do what anyone else would do without thinking twice."

Cora crossed in front of him and put her briefcase, with the copies of her plans, all the papers she had drafted for the campaign to win a zoning change, into the car. She did not get in. She rolled the window down, closed the door and stayed on the sidewalk.

(What was too hard, what seemed impossible, what the 1929 edition of the Encyclopaedia Britannica, the one jammed in behind the couch in the airy living room in their first nice apartment, what that Encyclopaedia said humans, the talking species, found themselves unable to say and what she could not, in the end, accomplish was to tell him exactly what it was she wanted him to do to her. So that she would be filled, expanded, exploded with pleasure. Even away from him she could not frame the words in her mind, yet she could imagine what the movements had to be, could feel them, almost, could sense her body hum beneath them as they were made—the exact perfect slow caressing starting gently here, yes, then moving there, too, there, that way, exactly that way, over and over, slowly, here and right there with the sensations from the movements, the slow stroking, echoing throughout her body, and she knowing all the while it would not be stopped but would continue, and continue, become unbearable and endless with that same slow relentless rhythm which would not alter, would not cease but go on and on and turn her, she imagined, yes she could imagine perfectly, turn her wild, make her sweat, make her sodden, sodden, everywhere, from the struggle and the pleasure as her body responded helplessly, witlessly, ceaselessly, no will left except for this one thing and her mind finally, at last, at last, like her eyes, gone blank and gaping and lost. Exploding.

If she could say to him, not there but here. This way, not that way. Slower, slower. If she could say it that clearly and exactly to him.

She had tried. *By God she had tried.* No one could say she had not tried. There were statements, pronouncements actually, she had made by her body's enthusiastic response, exaggerated sometimes, blatant, when his movements were right. And when those were not noticed or remembered, she had openly muttered words of liking this or that. Saying, "good, good." And, "that is *so good*." Then being absolutely silent, deathless, her body still, fled, gone, in reaction to movements he made which did not make her whole being hum.

He heard her. How could he not hear? He was smart. She heard him when he told her in that way. Once she had tried guiding his hand, his body, showing the right placings, instructing him in the right rhythm. He did not care enough to remember. He did not adopt what she had shown him, many times, with her body, her few words and the rare instances when she had indicated to him precisely what was most pleasing to her.

You could blow me apart, she would think. Thinking it angrily, for he had been starting to do that, then he shifted, stopped, changed pace, leaving her with her mind and body thrown completely out of what had begun exquisitely and left raging instead. Raging—go back to what you were doing. Can't you tell what you could do to me every time if you only kept on the right way? You could blow me apart.

There were times when she did come. Many of them. Even gorgeously, full blown and slow and mounting, prolonged to the final last long bursting apart. Times so good the feelings were a long time subsiding and were savored afterward in the languid humming all through her. And sometimes, a few times, she came more than once. She had. Only she was never certain how it would be. *He* came every time, no matter what she did. So why not tell him what she needed?

Because sometimes she was the one at fault. She knew. At some point, even far along in the pleasure building in her, all on its own, like an oven light shut off, the humming and responses in her body stopped and would not continue.

Not a good enough reason. What of the many times the shift, the shutting off, came from him? Because she could not imagine the words. Like the Encyclopaedia said. And when say them? At breakfast? Over their lunch? Before going to bed? A long disquisition ahead of time from her on her side of their joint act? She could hear his answer: Why did you wait all these years to tell me? Did you fake it before? What else have you lied about?

"Hmmmm," she murmured audibly. She wished she could purr. Wished there were a sound that distinct and recognizable so she could signal to him that now what he was doing was exactly right. "Hmmmmm," she murmured, into his neck below his jaw.

She loved the line of Alan's jaw, the skin beneath the bone there. A softer skin, a lovely welcoming burrow for her face and mouth. "Hmmmmm," murmuring the sound louder, near his ear. He *must* hear her, she knew he must, for what he was doing was so absolutely right. So right she could not believe he did not know.

No! Not right. He had changed. Not right at all.

Say. You must say, she told herself.

She did not say.

Instead she moved. Moved and lay dead still in such an obvious way he could not help but notice. He must notice this.

He did not notice.

She opened her eyes. She could see his face. His eyes were closed. He did not see that she had opened hers.

Say. Say.

He was so absorbed. She did not speak. His eyelids were shut, were closed and smooth. Not entirely smooth, for a line, a crease, ran horizontally across the center of each lid like a single lip. Closed eyelids and he absorbed behind them. He was getting lost. She knew. Knew by his breathing, by the nature of his body's movements and the sounds he made. So how could he not notice she was not?

And how could she tell him with his lids so concentrated and closed and behind them, she was sure, going farther and farther away? Rapt.

SAY IT!

She murmured noticeably, more loudly, in a questioning, urgent tone against his cheek. He could not help but hear. Yet he altered nothing, did not open an eye, and the line, the single lip across each lid, was undisturbed.

She questioned again, strongly, "Alhmmm?" Nothing. He was gone, striving, with closed lids.

Cora moved the position of her body. She arranged herself in ways she hoped would be good for her. He did not seem to notice. She altered the position of one hip and that side of her body, down there. She pressed her other leg further apart, opening it more. Not exactly right. She shifted again. Angled further out, more open, there. Maybe. Yes, maybe. Close. Close. Maybe with absolute attention on what she wanted there and if she did not switch off inside and if he would this time not alter anything except perhaps to move better and in better rhythm and not misalign himself with her again and if she focused firmly, totally only on this—nice, very nice—then maybe even though it was not exactly right but nice—nice—concentrate, just concentrate— oh nice—maybe she could get lost, too. Maybe she just might—nice nice nice—might get there, too. Maybe she could catch up with him.)

"Of course I can explain," Cora said to him. "Do *you* want to lie and say Haskell committed a deliberate fraud? We don't know he did, Alan. The truth is—we don't know."

"You're so blinded by a lawyer daring to question Haskell's legal tactics you can't think straight. You go into an emotional explosion. I told you from the beginning you mustn't let Haskell paralyze you. If you want this money, Cora, if you really do want it, then we have to fight for it just as if we were an institution, like Dawson. No illegalities and no lies, and no sentimentality. Haskell doesn't have any, why should we cripple ourselves?"

He had made her uncertain. Not turned around. Not ready to march straight back into Morand's office and agree, but he had made her uncertain. He could tell.

"You keep saying we'll charge Haskell with fraud," he went on. "That's your word. Morand never used it."

"He meant it."

"He said insufficient evidence. Nothing else. He probably struck you as some kind of gargoyle of a man. A clever lawyer plotting a case against your father. So you reacted like a whirlwind. It's a wonder you didn't blow him out of his office. That's the way you would behave, Cora. It's like you. But it's not clear thinking."

"He's too slick. I don't like him."

"I know you don't. How could you like him when you had to sit there and listen to him work out a case against your father?"

"Do you think that's why?" She asked Alan hopefully, and wistfully, asked him as if she did not already know what his answer would be, as if his answer could take away all her uncertainty.

He said instantly, immediately, "Absolutely. No question. No one likes seeing a parent put in a vulnerable position. Especially if you feel you're contributing to it."

"It wasn't fraud, what Haskell did."

"Of course it wasn't. No one says it was fraud. All we need to show is insufficient evidence. That's all Morand needs to win our case."

"You'd do it, if you were me, wouldn't you?"

But Alan surprised her. "I don't know," he told her. "You're incredibly durable, Cora. I'm not sure I would be. No one can predict ahead of time. I've never had a conflict that pitted me against my father, or Mike."

He was serious. He was not being superior behind a show of sympathy. He was grateful he did not have her problem.

"You believe we ought to do what Morand says, though, don't you?"

Alan concentrated on her, bringing every force he could to bear upon her until he seemed, almost, to be frowning at her. "I know you hate it," he said. "It isn't going to be easy for you. But you're an extremely intelligent woman, Cora. You know how to separate emotion from facts."

He could see from her face, somewhat loosened, somewhat softened where the most rooted lines had been, that he had won.

"I get back from my trip before you do," Cora said. "Do you want me to make another appointment for us with Morand?"

"You have too much to do already," Alan said. "I'll call Morand from my office. I'll tell him to speed up our case, that you don't want to spend extra time in the house because of your work. Look, if it will make things go faster, I won't go to France more than once this year. I'll tell Morand that. I'll stay here until our case is settled."

Neither of them moved to separate from each other. Cora reached in to put her handbag on the front seat of the car and then opened the door, but only ajar, not wide enough to get in. She lingered by the car. In the brilliant mid-afternoon sun her skin had changed color. A gleaming, rosy quality burned just below its surface. Her lips were moist. She must have run her tongue over them. More than once. Probably because of the heat.

"Are you seeing anyone?" Alan asked her.

IX

The plans were simple but the details made them complex. Cora would travel in the state for a week with Dawson's President and others from the college. Alan was to fly to see his father on the way to the international linguistics conference in Paris. He would return to France later, in the fall, but only, he promised Cora, if Morand agreed his going would in no way delay their case.

During the week Alan and Cora would both be gone. Ana was to stay in town with a friend, but not over the weekend. The parents might be out and, in any case, Cora was unwilling to leave Ana with another family on a weekend. She might see too much of Norris. Ana would have to spend that time, including Friday night, at her grandmother's.

Larry, on the other hand, could stay with his best friend in town for the weekend, including Friday night, but not during the week. His friend's parents both worked and refused to have two boys that age loose and on their own during the week. Larry would stay with his grandparents during the week, but could go into town for the weekend, starting Friday afternoon.

Nessie, of course, would be with her grandmother all the time. Except Saturday. Saturday she had been asked to a birthday party. The party was only two blocks from her home in town, but she would not be in town. She would be at her grandparents'. And Millie did not drive. Cora was adamant that Haskell not be asked to drive her children anywhere. If he chose to, if he offered because he wanted to drive them, that was his decision. But she was not going to ask him or make any arrangements which depended on his good will or made casual use of Ramón's time. Instead, Cora left money for a taxi for Millie and Nessie, both ways.

Millie put the money on top of the papers with Cora's pile of instructions: the time, place and telephone number of Ana's dentist for her appointment. The same for her piano lesson. The telephone number of the family with whom Ana would be staying so Millie could call to remind Ana of the dentist and the lesson, since being with a different family and on a different schedule, Ana might forget the appointments. A slip for Larry with the time of his dental appointment, which had been changed to late in the afternoon on Friday when he would already be in town and not need to make a special trip. He would have to be reminded, however, since he tended to forget dental appointments. The need to remind him had been written on his list and circled in red.

Also the name of the man Larry was to see Wednesday for his second St. Andrew's interview and the time. The place was at the Chamber of Commerce. Larry was to take the questionnaire along and be sure he read the questions again before going. He should be given enough money for lunch that day, in case the interview was delayed, but Millie was not to give him any other money. No extras. He already owed them work and he must do the work before he got more money. He could have extra money if he worked for Millie. He could ride his bike to town and back on Wednesday and into town Friday. He would not need many clothes for the weekend. He could take what he needed on the bike.

The name of the children's doctor Millie knew, but here were his office and emergency phone numbers. Not that one of the children was ailing. No one was, but in case.

Then there were the men working on the roof. They had been working erratically all summer, whenever they had time free from larger jobs. Millie knew the workmen. Pete had built the Bosks' new house. Pete told Cora they might be free to come Wednesday, or else Thursday, and Cora had given him the key. If they did come Wednesday, or Thursday, they had promised to call Millie. She did not have to do anything. Not a thing. Simply make sure Ramón stopped by the house on his way home to check that all the doors were locked and the curtains closed. Also, make sure the lights were off. The men came through the house to work from the inside of the attic, too, and sometimes left lights burning.

Cora wrote the word "lights," with an exclamation point, across the side of the note about the repairmen.

"And you better tell Ramón not to cut down the Riles Historic Landmark sign. He might think it shouldn't be there. Or does Ramón already know everything about it?"

Millie's eyes were settled on the pile of lists. Cora put the last slip on top of the others.

"Quite a stack, isn't it?" she said.

Millie tucked the lists and money out of sight in a counter drawer.

The kitchen was new and modern. The counters wrapped around three sides and were bare except for small kitchen appliances, a vase of salmon pink roses and a huge apothecary-style jar of hard, different colored candies.

"It's not too much, is it?" Cora questioned.

Millie shook her head. "Larry asked if he could use Haskell's tools. I said only if he was supervised using any of the power ones."

"And only if Haskell knows I didn't ask. He's not doing it for me."

Cora was sorry she snapped so frequently. It was not her mother she should be treating this way. But she was angry. She kept growing angrier about Haskell. A moody unsettled anger which kept expanding, ballooning since she had started the law suit against him.

"Forget about that," she said to her mother. "What brought Larry back to woodwork? He hasn't done any for ages."

Millie tilted the large apothecary jar toward her, offering her candy. "He wants to make a toy cart," Millie said, "like a miniature of his."

"A cart?" Cora stopped in the middle of unwrapping a candy. "For Nessie? It's bound to be for Nessie." She slid the lemon ball in her mouth then round to her cheek. "He is so sweet sometimes. He really is. And I've been going on and on at him about the work he owes us and how careless he is when it's our money. I've been so irritable with him, with all of them. He wanted Ness's old doll carriage for the wheels and I jumped all over him about that. I didn't even ask him why he wanted them."

Her mother took both their candy wrappers and crumpled them in her hand. "Is there anything else you want me to do?" she asked, moving typically, so absolutely typically, on to some possible action she could take to help. "How about Ana's skirt? Didn't you want me to shorten it?"

"Oh Lord, I forgot. She put it on the table by my briefcase and I walked off without it."

"Ana can get Norris to drive her out with it," Millie said.

"Absolutely not. We don't want her turning to Norris. She's doing that far too much since Alan moved to Austin."

"She could drop the skirt off at Haskell's office," Millie suggested. "He could bring it home."

"I don't want Haskell doing me any more favors. Haskell's favors turn out to cost more than I can pay."

Millie removed a cloth from the sink and wiped the counter mechanically, as if there were something on it to be cleaned. "Nancy Lou?" she suggested.

"I've asked her to do too much as it is. Take care of the newspapers, the mail, my car. I can't ask anyone at Dawson, either. You're not coming into town?"

Millie shook her head. She draped the cloth over the faucet. "Tell Ana to leave her skirt with the receptionist at the dentist's office," she said. "Ramón can pick it up for me on his way out Wednesday morning."

"We're beginning to sound like characters in a cop movie," Cora said. For the first time since she had arrived, she sounded relaxed, her voice open, lighter. "We talk like gang members plotting out our next drug pickup."

Millie's blue eyes shifted from the jar of candy she had been realigning. Her eyes were bright and startlingly, almost shockingly, intense in so pale a blue. "With Ramón as a mysterious stranger?" she asked.

"The dark foreigner, he'd be," Cora added, "with that finger joint missing, like the hoariest movies."

"Arriving after a night in town with his unofficial woman, and carrying a strange package," Millie said. She half-masked a side of her lips with her sturdy fingers; she was unused to such chattering and unaccustomed, ever, to saying anything speculative, especially playful, about Ramón.

"And with a package wrapped suspiciously in a plain brown paper grocery sack and he'll be coming out of..." Cora began laughing while she talked, "out of a... a dentist's office which is... is a... you know... perfect source..."

"Wearing the hunting shirt he uses workdays," Millie continued, her eyes fastened on Cora's, snared, both having hiccups of laughter erupting between words, and Millie, with her hand still half-covering, camouflaging, her mouth, saying, "with dozens of pockets for hiding."

"And he'll be taking it..." Cora leaned on the counter, "to a...to a...packing shed for...for...mailing things," she burst out finally before collapsing into laughter over the counter's edge. Both of them laughing. Both of them.

Millie reached for and pulled a tissue from a pocket and slipped it beneath her glasses to blot her tears.

"No one," Cora said, catching her breath, "no one would believe our real story, Mother. We couldn't possibly be innocent."

She stood up and took a tissue from her mother.

"It's been too hard for you," Millie said.

"I'll give you credit for one thing. You never once said I brought it on myself by insisting Alan and I separate. Only please don't start in telling me I could have it worse. I know. The carpenters could fall through the ceiling."

"Pete says they didn't find much rot in the ceiling."

"Mother, you are hopelessly literal. And I suppose Pete naturally tells you or Haskell, and not me, what he finds in our house?"

"He's used to us. And your father's paying him."

"You don't have to remind me. That's the main reason I decided to go on this trip. I hope I'll get a raise if I do more of this kind of work. The first thing I'll do with the money is pay Haskell for the repairs he's done on the house this summer. I intend to start paying for our gardening, too."

"Don't do that," Millie said. "You would never have put in all those gardens."

"I don't want any more help from Haskell."

"You're being childish."

"I should have been childish sooner. Getting ahead seems impossible without a childish self-centered devotion to your own interests."

"You do all right," her mother told her.

"I feel trapped. And not just by the house, either."

"Can't you find time to finish your paper?"

"I'm not working on it at all, Mother. Maybe I'm not meant to do research and write great papers. I'm better doing these jobs for Dawson's President. I'm good at it. I think I could turn that into something, move into a full position there."

"Do you have the right degrees?"

With an effort, Cora did not let herself smile. It was so like her mother not to understand that the degrees she had were more and better than any required for administrative work at Dawson. So like her mother, too, to ask in that staunch familiar way, meaning—if you don't have them, we'll see you get them.

"I'm fine on degrees," Cora said. "I'm over my head on degrees. It turns out I'm not interested enough, or not cut out for, research. But I like working for the college itself, administration, development. Who knows, if I could get where I'm not enmeshed by everything else all the time, if I could get free to work at it, I might get a big promotion. Get myself a double raise."

"What would you do with it?" her mother asked. "After the basics, what would you do then?"

Her mother's light acute eyes, bottled behind thick lenses, fastened on her. Cora felt a subterranean tug toward her, a strong unavoidable pull, more compelling by far than would ever seem likely from her mother's taciturn and unemotional surface, something inescapable as gravity.

"You mean what will I do for myself?" Cora said. "After the school for Nessie is paid and St. A's fees for Larry and even the taxes all paid?"

"Yes. Yes. After all those."

"Travel," Cora said. "Take a trip. Anywhere. No careful plans and without kids. Once I'd have said with Alan but without the children. Now I have to think of things just for myself. I'd travel alone. And buy a car. Get myself a car with automatic transmission. That's practical since we need it, but the real thrill would be travel. The way Alan does, or Haskell. Get up in the morning, pay for domestic help, arrange superb meals for the kids, pack my bag and go. Only one bag. Carry-on. Then out the door and off. Just like that."

"And go away," Millie said.

"Sure. Everybody wants to. What about you? Your business is growing. Suppose you take in more money than you expect. What would you do?"

"Buy indoor-outdoor carpeting for the greenhouses," Millie answered immediately.

"You're serious? No trips?"

"A small check pattern in orange and brown or a mixed tweed green. Carpets where the dirt won't show. In all the greenhouses. Even the half open one."

"Nothing else?"

"Nothing else."

"No clothes?" Cora pushed her. "No new car? No, you wouldn't want a car. No porcelain flower baskets or lovely crystal vases for the house? Only carpeting in the greenhouses?" She already knew what her mother would reply but she relished all over again this surprising and yet familiar aspect of her mother, this literal, concrete, indoor-outdoor carpet attitude to life.

"I'd help you," Millie added.

"Don't say that. I want you to buy your carpeting. All of it you want for all the greenhouses. If I get a raise, I'll contribute. Agreed? Come on, Mother, let's make a deal. Agreed?"

"Agreed," her mother said.

~~~

What of the house, then? The house itself?

It was old. Old. Started before the Civil War, records showed. Or immediately after. There was no knowledge of the exact date of the first construction. Originally built to be a small practical hospital and midwifery, the house was useful later as a home, and was pleasant in many ways for its inhabitants. The two story gallery, that expansive porch with thick white columns on both the first and second floors and stretching all along the front and one side of the house and half of the back, caught every breeze and gave shade from the sun. In the hot summers they could sleep on the part of the upstairs porch which had been screened. They would be cool there in the night air, protected from mosquitoes, and relieved of the motionless heat indoors. Still, there would be muffled laughter at the possibility they might slide right on off the old porch, which over time sloped down like a diving eagle's wings from the solid center of the house.

Millie never liked the house the way Haskell did. Because not enough of her children lived to fill it, Haskell believed. The empty bedrooms reminded her. The only child she bore who lived to grow was Cora. The first had been stillborn. Twins, a boy and girl, died within a month of birth, the girl in the first week, the boy later. The last child not to live, born almost two years before Cora, died when he was six months old of a malignant lymph disease. No more children after Cora. No son to rattle through the rooms, to learn from Haskell how to whittle wood, to carve his own and Haskell's last initial on any tree.

What Millie did like was the open space between the house and the neighboring one, their extra lot which she festooned with a variety of gardens. She liked their front street, too, lined with old trees and along which she would take Cora, when Cora was little, to meet Haskell walking home from his office. Coming back they would swing Cora up in the air at every other step and Haskell would point out to her the house's highest windows and tell her they were elves' windows, for swinging in and out of on magic threads.

Those small high windows opened out from the partitioned attic rooms that were intended, by the first owner, to house the nurses at the hospital. And one of the larger second story rooms was partly rounded to catch the light for operations. Cora's baby nursery had been the room adjacent to the operating room, a tiny space originally meant for storing linens. But during the early weeks, until into the third month of Cora's life, Millie was too worried to let Cora sleep so far away from their bedroom. Not until Cora was older and securely established in living, did she sleep far from her parents and then only one year in the nursery before she was thought active enough, and real enough, to be moved into one of the bedrooms.

After Haskell realized they were not going to populate the house with a stair-step range of little Bosks, he had tried to use the operating room for his study. He found the light too glaring and the room too isolated and went downstairs again to the large back room, the one he had panelled in a style used in homes built when the house was first constructed.

When Cora was nine she took friends into the operating room and told them imaginary horror stories of its early days and explained—accurately—that the floor was made of tile to make mopping possible, because of all the streams of blood—which was a good deal less accurate. When she was much younger, just starting school and unusually tall for her age, she had wept inconsolably on the wide half-step-high stairs of the house.

"Because the house was built as a hospital, that's why these steps are low," Haskell had consoled her. "They are *not* baby steps made because you're too clumsy to climb big ones."

All to no avail because no other child in school lived in a home with baby stairs, or had huge bathtubs with ugly clawed feet.

"This was an honored place for helping sick people get well," Haskell told her. "This house was revered."

Reverence was no consolation for the betrayal by her friend, pretty petite Marianne Jenks, who spread the story of those baby stairs and ugly feet on the bathtubs to all the others in the kindergarten.

Later Cora would brag to schoolmates about the house's history. About the extra, partly open, summer kitchen used in long-ago days of wood stoves, which gave off too much heat to use indoors on hot days. And the pantry-way to store food before refrigeration. The tarred rope, now gone, used to suspend the screened box of food because the tar's thick gummy texture helped deter insects.

Nessie had been conceived in the house, on the sloping upstairs porch, one summer night. Cora and Alan kept laughing while they tried to quiet the noise they made on an old cot and laughed all the more from trying unsuccessfully to stifle their laughter, ending up shaking the cot until Cora said, "What if we slide off?"

"I'd grab the pillar and hold us."

He would, she thought. He would. He was strong enough.

"Hush," he said, "think of your parents."

"At our ages? Much less theirs. Why?"

"Because making love's not supposed to be hilariously funny."

Nessie had loved that sloping upstairs porch from the first, especially at the back of the house. There it was unscreened, but had a wooden trellis and heavy vines. She kept her favorite toys there and when she was supposed to be napping she would frequently slip out to that part of the porch and entertain herself by rolling anything she could that would keep turning over and over on the tilted floor. But nothing noisy enough to be noticed.

Like her grandfather, Haskell, Nessie prized everything about the house. She had crawled up the wide safe half-step stairs on fat legs when she could first crawl and on the next visit had learned how to walk by clinging to the wooden trellis of the downstairs back porch. Later she had asked to be allowed to open each of the small doors to the storage cabinets under the eaves in the attic and had stood at each doorway, peering in, but tightly clutching hold of whichever indulgent adult had carried her up the steep flight of stairs. She had filled the old empty iron bird cage, which Larry later sold, with stuffed animals who had been bad, and she learned to tell time by turning the hands on the foot high, inoperative family clock, which Larry also sold. After her parents bought the house and they had moved into it, Nessie went through all the rooms afresh on longer, less chubby legs, and chose the upstairs back porch for her own private storage place, and would not change her mind, even though the spot was not protected from rain.

"Don't leave any stuffed toys here," Cora told her. "Or books. Never anything which can be hurt by rain."

Usually, Nessie obeyed, and the time she did not, and a book Haskell had given her was drenched, no one complained severely, not even Haskell. Nessie was never seriously spanked in her grandparents' house.

It was in this house, the Christmas after Nessie's summer conception, that Cora, heavily pregnant with this last child, had coped with Christmas and Ana and Larry and tried to write a second paper from her unpublished dissertation. A paper that, in the end, she would also never publish.

Millie found her one morning in the main guest bedroom, originally the operating room, seated at the table with her papers and wrapped in a blanket. There was no adequate protection against cold in this house built for a hot climate and in the winters the remote operating room was chilly.

"You don't have to be cold," Millie said, tugging pointedly at the blanket. "I'll loan you a sweater."

"I'm bigger than you, remember?" Cora said. "Even when I'm not pregnant."

There was a wealth of affection in her voice. From pleasure at her mother's concern. She added, for the first time in her three pregnancies, "I hope this baby has your eyes, Mother. I'd love to have a child with eyes the blue of yours."

"Mmmm," Millie said. She had started making the bed. "I thought Alan helped you with the bed?"

He had. He had when they were graduate students and before there were any children. He had shared fifty-fifty in all the domestic chores, as he often said. He had said it, in this house, in Cora's home, to her father, before going upstairs after Cora one morning to help make their bed. Yet once the children came, the work became so great that doing any reasonable fair share of it would take a serious amount of time. So Alan gave up helping at all. Cora made their bed, now, and also the children's.

Of her two older children, Ana was the one who always wanted most to visit her grandparents' home. And Ana was ecstatic when her parents bought it. It was the most romantic house she had ever heard of. Not the operating room or the broad half-step stairs of the hospital days, but the lumber lavished on it by the lumberman owner, a man named Garnett, so in love with a Riles woman—the story went—he had lined part of the house with the most exquisite wood to persuade her to marry him. Lumberman's Folly, it was called, since only imported lumber was used. This part of Texas did not grow the woods he wanted: oak, in long unbroken boards, birch, maple. No one had ever seen such maple laid in parquet style along the sides of a stairway.

Much less placed on the ceiling of the stairway, turning it into a tunnel of warm inviting wood. He remade the banisters, too, converting the uninteresting original handrail into one long sensuous flow. Perfect to walk beside, Ana thought, perfect, coming down to one's wedding.

It was the wood on the stairway and the panelled walls of the dark upstairs bedroom, used by her grandparents, which Ana showed her friends. Alone in the house with Norris, she took him to all the choice places, one by one: the minute formal front sitting room with leaded windowpanes, the elegant arched entrance to the dining room, upstairs the open sitting room that led straight onto the screened porch and her grandparents' bedroom with polished panelled walls, then back down the stairs again to see the French doors leading from the dining room to the raised brick walkway and best of all, at the very last, the heavy glass chandelier above the dining room table.

"Isn't it fabulous?" Ana said to him. "Imagine how they must have lived. They must have had dinners in here after it wasn't a hospital. I mean real dinners, with long dresses and gloves with tiny buttons and lots of maids. Probably six courses for a meal. And ices for dessert."

Her eyes were wide, gazing past everything in front of her, imagining ices.

The first owner to convert the house from a hospital to a private home had been a wealthy German who was a citizen of Mexico. To the amazement of the neighbors, he had intended to spend his summers there, partly on business but partly taking a vacation in the house with his large family and numerous servants. He wanted to be in an area close to streams and a lake and hills, and perhaps with German names of towns, and away from the dry winds of Torreón. But the house, or the life, had not been satisfactory for his business or his wealthy Mexican wife. She did not care if the servants were happier sleeping in their tiny hot attic rooms than on the floors in the hallways as they did in Mexico. She wanted to go home to her own country.

So the German had managed, in a business deal, to transfer the house and its extra lot to the lumberman, Garnett, who spent himself into bankruptcy improving the place—it was said—and lost his lumber company. The house was bought at a bankruptcy sale by an ambitious young man who was starting an insurance company in Riles. He had thought of the house with its extra lot as an investment, for he was sure the town would explode with growth. When it did not, he joined an established insurance company in "finally, a civilized place," as his wife announced when they moved away.

He had sold the house to an able and artistic banker, part-Mexican. The banker relished owning it and filling the rooms with his many children until they, like typical upper-middle-class, one hundred percent Americans, began growing up and going off to eastern or midwestern colleges and after that never giving a thought to coming home to live in a small Texas town.

Haskell offered to buy the big, emptied house from him.

"Why?" the part-Mexican banker had asked. "Why the biggest house in town for so young a man? And with no children yet."

"Why shouldn't I?," Haskell asked him. Then, more congenially, with less of the prickly air of a young man set on achieving every goal, "No, hear me out. I love the house with all its different sized rooms. And that space next to it. My wife, you see, is an avid gardener." He did not say that he, too, planned to have many children to fill the house, and at that time he could not imagine, not even had he tried, that any child of his might grow up and think of moving away. "In any case," he had added, a short sweet smile sneaking out and brightening his face, "I could put up with owning the biggest house in town."

In the end the banker and his wife were delighted to sell to this young man. He was so interested in the house and its history and all the records they had saved about it. He was a man who obviously meant to care for it. They sold Haskell the empty lot, as well, and the tools in the shed, and over half of the Mexican furniture the banker had shipped up from Mexico. But the rugs and tapestries hanging on the walls Millie did not keep.

They would require extra time to clean. Millie had no interest in unnecessary inside work, nor would she pay for anyone else to do it. She was used to a farm and hiring outdoor hands but never, ever, anyone to help in her own home. She refused the hangings on the walls, including those in the heavily draped, oasis-like back room which Haskell converted to his study. He replaced the tapestries with floor to ceiling bookcases and wood panels which he made himself.

Ana kissed her Norris for the first time in her parents' house, formerly her grandparents' house, in that study. On a night her mother and father were out. Cora had never kissed a boyfriend in that room, or any other room, nor on the porches of the house. Certainly in cars on dates, in other homes, or out beneath the cottonwood trees on walks home, but never near her home. Never near Haskell or Millie.

In the richly panelled study Haskell had begun a draft of one of his *amicus curiae* briefs which went to the Supreme Court, working in the evening, with windows wide open and the fresh smell of jasmine coming in and Millie off somewhere in the house, reading probably, about gardening maybe, and Cora on a date or with a friend, though Haskell would not have known which.

Alan had preferred working in the dining room. He finished a talk for a seminar on the long dining room table during his first visit to the house, over spring break, and he made corrections on the proofs of his third book at that table during one Christmas vacation, when Cora was pregnant with Nessie and making all the beds. And on his last day as only a visitor in the house, one year before he and Cora bought it, Alan had settled himself once again in the dining room to work. Nessie slept beside him in a bassinet, her fist squeezing and unsqueezing her baby blanket as she worked hard at sleeping. Larry had gone outside to break in his new mitt and had persuaded Ana to do it with him. Cora was packing for all of them and Alan, pressured by a close deadline, worked quickly yet with his usual clear concentration on an abstract of the paper he was to give at the conference in Denmark.

Earlier that year Millie had studied the architect's drawings for her new house on the same heavy Mexican dining room table. She had drawn her own sketches there for the first greenhouse she would build. Cora had been visiting for a few days only, having come alone, except for Nessie. Cora knew nothing of greenhouses, but she made suggestions about changes in the plans for the kitchen. She had lived in far more kitchens than Millie and had firm ideas about the best three point balance between stove, sink and refrigerator.

One of the last tasks Millie had finished at the same useful table, protected while she did so by a heavy plastic cloth, was to wrap the treasure boxes she had made for the children. She had lined each box with distinct material and decorated each differently: Nessie's by attaching three flat, decreasing sized, velvet teddy bears and a yellow duck; on Larry's chips and small fragments of broken arrowheads he and Haskell had found and would have discarded, glued on in the pattern of a tepee; Ana's with a perfect sand dollar from the beach set in the center and surrounded by tiny delicate sea-shells with pink and mauve and even coral insides. Ana's was the largest.

And it was into one of this dining room's high-backed Mexican chairs, by the table, that years before Larry had been carried when he had fallen down the length of the many half-step stairs, screaming all the way, one leg snagged in a batch of clothes hangers he had found. He was three. His accident-lover's summer, Alan described it, yet gratefully acknowledged that Larry was never badly hurt. He could not be stopped from opening every door or drawer, lifting every lid, turning over any object, trying to make use of anything he came across while exploring his grandparents' house.

On the Fourth of July during that same visit, out in the vast backyard, Alan taught Larry how to hold sparklers and not be afraid, and that the fiery fascinating sparks were not harmful, only the hard stem was.

X

That bleak look which came upon his face when someone else was being praised settled around Alan's mouth and eyes. Nor was it masked or softened by his being the one to do the praising. The man standing next to him in the group, paying no attention to Alan, had assumed he was as enthusiastic as the others, and nudged Alan with excitement.

Unspeaking, Alan disengaged himself. He moved toward a group on his right. They, too, were talking of DuBost's French protégé and the paper he had presented. It was a triumph, they said. Doubly astonishing from one so young. He would be made a member of the Academy if he continued with such high quality work. He would be elected at some absurdly young age.

The vast decorated room in which the aperitifs were being served had an enormous Oriental rug on the floor. Reds, corals, deep golds and blues. You forgot, if you did not live around such places, that a single rug could be so large, Alan thought. He was still treading on it as he came to linguists surrounding the protégé. Alan edged close to the crowd and, like the others, examined DuBost's new find. He looked oddly wizened for a man so young. He had heavy angular bones with little padding to them and his body was drawn inward, his shoulders seeking each other for safety, and the inner parts of his arms pressed protectively against his ribs. He wore steel-rimmed glasses with a left lens so thick it seemed it should weigh down his head on that side, but did not. When he lifted his gaze, that eye, exaggerated, like a flashlight, blazed at them. In unpleasant nasal French he was saying that most unfortunately he had the need of departing before the lunch was to be served. He had innumerable important telephone calls he must make immediately.

"What an act," an American voice, close to Alan's ear, spoke in muttered English words. "Like shit he does."

Alan spun on him.

"Wouldn't you, if you'd given that paper?" Alan demanded. "He's got a right to make all the calls he wants. To brag about it to everyone. We have to bring him to the States."

"Come on, Belknap."

"He was sensational. We'll arrange financing for him. We should put him up for a Henderson Fellowship."

"A Henderson? You're crazy. He's just starting. You haven't had a Henderson."

"He should get it because he is starting. When he's really talented. He shouldn't blow his time teaching or consulting or anything else. Tell Crimmins about him."

"I know ten other people I'd rather see get Hendersons."

"Then I'll write Crimmins. This kid shouldn't be wasted."

"What's got into you? Just because your paper had a rough time, don't turn this French snot into a frigging genius."

"You heard his paper. What more do you need? I'm going to make sure he gets what he deserves."

Alan pulled away and as he did that bleak look settled on his face again. He searched for a place where he could put down his glass and found a small table that was clear.

Outside the room, Alan looked for an attendant. Deliberately he would not let his eye be caught by any of the linguists chatting in the hall. He crossed to a newspaper stand and as he approached spotted a small young attendant. Alan asked him where overseas phone calls could be made.

There, exactly there, the attendant told him, and leaned forward to stare at Alan's name tag and shook his head, deciding that was one name not worth trying. There, he continued, exactly there, where it says above in *plain letters* that you can telephone to other countries, the Frenchman finished, rudely.

They must train them to be insulting, Alan thought. That under-sized chinless wonder learned fast. Probably doesn't have to shave yet. Not even the age of DuBost's protégé. The protégé was no kid, though.

Not as young as he looked, probably. At that age, you always look younger than you are. Especially if you live in a two-bit French town in the middle of nowhere. "City," he most likely called it. But not Paris. Not yet, anyway. No distractions to bother him there, though. Nothing but time to work. Emile Guy Laposteneau. Must be over twenty-five, at least. Thirty? No, not thirty. No major obligations where he taught probably. Come off it, it was not free time or living outside of Paris that produced that paper. Time wouldn't do it. Talent did. He probably wrote it in a month. Time helped, though. Having a whole free month would help.

Alan closed himself into one of the formal, antique-looking booths set up for international phone calls. Even the kidney-shaped stool was heavily cushioned and covered with green velvet. Alan took out his magic plastic phone card. To his surprise, there were no difficulties. Surrounded by the imitation antique fixtures, he had expected anything technologically sophisticated to fail. Leave it to the French, Alan thought. Just like their state-of-the-art cooking utensils in old kitchens. The fake gold telephone beeped all the numbers, clicked, paused, then rang. It was his home phone.

He might wake Cora. It would be six, or would it be five there? Six. She would almost certainly be sleeping. He returned the plastic card to his wallet.

The phone rang again. There was a phone beside their bed. She was slow waking, Alan thought. Deep asleep. But she wouldn't mind because it was an overseas call. The phone drilled again. She might be showering. Could have got up early for something and be in the shower.

The ring sounded another time. A fourth. Answer, Alan thought, and in the same instant realized, taken aback, that Cora was not there. She had gone away for the week. She was in Corpus Christi, or Galveston. She was in one of the cities on the Gulf, raising money for Dawson's endowment.

The phone rang on. There wasn't supposed to be anyone in the house. She was in Galveston, he was sure. Not Corpus or Houston. Galveston. The children were at Millie's. No, with friends, she had said. Well, somewhere. But Nessie would be with Millie all week. He knew she had said that. Except for some party or something one afternoon.

The ringing continued.

Galveston. Right. Narrow tannish beaches. And those pulverized white-gray shells spread all over the place, in flower beds, around oleanders in parkway centers, around city trees, making everything look ocean washed. Cora had hoped a rich alum would take care of the bill so they could stay right on the beach in a swank hotel. She adored ocean swimming. She always laughed, standing in the ocean breakers. He loved her laugh. Would she be with someone, Alan wondered. That's what she's there for, he told himself promptly. Oh, not that way, but would she be *with* someone? With some man? Seeing someone on the beach, for example? Or somewhere else? Say that tall man, Poinsett? He was connected to the school. No, he was a regent for the University, you idiot, not Dawson. He had a daughter in Dawson. He told her he would help raise money for Dawson. He had been hanging around Dawson since spring. She talked about him all the time. OK, not all of the time. Most of the time.

He fit the receiver back in its elaborate cradle. There was no point having the phone ring in an empty house.

He could call someone else, he thought. He could call his brother. And scare him to death? They never woke that early. It would be five there. Five fifteen, now. So call and ask him about Dad? That would scare him to death. What if Mike were awake? He might be awake. Then he could talk to him. Tell him....what? That he had given his paper yesterday? He did give his paper yesterday. At the major afternoon meeting. His big paper. The one he'd worked on so damned long. He should have worked on it more. When? Just when? It doesn't matter how or when, he should have done more. Then it would've been all right. Forget it, he told himself. Call Mike and talk about nothing. It's too early to talk about nothing.

He could call Nessie. What an idea. Just call her at Millie's, he supposed. Nessie woke early in the summer. Yeah, but Nessie never answered the telephone.

Alan's attention was struck by a sharp noise. That same near-dwarf attendant tapped on the glass part of the door with a coin. From

Alan's angle, looking up at him, he was like a toad with his absence of chin and narrow lips which, like a toad's, wrapped far back around his face.

Alan slid the door ajar.

There, there, the attendant said to him in exaggeratedly careful French, as if Alan did not understand a word of it, over there. Not trying to say Alan's name. Not here, but at that one which is there, he said. This is not correct, but a call is entered for you there. And he pointed with the coin to a different one of the cubicles for overseas calls.

For you especially, the attendant repeated, there.

Alan listened without at first comprehending, and the attendant tugged his sleeve and pointed with the coin to the other booth. There, he said slowly, his lips laboring with exaggerated emphasis over the French words. Not here, but there.

Alan moved to the next booth.

It was Haskell. Haskell had telephoned him, and the satellite connection, once Alan shut the door, brought in the call undistorted, deceptively, as if it had been placed from the next cubicle.

"The house is burning," Haskell said. "Alan? Have I got you? The house is burning."

Haskell's gravelly voice was perfectly clear. In that strange way of familiar voices, simply hearing the well known tones instantly brought back a sense of the whole person: of Haskell's size and powerful stomach, of his short legs pounding determinedly across a tennis court, of the force of his personality.

"There are two fire trucks," Haskell said.

"The old house is burning?" Alan asked. "Your old one? Ours?"

"Wardlaw…" Haskell began. Who was Wardlaw? A fireman? Yes, a fireman obviously, as Haskell continued, "says he hopes to contain it." The fire chief, then. "He needs to get another truck. He needs longer hoses."

"How much has gone?" Alan asked. But before there could be time for a response, he spoke loudly into the phone, shouting against the distance between them as if it were not true they could hear each other easily, "No one was in it? The children weren't in the house? Haskell?"

"I would have told you immediately if the children had been in danger," came back to him in Haskell's assured, somewhat arrogant manner. "The children are all right. That should be obvious. Surely you're aware you planned to leave the house empty?"

So it was not simply the house's burning that caused Haskell to search him out in a conference and have him brought to the phone out of a pre-lunch gathering.

"How did you get hold of me?" Alan asked.

"I tried," came back. "The other truck is coming from Layton. They have longer hoses. That's what the firemen need."

"Can you see the house?"

"I can see it out the window. I'm at the Mayhews'. They reported the fire. If they hadn't come back early from camping, who knows what would have happened."

"But the kids are safe? All of them?"

"I told you they were." Then speaking differently, with an air both of interest and surprise, "People have come out to look. Naturally. The neighbors are standing in the street in their nightclothes, watching."

Alan stood up slowly in the small ornate booth. With his free hand, the hand that did not hold the receiver, he reached slowly for the top of his head, not sure where it would be.

"How much of the house is left?" he asked.

"Wardlaw says they can't tell what they'll be able to save until they stop it. He says it must be electric in origin. The fire seems embedded in the walls."

"Does Cora know?" Alan asked.

"We haven't been able to reach her," came back to Alan from across the Atlantic. "There's a call in for her but we had to know if there was anything essential that should be saved. So I phoned you. Wardlaw tells me he can still get a man inside to some of the rooms. Is there anything he should save? The mortgage papers and deeds are in the bank, aren't they? Or with your lawyer?"

He would add that touch about the lawyer. "Yes," Alan said.

"How about your manuscripts?" Haskell went on. "I've seen some notes and computer printouts. Do you have copies? Is there anything essential there?"

"I moved everything important," Alan answered. When he moved out himself, he meant. He was trying rapidly to remember what printouts Haskell might have seen and were they his and did he have copies of everything on paper or disks? He must have. Was there anything important left? Anything he could not do without? "I don't think there's anything crucial," he said.

Then, "Listen, Haskell. Listen. Don't hang up. Can you still see flames?"

"Along one corner."

"Which corner?"

"They evidently haven't been able to slow the fire," Haskell's voice came back to him, still assured, still calm. "Even with all that water."

"Are the kids with one of you? The kids should be with you or Millie."

"I told you, the children are all right. Nessie and Ana came into town with us when the Mayhews phoned. Ramón heard somehow, you know the way they do, and came over. He's been helping."

"Who's taking care of Nessie? She doesn't like Ramón. She can't understand him. She doesn't know any Spanish. Who's Nessie with?"

"There are more than a dozen people on the street in nightclothes now," Haskell said. He added, with contempt, "There's a man in his bare feet."

"Where is Larry?"

"Oh, Larry's dressed. He got into his clothes fast, unless he was up and dressed all night. I suppose he could have done that. He spent the night in town."

"Where is he?"

"He's with the Deemer boy. They have that make-believe cart."

"It's a real cart. They haul things in it."

"He and the boy were pushing it between the fire trucks."

"For God's sakes," Alan said, "keep them away from the house." He turned around inside the tiny booth as far as the phone cord would let him. "Is it still burning?"

"Yes."

"Damn it, why can't they stop it? Listen…" and he broke off talking, for he was breathing so heavily through his mouth he had to pause before he could resume speaking. "Listen," he said, "get the children away from there, Haskell. I don't want them near the house."

"Don't worry," Haskell's voice said.

"Do you think Nessie's with Millie? Nessie's young enough to run inside the house to get some toy. She wouldn't realize there was any danger."

"I see Ana. Ana and that young man she's always with."

"Is Nessie with her?"

"They're trying to get water up to the roof," Haskell said. "They aren't waiting for the longer hoses. They're joining two hoses together. If they can just get enough pressure from the fireplug near the house."

"The roof's burning?"

"It's starting."

Alan sat back down on the cushioned stool. Though he did not speak, his mouth stayed open, taking in and expelling air.

"Hear that?" Haskell's voice asked, excited. "That must be the siren of the fire truck from Layton. Can you hear it?"

He could hear Haskell's voice and nothing else.

"Is it the truck?" Alan asked him.

"Yes. They'll try to hook up from a farther fire hydrant and get a stronger stream of water with the longer hose. Larry's helping them unwind the hose. He's right in there."

"Keep him away, Haskell."

"Wardlaw will watch out for him. *Don't worry.* Wardlaw knows his job. He wanted me to ask you—about the fire starting—did you have rewiring done? He thinks the fire started in the wiring."

"No. We didn't ask them to do any rewiring," Alan said. Right, right, he'd expected that—there *had* been another reason for Haskell to call. And they were Haskell's workmen.

"I understood you and Cora were going to have new wiring."

"Later. All we did was get the chandelier fixed. We did that before. We used your electrician, remember? That was way before your men started working on the roof."

"They have the new hose hooked up. Larry's still out there with them. He's very active. He's been all over the house this summer, hasn't he?"

"Larry would never touch anything electric. He doesn't know anything about electricity."

"Why would that stop him?"

"Your repair crew was working on the house, Haskell. They probably fouled the wires."

"They're professional construction men. Anyway, there wouldn't be any benefit to them from a fire."

"What the hell are you saying?" and Alan jumped up in the small closed box.

There was no reply to his question. When Haskell's voice returned, it was changed, astonished, right there in Alan's ear despite the ocean between them.

"There are flames at the study window," came from Haskell.

"The study?"

"Yes," Haskell said. His voice was deep as ever, but odd, hollowed. "They're different colored flames," he said without his usual certainty. "Do you suppose the panelling or all the books in the study cause a different color? Or those funny cardboard files Cora uses?"

"Where's Larry? Is he still with the firemen?"

"The flames are oranger," came back to Alan. "It must be the wood. They're unwinding another hose. They've got plenty of hose now. Larry's there, with the other boy, on the far side of the street. Oh..." he stopped, "I see. They're going to flood the study." And in the same rough-edged hollow tones Haskell asked, "Do you have many of your books in the study, Alan?"

"Not anymore. I keep my books in my office." After a second, "What about you?"

"I had a shelf of old law books I hadn't moved. Some very old ones. I'm not sure I can replace them. There's Wardlaw. He's moving people away."

"Hold on," Alan interrupted him, "hold on a second."

For the impossible runt attendant was clapping on the glass again with his damned coin. Alan shoved open the door and glared down at him. Was the telephone call as it should be, the attendant asked Alan. Was the connection exact?

Alan gestured him away and jerked the door shut.

"What were you saying?" he yelled into the phone.

"Could you hear?" Haskell's voice came against his ear, animated, louder. "That was glass shattering. Did you hear the glass shattering?"

"Glass from the windows?"

"They've moved people back. Two of the second story windows went. Could you hear them?"

"Can you see the kids, Haskell? Someone ought to be with the children. It's their home, for God's sake."

"They're getting the longer hoses up to the roof now," Alan heard in reply.

He turned in the decorated space and then twisted back. He rubbed his free hand across his eyes and slowly once again reached up and laid his hand, consolingly, on the top of his head. "Has it stopped now?" he asked into the phone.

"No."

"It's got to stop sometime."

"Wardlaw needs me," came Haskell's voice, changed again, efficient.

"You can't go," Alan said.

"No, something's wrong, Alan. I'm..."

"Haskell, wait. Wait. I'm coming home, Haskell. Do you hear me? I'm coming straight home. Don't hang up. Put someone else on the line. Haskell. I have to know what's going on."

No clicking or sound of hanging up came to Alan, but he could tell no other voice was going to be on the line any longer. No one was there.

~ ~ ~

Earlier than Haskell's call to Alan by almost an hour Cora had slipped out of her hotel room and walked down to the beach. The beach was narrow. The color was tan and sometimes beige, until closer to the water. There the sand had been hard-packed by waves, made excellent for walking and turned a darker, browner color. In the distance the hazy early morning light merged with the beige and tan and darker sand, but Cora could make out a seemingly endless line of graceful curves of foam stretching ahead. Waves which had rolled far up on the slender shore before sliding down into the Gulf had left soft lips of froth behind as markers of the distance they had come.

She could not sleep. There had been a celebration with representatives from business companies and nearby Dawson alumnae who had helped solicit funds, and they had ended praising her, *her*, for the money raised.

They would never have been given this amount but for her, they said. Repeatedly. They said it to each other, to the President, and to her.

She walked vigorously, at a determined exercise pace, but stopped now and then and swung her arms wide, stretched them out, then wrapped them in a tight hug around her body.

They had pointed out that she, *she*, was the one who had established connections in each city before they arrived. *She* had guessed who might respond to an appeal from a private college. *She* had been excellent dealing with big companies. She had not been overawed or too aggressive. She had been easy. She was good at this, they said. Skilled. And look at the way she had approached those with big money. She had a way.

A position should be created for her, the President was told by the CEO of an oil corporation. Would she be interested in such a position?

Cora paused before a smooth water-worn piece of wood. She shoved it with her foot and found it to be longer and sunk deeper in the sand than she expected. She stepped over it.

Such a position, they had said, would require her to travel. Could she do that? And there would not be as much time for her research, a dean said. He knew how much her research meant to her, he told her.

The air on the beach remained hazy although the sun was rising. In the uncertain light the gulls all seemed a uniform muddy brown. They were beginning to circle and land around her with lively double bounces as they hit the sand.

Maybe the President was being pressured. Maybe he was only being agreeable because the contributors were enthusiastic. Yet it was the President who suggested they might create a vice-presidency for development. He didn't have to say that. A vice-presidency. Cora stopped walking.

She *had* raised the money, just as they said, she told herself. She had made the arrangements and spoken on the phone ahead of time with everyone they were to meet. She had done all that at Dawson, when there had been time, and when there wasn't time, at night from Haskell's, no her, study. And on weekends. Every weekend.

She began walking again, veering closer to the water's edge where the sand was firmest.

She must keep in mind that a vice-presidency was by no means certain. Establishing new positions was hard. For anyone. Look how much trouble it had been for Alan to get his. They hadn't been sure until he got his first check. And you could never tell how enthusiastic the President really was. That mattered because she would have to work with him. But he had brought it up. It had been his idea. Then travel. Nessie was young. Millie could not be expected to take her every time. Once or twice, no more. But the salary would be greater. Double. Maybe more than double. Alan said the only serious money in academic life was in administration. Where all the incompetents were, he'd added. If the money were double, or more than double, she could hire someone full time to help with Nessie.

She would need new clothes. Meeting people, business people, people with money and not only academics, she would need really good clothes. Chic clothes, from Austin. Or Dallas.

And a car. Maybe Dawson would lease a car for her since she would be traveling for them. Dawson might even buy her a car. Or help her buy a car. Unless she flew all the time and that didn't seem likely. If Dawson bought her a car, could she say what kind? Could she get automatic transmission?

She had to have a respectable car to go with her vice-presidency. Not their old car. Even at Dawson, a vice-presidency was something.

Coming into sight on the beach was a stranded Portuguese man-of-war. As she drew nearer she could see its wobbly translucent body shining a dark purple blue in the morning light. She shifted her direction to get closer and once near she scraped a handful of sand free and tossed it lightly against one trembling side.

As a child, on a beach not far from this one, she had gathered with other children of varying ages and popped stranded men-of-war. A fat satisfying pop resulted when a man-of-war burst and she and her friends learned to be careful, for even the stranded men-of-war were virulent. A touch of the splattered juice raised painful red welts. Too much could make you ill, put you in bed, deprive you of the beach and water and days with friends.

She had also, with the others in that summer's mixed age gang of youngsters, systematically covered the jelly fish with sand, hoping some unsuspecting tourist—as if they themselves were not tourists— preferably a barefoot tourist, would step on one. None ever had.

Kids, Cora thought to herself, remembering the sharpness of the disappointment they felt because no adult trod on the carefully concealed lumps of poison. She wondered how they could have cared so little that they might hurt someone. Or how they could have only longed, truly longed, for the outcries and frantic antics they imagined coming from their deceived victims. Cries and antics they had play-acted out among themselves as a substitute, had done so with absurd exaggeration until they were weak from the exertions and from laughing.

Kids, she thought again, remembering acutely not her children but those with whom she had played, remembering herself, on that other beach, seeing as clearly as the curves of froth ahead how, with utter and undeviating application, more devotion than they ever gave to any school work, they would delicately cover those quivering noxious bodies with sand.

("Cora, don't forget," her mother had said to her, the day she went off to college. Forget what? Her ticket? She had her ticket. Had given it to that prissy stewardess with her belt pulled tight to show off her tiny waist. "Don't forget..." What? To write?

Her mother knew she would write. Cora stuffed her carry-on bag beneath the seat in front of her. Haskell had already told her, when they started to the gate, to write every week and to call home, collect, any time she needed to. He had given her extra money for the first month and would send more before the month was quite finished, because managing money on your own could be tricky at first. And she must not worry, Haskell said, about how she would do in an eastern college. He could assure her she would do well. He had been having discussions with her for years and he could promise her she would do well. It was then, as Haskell finished saying how well she would do, her mother touched her, gripped her, really, in a solid clasp, like a handcuff, a manacle, and said, "Cora, don't forget..." What?

Fastening her seat-belt, Cora was irritated that she could not, at the moment, remember the end of her mother's sentence. It would come to her. There was no reason for her to be nervous. Or to worry about it, either. And she had flown before. Dozens of times. Four, anyway.

Her mother's eyes had been damp. She had seen them. "Don't forget..." Millie had said. Then a burst of words had come over the airport's public address system, and Cora, along with the others holding tickets, had rushed through the gates to board the plane. To climb the steep steps to the platform at the top and once there turn round to see and wave to those you are leaving. She had done that, waved at Haskell and Millie while clutching her carry-on bag and her ticket, her handbag slung over her shoulder and inside the handbag the suede cosmetic bag which Nancy Lou had given her because she was going east to college.

She had ducked inside the plane, bumping her bag in front of her along the aisle, feeling hot and cold at the same time.

It's only college, she told herself, fastening her seat belt. She would not forget whatever it was her mother told her not to forget. It was obviously not important. Then what? Her manners? Come on, her mother never would say anything that dumb. Her mother would have been thinking of something sensible. Like make good grades.

Her mother never spoke about grades. Her mother believed she was effortlessly and magically intelligent, like her father. It would not have been grades. Probably something boring. Like keep regular hours. Or eat her salads. Or keep her room clean and tidy. Come on, stop it, she told herself. Stop. Why are you being so bad about her?

She rubbed her eyes once, quickly, crouched over and unzipped the carry-on bag. She would get a book. She would refuse those silly magazines the prissy stewardess was offering. She pulled from her bag a slender book on Buddhist philosophy.)

Cora glanced at her watch. Too early for breakfast with Poinsett. She circled around past the man-of-war and walked on along the beach.

She would have to think how much it would matter if she didn't do research. What the dean told her. Lack of time and so on and so on. No more trying to publish that paper, or revise it, or write a new one. She didn't have a new one. That took care of that question. But she hadn't thought of a new one. She could work on one. She wouldn't have time. Not if she took the vice-presidency, for sure she wouldn't have time. Don't take it then. She was smiling. She was smiling broadly and she knew she was.

Come on, she said to herself, who was she kidding. She'd take it. She'd kill for it.

What about research then? It could wait. What about administration, simply going into administration? A vice-presidency wasn't just administration. True. Even Alan would allow that. And Haskell. He would, too. Alan might laugh. He would laugh. But he'd be pleased. He'd brag, too. He'd brag to Mike. And he'd like more money. He'd like her being a vice-president. So would she. God, so would she.

There'd be a problem coping about travel. And Nessie. She'd make arrangements. Problems like that could always be figured out. Have a student from Dawson come to the house, maybe. Even live in the house. An older student. Some bright girl. Some girl who'd get on with all of them. Especially Ana. Then Ana wouldn't spend all that time with Norris. That was it, get someone level-headed. And when she traveled for any length of time, Alan would help. He could take one of the children. That way he'd get to see more of each child alone. Definitely. Cora turned to start back. Someone had come out from the hotel and walked down the beach and was waving to her. Not anyone tall enough to be Poinsett. It was a hotel porter. She could see his uniform. He kept on waving and it must be to her. There was no one else on the beach. He was waving her in with both arms.

XI

M~ike,~

I'm writing because I can't sit doing nothing all the way
back across the Atlantic.

Like I said on the phone, I don't know how the fire
started. Did I tell you it was burning while Haskell was talking to me? He described it room by room, down to the color
of the flames. And I wasn't sure where my kids were. I could
have strangled him.

He was dead set on telling me the fire was electric. And
he kept hinting Larry was responsible because the kid's adven-
turous.

Larry wouldn't touch wiring. He doesn't know anything
about it, so he'd leave it alone. He's got his head screwed on
right. He reminds me of you, Mike. He has your ability to
make things. You should see the cart he and his pal built. It's
insane to think he did anything that caused a fire. After this
loving insinuation, Haskell hung up. He claimed the fire chief
wanted him. Haskell has connections with every official in
town. He could be conniving with the fire chief, or someone
else. That's why I'm flying home.

I couldn't get Haskell back on the phone until I was at
Orly with something like nine and a quarter minutes to spare.
I asked him about the children. I wanted to be sure they were
all right. All Haskell wanted was to make more accusations,
this time about gasoline. Gasoline!

By now the firemen had decided gasoline might be responsible. Haskell seems to be trying to tie this on Larry because
the boy uses gasoline to mow lawns. So does half the town.
Haskell's off his head. He can't stand to see me make a profit

out of his old home. He'd rather blame his own grandson! So
I phoned you from the plane. Sorry I woke you. But you can
see I couldn't have Larry facing Haskell alone. The kid's
smart, and he's independent as hell, but he's only twelve. I
knew you'd help him, if only by talking to him a couple of
times. Haskell will find out you called. And it's important the
boy doesn't feel alone.

Yeah, you're right, it's a bad time for Cora to be in
Galveston. She'll get home before I do, but not until midday. I
won't have Larry harassed by Haskell and some half-wit offi-
cials in that town. What's more, I don't want Larry thinking,
even for a minute, that anyone else in the family believes
Haskell's charges. Larry's a fine kid, Mike. He mustn't be
turned into someone's victim.

Thanks, brother.

Sleep late tomorrow,

Alan

PS. Tell Dad I will write, SOON.

~~~

Alan folded the letter. He switched off the reading light and tipped
back his seat. The man next to him was snoring. The man farther over,
on the aisle, watched the movie. The window shield on Alan's right
had been pulled down to darken the plane. Alan shut his eyes. Then he
opened them. If he were going to sleep, he should take out his contacts.
He closed his eyes again and leaned on the tiny airplane pillow.

He did not expect to sleep. Rest his eyes was all. The engines made
a steady drone. He was not sleepy. What was it, 5:00 PM Paris time?
No one could be sleepy. Land in St. Louis at 4:45. What time would
that be? Getting on toward midnight, Paris time. Catch a plane to
Austin if he was lucky and got a standby seat. Three hours' wait in St.
Louis even if he did get the first plane. Hit Austin at 9:34, they'd said.
4:34 AM Paris time. Wow. No night. Be 8:34 PM at Mike's, on Den-
ver time. And 4:34 in the morning in Paris. And he still had the drive

to Riles. No chance to sleep. Have to tell Mike that. Tell Mike the trouble with chasing the sun is you don't get any night.

The engines switched tone. Different winds or a change in altitude probably. He had not felt the plane go up or down. He opened his eyes. Same semi-dark, semi-light, same heads watching the movie or sleeping. He'd rested his eyes enough. He pulled the pillow from behind his head. He would use it as a desk again. He switched on the light and wrote another letter.

Dear Jamie,

We should bring that Laposteneau kid to the States. Wouldn't you know DuBost would discover him? Whatever you might think about DuBost as a person, he has a genius for finding talent.

Laposteneau should be put up for a Henderson Fellowship. What he needs is time now, while he's young and doing first-rate work. He may never do work this good again.

Why don't you bring this up with Bob Lehrman? I'll write Crimmins. I'll be an adjunct advisor to the committee this coming academic year so we ought to be able to swing it.

Thanks for your thoughtful comments about my paper. Your points were sound. I think you're right about the structural shift. Shades of old Saussure!

That talk was one time when I welcomed a friendly face in the audience. Also someone interested in the basic issue instead of simply joining in to rip up my example. I've no idea what was bothering DuBost. He was excited about the first draft. I can show you a full page covered in his spidery Gallic hand. I guess he forgot what he thought before. I'll have to make my point clearer and make the example work. I know what I'm discovering is valid and, as you said, is a real contribution. I've just got to get the model right.

Call me,

Alan

Across the bottom of the page Alan wrote a note to his secretary at the Institute:

Phyllis,

This goes to James Rayker, obviously. Get out a reprint of the last review I did for the JL and send it along with the letter. Remember Jamie's moving. Send this to him at MIT.

AB

~~~

Alan was right. Cora did get back before he did. By the time she rented a car and drove out of the city through the hills and reached Riles, it was after one o'clock. It was a few minutes past one when she turned the corner into their street.

From a distance the house looked the same. It had been a blue-gray color all the years Cora could remember. With a roof so dark a gray it could be taken for black. As she got closer the house still seemed as before except that Cora could begin to tell that one, no several of the windows had no glass. They did not glint in the sunlight. They were square vacant holes.

The street in front was empty. She had expected cars to be there. Without actually listing them, she had expected a fire truck, or some sort of fire department car, as well as the police, or the insurance people, or their lawyer and certainly, unquestionably, some car from the family. There were no cars. None.

Swatches of mud which had run down from the carefully designed raised flower beds coated the street close to the curb and streaked the sidewalk. And mud from the long beds running on each side of the walk up to the house lay in wide swirling patterns on the concrete. Farther away, back on the lawns, were piles of debris.

Cora pulled the car over to the curb and stopped. She reached forward and turned off the engine. As she did she noticed the black streaks running down from the upper part of the house and merging with the remainder of a charred post which dangled from the upper rim of the second story porch. Near the post was a gap, an entire section of balcony, gone.

Cora's lips parted and she leaned farther forward, pressed against the steering wheel, staring. Her eyes moved to the chimney. The base had been burnt. A chunk of roof, like many of the window panes, had disappeared, leaving a dark irregular hole. Remnants of attic beams, heavily blackened, poked out from the edges of the hole like scorched fingertips, holding nothing.

Someone was there. Millie. She came from the far end of the yard along the strip of lawn between the house and one of the large gardens in the empty lot. She stooped to pick up something—the torn branch of a damaged plant—and tossed it onto a pile of trash.

Cora got out of the car. Millie stopped again and bent. She was restoring a battered plant. A number of the leaves had been stuck into the clammy earth. She freed them, straightened, wiped her hands on a rag dangling at her waist, and solid, short, sausage-like, moved toward the muddied sidewalk and her daughter.

Cora asked where the children were, where was Nessie, where was everyone, and how much damage had been done inside the house and why weren't the empty upstairs windows boarded up the way the ones on the first floor were?

Millie said Haskell had taken the children to town for lunch. Yes, Nessie, too. All of them had been helping clean up the yard. The fire department had not boarded the upstairs windows because they were upstairs, but Ramón would take care of them later. He had brought the ladder and could do it from the outside. No one was allowed to go inside. The fire chief had sealed the house.

"Why?" Cora asked. "Isn't it safe?"

Millie shook her head. She had approached so close that Cora saw the perspiration on her forehead. Could see that Millie's eyes were red behind her rimless glasses and that the edges of her eyelids were inflamed and sore.

"You've gone inside," Cora said. "I want to see it."

She loosened the collar of her dress. She, too, was sweating. She started to go around her mother but Millie stepped squarely in front of her.

"You can't," Millie said.

"I have to see it sometime."

Her mother did not move. The light blue searching eyes and hot damp face seemed to Cora to be bursting to convey something to her.

"Don't worry," Cora said. "I'm a big girl, Mother. All grown up."

Millie still did not move but stayed directly in her way. Cora put a palm on her mother's arm, to assure her, to thank her for the concern, to push her gently aside and move around her.

"Remember, no one was hurt," Millie said. "None of the children; not you or Alan. No one. That's what matters."

"I know," Cora said. Don't worry so about me, she felt like adding. She felt like hugging her mother close, too, hanging on to her for a moment. And felt as strongly, at the same time, a wild desire to burst out telling her mother, now, face to face, in the middle of everything else, that she had been offered a vice-presidency at Dawson. Grinning ear to ear while she did.

Haskell's car appeared around the corner. Norris's car followed, with Norris driving and Ana sitting next to him.

Nessie jumped out of Haskell's car and ran to Cora saying she had stayed in pajamas all day until they went to town for lunch but Grammer made her wear shoes with her pajamas so her feet wouldn't be hurt when they watched the house burn. And wasn't it a good thing she had Puddles with her because they never let her go in her room and did Mommie know they saw the windows all fall out so no one could get close anymore, not to get anything, no one, not even Haskell?

Cora grabbed her daughter and hugged her tight. She smelled sweetly familiar, and her skin was cold from the air conditioning in the car. Cora heard herself saying in cheering confident tones that it was right they could not go inside the house. They had to be sure no one could get hurt first. Not being hurt was the most important thing. When the house was safe they would all go in and Nessie could come, too.

Nessie wanted to get down and Cora set her on the damp lawn.

Larry had approached behind Nessie and waited, watching Cora. Cora did not focus on him. She was distracted by Ana and Norris holding hands on the sidewalk next to Haskell. They had been taken out to lunch by Haskell. They had driven back together in Norris's car. They held hands on the street openly, in front of everyone, with Ana not looking at her and Ana's righteous stony face saying, if you go away, Mother, and the house burns and Norris has to help when you're not here, well, if you go off and do that, what do you expect?

Larry took Cora's hand, tugging at it. In a voice tighter than this summer's usual reedy, uneven, not-yet-broken one, he said, "Mom...Mom. I didn't start the fire, Mom."

Cora turned toward him and he held on to her hand and rushed on, "I had to tell them Grammer was wrong about what she said. I didn't mean Grammer was lying or anything, but she said I couldn't have been near the gas can. Everyone knows me and Kyle use it, Mom. I know, *Kyle and I*. Kyle and I use that gas. I had to tell them or they'd think I was keeping it secret because I was the one who started the fire."

Cora was stunned. Stunned. As if she had stumbled suddenly and the hole was unexpectedly a pit, enormous. As if the ground beneath her had gone way.

(Another time, not here, not in this house or near this house but back East, in a tiny apartment they were renting, after a dinner party celebrating their wedding anniversary. Ana, a baby, whom everyone had seen put to bed. Larry not yet due to be born for two months. She, Cora, gloriously pregnant, glowing from having served an elaborate dinner with a rich home-made dessert. Beside her a graduate student, Alan's first disciple, who had separated himself from the others to be next to her all evening, had followed her as she carried dishes into the kitchen no bigger than a closet and stood there talking to her with his eyes shining with admiration, saying, "It was kind of you to invite me. Your husband, Professor Belknap...Alan, I mean, is amazing, isn't he? The way he mimics voices. He can mimic anything. Everyone knows about his climbing but I just found out tonight he played tennis for his college team. And published his book one year out of grad school. One year! He's quite a catch, isn't he? I mean," his eyes simply glowing at her, "what you've got, Mrs. Belknap...Cora, what you won must be about the best catch of all the rivers."

And her shock. Her dumbfounded shock. With her looks and her hair and her full stature, with one gorgeous baby already here and quietly put to bed and another on the way, with that dinner and dessert and her academic grades and the talk about her in her department, the plans for her in her department, and this punk kid student who had been following her and sitting next to her and talking to her and gazing at her all evening with shining eyes, didn't he know—she had been the catch?)

(Another time, also in the East, and several years later. This time Alan. When he was an associate professor and Larry had been born. After another, larger party, so crowded the rooms were jammed until near the party's end when only the last die-hards remained.

"...what women do is pretend a talent they don't have." She heard Alan's voice. She was sure he was joking with the men beside him in the doorway. She caught his eye and saw he meant what he said. Saw he meant it for her, too. Maybe particularly for her. When the guests had left, Alan went on, as if the conversation had always been with her, "That is what women do, don't they? Pretend a talent then assume the role that goes with it? They put on an act. Women students who come to us from the English Department do. They want men to play a worried Leonard Woolf to their genius Virginia. That's their theme song: play Leonard to my Virginia. Any talent they might have gets used up in the posing. Only pose produces no prose."

He laughed aloud, enchanted with what he said.

"You're soused," Cora told him. Even a small amount of alcohol could sometimes do that to him. Tip him over the edge of his babble point, as he himself said.

"Clear your head," she went on, "and help me with these dishes."

He did not stir.

"How about it?" he went on. "Do you agree? Men don't get such options. I never get to say, hey there, would you be Mrs. Chomsky so I can play at being Noam? Ole Noam of the lowering dome? Or how about..."

"Alan."

"How about Mrs. Starobinski? Would you call yourself Mrs. Starobinski so I can be Jean? Except...I'd have to start writing articles about psychoanalysis and Rousseau and 18th-century French culture as well as linguistics. Oh, no, I forgot. The pose is enough. The pose is all. I could get away with doing nothing, too."

"Alan, I'm going to clean up this room."

As if he could not stop himself, sprawled on the long narrow couch where when one of the children had been ill either he, or she, had both, at different times, caught up on sleep. Slouched on the couch, with an almost full drink in an exaggeratedly casual hand, Alan kept on, "Or there's Mrs. Whorf. You could be Mrs. Whorf. Then I'd get to be a distinguished founder of the subject and not have to submit another grant appeal to some government nudnick. I don't know much about Mrs. Whorf, but we could research her. Get the part right for you. The way earlier women researched Edna St. Vincent Millay or earlier than that all dressed in white to playact being Emily Dickinson. I'll bet droves of them came dressed all in white. I know, better idea, maybe you could take up weaving to go with Whorf," and he ended with a loose, slovenly grin.

She was sure he was pretending to be drunker than he was. With the fatuous smile and the over-acted, deliberately inept fingers holding his glass. False. Exaggerated. A pretense put on so he could say anything he wanted under the cover of seeming drunk.

Cora placed the stack of plastic glasses she had collected on the littered table, reached back of the couch to the encyclopedia stand and took a square heavy ashtray they called the pipe-lovers' depository.

"All right, Alan. If you're dead set on your 'look at us poor mistreated men' act and determined to go about in sack-cloth, let's add real ashes for verisimilitude."

She tipped the ashtray so a flutter of dark pipe ashes spattered across his knee and others, from the opposite side of the ashtray, floated down to the side of his head and settled there, standing out poised and prim in dark gray contrast against his straight, light brown hair.

Alan dropped his glass. Maybe he was drunker than she thought. His tumbler clumped on the rug while he rolled to his right catching her below the hips with his left arm and bringing her down beside him. The heavy ashtray slipped out of her hand, bounced off the back of the couch, and crashed, ringing, on the bare floor behind. She and Alan both sprawled half on the narrow couch, half off, with Cora trapped by his leg and arm. She started to laugh. Alan did not.

"Don't ever do that," he said. He *was* drunker than she had thought. The fragile bits of ash stood out like tiny petals on his hair. Flecks of ash perched on one eyebrow making her, even now, want to smile, to tell him about it, to reach over and gently brush them away.

"Don't ever trash me," he said. He pressed them both harder into the couch. His arm ground down achingly across the point of her hip-bone. Her leg hurt where it was trapped between the floor and the edge of the couch.

She made an effort to move and by moving shift herself, or Alan. She was still close to laughing though vividly aware of all the places where his body was fully against hers and of the two where she hurt—her hip bone and her leg.

Alan looked different, close and alarmingly intense. Quite possibly very drunk. His nose was red and the skin across his lovely gently raised cheekbones, each like the outline of a dove's folded wing—so Cora had thought of them—that skin, too, was flushed. Yet Cora was surprised, as she had often been before, by his strength. He was not much larger than she. He often needed more sleep. If they caught flu, he was the one who was in bed longer. But she could not begin to move him. He had trapped her with his left arm sloping across her body from the waist and especially over that hip bone.

"Alan," she said. She would not say please to him. She would not say come on, stop, that's hurting. She would not say the ashes were only a joke or were an accident or meant nothing serious.

His eyes had fixed on hers. They were fervent. The whites definitely damp. Had he lost his contacts? He was so near she could see the different colors in his irises. As she looked at him, he pressed them both deeper against the couch. Her shin was bitten into by the wooden edge of the base and her hip ground by the bone of his arm. She could not twist away from the pressure of his body which lay across her. Her left arm was caught helplessly between them and her right, which he had snatched as she poured the ashes, he pinned beside her head with his right hand.

But her head and neck were free. Cora raised her face closer to

Alan's, right against his. She could smell what it was he had been drinking. Could feel on her lips the salt from the pretzels he had eaten. She touched the tip of her tongue to the rim of his upper lip and carefully, slowly, traced the outline of his mouth, starting in the center and moving by minute degrees to his left, her right, until she reached the corner of his mouth, turned down, around, then along the bottom edge of his lower lip, moving slowly to her left, and his right. He was immobile, focused on her, unsmiling, but his eyes were less vehemently clear.

She moved her tongue leftward, slowly, to that other tucked-in corner of his lips. He was not loosening her, there was no releasing, the wood still bit into her leg. Slowly her tongue negotiated this second corner and up along his lip's upper outside edge to the center. At the center of his upper lip, below his nose, she paused, hovered, then edged her tongue tip higher, gently up that twin ridge from his mouth to the base of his nose, and poking, trembling, into his left nostril, farther in, against the small moist hairs.

He shuddered and exploded back from her, releasing them both and shaking his head, snorting, half sneezing. He rubbed his nose from side to side.

"Yuugh," he said. "That's disgusting, Cora."

Ticklish? she was going to say. I thought you might be ticklish, she was going to say. And wanted to add, but could she without saying please to him? without placating? let's make love tonight, Alan, let's make love.

"You always win," he burst out at her. He got up, took out his handkerchief, and rubbed his nose. He stood away from her, separate, his eyes furious as he repeated, "You always win."

She was floored. She could not even take away the smile on her face. Didn't he know she never won? Never. He was the one who always won.)

"Mom, you can see I had to tell them," Larry was saying to her, squeezing her fingers tightly between his. "I didn't mean to cause extra trouble. Everyone else was going to say it anyway."

"Someone started the fire," Cora said stupidly, absorbing the words and the meaning of the words—that was the reason the house was sealed; that was what her mother had been trying to tell her—and while she did, quite witlessly, for no reason, she smoothed the hair on Larry's forehead.

XII

What no one had expected was the smell. By the time Alan arrived at the Bosks' it was almost eleven o'clock at night. He looked worn, his clothes rumpled. His eyes were bloodshot, more even than Millie's. Yet he came in alive with energy and announced they were going at once to the house. He would not listen to protests. He gathered up Nessie, who had sleepily but doggedly remained with the others in the living room, and he told Larry to ride with him in his car. And after they had driven into town, all the way to the house, got out of the cars and climbed the steep stairs to the porch where Haskell said again that the fire chief had sealed the house, Alan simply kicked open the front door.

The kicking was not necessary. The seal was nothing but a strip of red plastic tape stuck across the crack between the door and the frame. Alan entered, holding Nessie in one arm. He turned on the light although Haskell told him not to do so. The lights needed to be checked first, Haskell said. Alan left the light burning. "I just checked one," he said.

Still, no one had expected the smell. It was strong, pungent and acrid. Powerful enough to leave the taste of it against the roof of the mouth and clinging to the tongue.

"Yuck. Stinks," Nessie said. She made a face and squirmed in Alan's arm until he let her slide down to the damp hall rug. It was a smell of burnt wet wood and scorched, water-logged materials—drapes and stuffed chairs and rugs. And there was an unmistakable odor of burnt electric wiring.

"Yuck," Nessie repeated, shaking her head. The smells were denser near the floor. She squinched up her face and rubbed it back and forth against Alan's expensive gray trousers, one of the pairs he kept for travel and conferences.

"Come in," Alan said to the others.

"The fire warden sealed the house for safety," Cora said. "And they have questions about the fire they haven't answered."

"He sealed the house because no one stopped him," Alan said. "There's no law against breaking and entering your own home." He flipped on the porch light so those outside on the porch were visible. Haskell was in front of the screen door. Millie had climbed the stairs behind him, and her stalwart head and firmly placed rimless glasses were visible to Haskell's left. Ana waited beside Norris, who, so far as Alan could tell, seemed to have moved into the family on a permanent basis. Cora was on the other side of the entrance, tall, statuesque, her attractive face worried and controlled. The yellowish overhead light picked out the brighter reds in her hair, somewhat in the way the sun could do. With one arm she held on to Larry.

"Get on inside, Larry," Alan said to the boy. And to Haskell, "I talked to Wardlaw from St. Louis."

"You called him from St. Louis?" Haskell asked, surprised.

"While I was waiting for my plane. I reached him at his home," Alan said. "I didn't have time to call him from Paris. He agreed to meet us here tonight. Come along in, Larry. Don't wait. You can't trespass in your own home."

Alan forced the screen wide, scraping it on the water-swollen sill. Nessie had wandered farther into the hall, squatted down and was pressing her thumbs into the spongy hall rug, watching the small pools of wet which formed each time she did. When Alan opened the screen wide and invited the others in, she edged nearer the wall to be out of the way of incoming traffic.

"Move, Larry," Alan ordered.

Either Cora released him or Larry pulled away, for he stepped across the porch and into the house where he, too, made a face at the smell.

"Jeez," he said. Then, "Jeez, look at the wallpaper." The delicate white and lilac flower-patterned wallpaper Millie and Haskell had selected to give the long dark hall sweetness and an appearance of an arbor had pulled away on one scorched side. Detached strips curled down into brown rolls dangling like enormous hair curlers above the baseboard. Nessie began tentatively touching a coil, seeing what would happen. "Are you coming?" Alan said to everyone on the porch.

While he waited they all heard a loud splat. Then another. And a third.

"Didn't they make sure they took care of any water before they sealed this place?" Alan demanded of Haskell.

"They didn't want to touch anything until experts could investigate." Haskell said. "We aren't supposed to be inside."

"They'd rather let the house be flooded?" Alan said. "And they left the electricity on with water running? That's criminally negligent!"

He strode into the dining room where the splattering noise was based. In the doorway, briefly, he hesitated. He checked the floor on which he stood to be sure it was dry, then smacked the wall switch swiftly with the bottom of his palm. The ornate crystal chandelier flashed on. There was no sign of water near it but several feet away, close to the window, the ceiling sagged in a long narrow bulge. A drop of water formed slowly and elongated in the center. A pool of water must have accumulated on the floor above, soaked into the ceiling and begun splattering on the round brass platter set as a decoration on the buffet.

"I'd say we're lucky we burst in," Alan said. "Saved the ceiling from collapsing." What he said was meant for Haskell but he glanced at the others. They had all followed him into the house.

"You said you talked to Wardlaw," Haskell replied, his gravelly voice resonating in the acrid-smelling hall. "No doubt he told you they need to establish exactly how the fire started."

"Listen, Dad," Larry said, "Grammer wasn't right telling the fire chief what she did about the gasoline drum."

"Dumbbell," Ana said to him, spitting the word at him in low tones, beneath the adults' interest.

"We have to take care of that water first, Larry," Alan told him, "but you stay with me. I need you to help."

And Haskell, pointedly, "Have to have the boy where you can watch him all the time?"

Alan ignored Haskell and went past him to the front of the hall for Nessie. She was still concentrating on the dismantled wallpaper. She had begun to unfurl one loosened strip, with the burned delicate flowers face down on the wet muddied rug.

"That's enough down here, Nessie," Alan said. He scooped her up and when she wriggled to get down he held her firmly with both hands. "Let's go upstairs," he said. "Don't you want to look around upstairs? We'll do some tidying there."

The stairway was sodden, too, but little harmed. The banisters had been badly scratched by some piece of fire-fighting equipment but the stairs themselves were untouched.

Alan took the shallow steps two at a time. At the top Nessie demanded to be put down and began drumming her feet against him, her feet in the shoes Millie had put on her in the car. Alan held her away from him, then set her on the floor and gripped her hand and started down the hall.

He had meant to examine the master bedroom, which was directly above the dining room and must be the source of the leak below, but straight across the hallway before them was Nessie's room. He could see that her bedroom had been devastated by the fire. She could see, too.

"Nessie, sweetheart," Alan said, and pulled her against him, "don't go nearer." He put a hand on her head, pressing her face into his leg to shield her eyes.

She twisted her head down and free, her soft curls ruffling beneath his palm as she once more peered into her room. "Sweetheart, no." Alan picked her up. She was transfixed by what she saw and stayed motionless in his arms until Alan turned away. Then her head spun, like a burst spring in a wind-up doll, her pointed chin digging into his shoulder as she gaped back into her room: at the miniature desk, once pink and blue, reduced to an unrecognizable outline of solid black; at an edgeless, congealed wet heap of what had been stuffed animals at the bottom of her bed; at her bed—black, burnt, soaking, raw springs glaring out.

"Let me see," she said to Alan as he walked away. "Daddy, put me down, Daddy."

"You take her," Alan said, handing her to Cora, who was coming down the hall toward them. "She shouldn't see her room like this. Take her downstairs."

"I told you we shouldn't bring the children," Cora said.

Nessie was inching higher in Cora's arms to look over her father into her room.

"The children have to know what's going on. They should know," Alan said. "But Nessie's too young to see her room like this."

"Let me down, Mommie," Nessie said. "I *want* to see my room."

Cora encompassed both of Nessie's legs under an arm.

"Take her to your mother," Alan said. "Your mother's always able to entertain her. Just so it's downstairs."

Turning to Larry he said, "You help me with the flood of water. Get the mop and bucket from downstairs."

"The bucket's not downstairs," Larry said.

"Where is it?" Alan asked.

"In the attic."

"What did they do, carry water up to the attic by bucket?"

"No," Larry said. "They didn't. But I know it's in the attic."

Because he put it there, Alan was sure. And made himself continue talking immediately, for Haskell was there, too, in the hall. Haskell was listening. "We'll do this without a bucket," Alan said. "We'll do it faster. I'll show you how."

He had thought he would throw the bed covers on the floor to soak up the water, but the bed was burnt. Not the way Nessie's had been, not totally, but the bedspread had been seared by flames and the pillows had been, too, so the air around the bed was filled with the hurt smell of burnt wet feathers, and when Alan tried to toss the bedspread onto the floor it ripped loose in his hand.

"I know, Dad," Larry said to him, "I'll get towels."

He was all at once alert. He was lively again, looking more full blown, released by his good new idea.

He ran to the linen closet. The towels were not burnt. Some had smoke stains on the edges but they would still soak up water. Larry pulled out a pile and rushed back into the master bedroom, where he and Alan began spreading them on the pool of water on the floor.

Larry tossed one towel beneath the bed and bent down to shove a second underneath.

From there, from the floor beside the bed, he called up, "There's a ton of water underneath. All the way from me to you, Dad. It smells like the dead goldfish that time the bowl broke."

He popped up. He was unsmiling, his face strained and anxious. "That was kind of funny, then. But I know this isn't funny, Dad."

(For nothing that had happened was intended. All that was intended was to have a lark, was to have fun mucking about in the dark alone, feeling for your way with eager outstretched hands as you went from one room to another in the big old totally empty house and all the time maybe almost not breathing because you knew you were where you had no business to be.

No one was supposed to be in the house. Even the men working on the roof stopped at five and no one ever was to be inside at night when the grown-ups were away. To be there when you were meant to be somewhere else, being watched over by some other grown-ups, like the Deemers, and you weren't, but were here instead, by yourself, because you were clever and had sneaked away so you didn't have to follow any rules but could do exactly what you wanted and whatever would be most fun: spitting a few times for the hell of it on that stupid love seat in the living room that always had to be kept so special; cooling off in front of the open refrigerator and getting plain cold standing there but not caring how long the motor ran on and on against the house's closed stuffy heat and pleased you were smart enough to keep the refrigerator light turned off by pressing on that little switch you found so fast in the door frame. That was good. That was super smart.

Then going upstairs and lying on the large master bed. But that wasn't fun so getting up quickly. Touching everything on Mom's dresser and Mom's bureau and feeling what was on the top of the bureau that had been Dad's but not opening any drawers because you never had and once when you started to, right after Dad left, you felt kind of sick and closed it. Going into all the other bedrooms, even Ana's. Feeling all the jars and bottles on her dresser and the books on her desk and by God, there, right in the middle shelf back of her books

155

was her treasure box. With the shells on it and a sand dollar smack in the middle.

Why hadn't she taken it? Didn't trust Patty Ann Lewis? Sure. Sure. Better to leave it than risk taking it along. Didn't want anyone even a friend to see what was in it. He didn't know what was in it.

He breathed in a mouthful of hot motionless air. They had a pact, he and Ana. A double pact since Dad left. No telling on each other. Number one. Never tell on each other and never to a grown-up. Number two was don't get into each other's hide-aways or hidden treasures.

His fingers ran over the shells, their patterns, the sand dollar. He'd never thought very much about what Ana kept in her box. Letters maybe, or pictures. From Norris. From someone else, maybe? Because she wouldn't leave it at Norris', either. Why not? Someone else? Someone not Norris? Money? She was going to go off and live on her own. She said so. She'd have her money in the bank, like a grown-up.

He sighed. But it was a double pact, a twice-sworn pact, since Dad left. You don't get in each other's treasures.

The excitement was beginning to wear thin except when a car light ran like liquid across the windows, giving the fear and the thrill of discovery. The house was too quiet. Empty. The house was becoming boring.

There was the attic. The attic had been a forbidden area all summer because of men working there. The carpenters must have rearranged everything in the attic. They may even have opened up the back sections underneath the eaves, the ones which had always been closed and had no little doors so you could see into them.

But there were windows in the attic. And a skylight. And there weren't any shades on any of them. If you used a light to see, it would show outside. So how look around up there in a space that was maybe all torn apart and find what was different and still keep the light hidden?

The problem turned round and round just as the china knob to the attic door rotated round and round under his palm. Then the answer came. Cover the windows. Right. Cover the windows the way they did for those black-outs in the movies about that old war.

What could he use? He needed something like the black sheets in the movies. He'd get tape from the kitchen. But the sheets? And something to stand on so he could reach the skylight. And a flashlight, sure. For he wasn't going to be dumb and turn the attic lights on since there might be a hole in the material, whatever kind of sheet material he found. Or a crack left somehow by the workmen. He would use a flashlight. Right. Great!

And he knew all about that skylight. The skylight pointed up and sort of sideways and was high. To cover that, he was going to need something solid to stand on, something higher than a chair. The ladder was at Grammer's for trimming. No sweat. He'd get a box instead. But there weren't any strong boxes in the attic. Not even a little one to put on the trunk. He'd check the garage. He was sure to find something in the garage.

He bounced up and down in tiny jiggling movements. He would get two solid boxes out of the garage and use both of them, or else move the trunk over for a base and add one box. And then climb up and mask the skylight.

He was thinking out how he would tape that skylight all the time he was feeling his way, quickly, down the stairs and into the kitchen. The second drawer to the left of the door had what he wanted. He opened the drawer and found the masking tape. Right. He left the tape in easy reach, near the edge of the counter and went out through the screened back porch. The yard was brighter in the faint moonlight. He could see better. And be seen, too. Remember that. Only don't rush, either. One easy quiet dart, like a fish.

There, there, he was inside the garage, almost smiling, for it was dark and he would not be visible. Garage smell—gas and oil and dust and mothballs. *Mothballs.* He stepped carefully—sneakers can catch on things. But he had been smart not to come barefoot at night. Couldn't tell what he might step on at night. He moved toward the corner and the smell of mothballs and found a large storage bin and raised the lid.

Right. Perfect. Side by side with old mothballs rattling around in punctured metal mothball containers were those dark gauzy sheets Grammer used to cover plants when an early freeze came. They would be perfect. Not too heavy, either, so masking tape would hold them. Oh, he was clever, really clever.

Now he needed something to stand on. The storage bin was immobile, built into the garage. A chair too low. A chair set on the trunk would be way too wobbly because the trunk lid was rounded. He had thought of a solid box on the trunk. But he hadn't found a box. Maybe there was a smaller ladder or a strong box in the tool shed.

Quickly, yet not being foolish, not tripping, he dodged across the narrow open space and between two bushes to the shed. He let the shed door stay a touch ajar so the moonlight could seep in and let him see.

Rakes, clippers, pots for plants, an outdoor grill which was too unsteady to stand on. Tools Grammer kept here, the old mower he used because the new one was at Grammer's. More tools, bigger pots, wicker baskets, twine.

And oh yes, Grammer's small metal drum for gasoline. Got from some farmer living on one of Haskell's farms.

Ramón must have hauled the drum into town to get more gasoline. Probably take it back Monday. They didn't use much gasoline in town, but Grammer used a lot in the country, clearing and all. He had plenty of use for it, too, mowing lawns, and Grammer let him fill his lawn mower from the drum if it had any gas left before Ramón took it away to refill and then take back out to the country.

He pushed on the top of the can. About chest high. Pretty much empty. He could rock it easy. Must be hardly anything in it. Absolutely time to refill. Pretty light, probably. The drum would be awkward. He reached both arms around it as far as he could. He could lift it. Carrying it would be really awkward. But he could do it. And the drum would be steady. He bet he could stand on it easy. He gripped the ribs of the shed for support and hoisted himself up and found that the drum was perfectly secure underneath him.

Excellent. Fantastic. He would carry it behind the bushes and the garage to the back porch, going as fast as he could so no one would see him, but being careful. Then carry it through the house. Yeah, it would be clumsy, but he could manage. And he knew exactly how the drum worked for he had used it lots of times. He'd just be extra careful not to open the valve or something dumb like that and stain anything in the house when he carried it to the attic. All he needed the drum for, anyway, was to stand on.)

"I know you don't think the fire is funny," Alan was saying to him. "And you're a great help, Larry. Wring the towels out in the bathtub. We've got to keep using them to mop. We don't want the water to bring down the whole ceiling."

Haskell's figure appeared in the doorway of the bedroom.

"Hasn't Wardlaw showed up yet?" Alan asked him.

"No," Haskell said. He stepped into the room and surveyed it. His and Millie's bedroom for decades. He looked down at Alan, who was stooping over to use the towels again on the last of the disappearing film of water.

"I didn't think you'd be that energetic about taking care of the house," Haskell said.

"I don't want anyone hurt," Alan said. "If you consider how fast this house burnt, we're lucky no one was in it. The place should have been sold long ago, Haskell. Then none of this would have happened."

"If someone had stayed in the house and taken care of it, nothing would have happened," Haskell said.

(Nothing happened getting to the house, and once inside, with the clumsy old drum finally settled on the attic floor, Larry went down to the utility closet and got the bucket. He had not been able to find the little footstool, which was usually in the study for reaching books, and he needed something to stand on before he climbed up on the drum. He wouldn't have the ridged walls of the shed to help this time and he had to make sure he got up on the drum without toppling it. When he couldn't locate the footstool, he decided to use the bucket. He knew where the bucket was. He could turn it upside down and climb on it first and then step securely onto the drum.

Clear thinking, he told himself, clear thinking to plan it out ahead of time. He got the bucket and that gauzy material of Grammer's and the tape and flashlight, and though he stumbled once in his sneakers on the kitchen's uneven floor, he didn't drop anything.

Once in the attic he needed to move carefully. There was less light in the attic than in the rest of the house. And tools might have been left on the dark floor by the carpenters. Or the carpenters might have moved the cardboard cartons or the trunk.

Think it out, Larry told himself. The hardest part would be getting that gauze stuff up over the skylight. But he could use the light coming in the skylight for that window and the light from the side windows to cover them. What he had to do now was move the drum where it belonged.

As he felt the floor in case he bumped into anything, he was again eager and pleased with himself because he had just decided he would double the gauze sheets to be absolutely sure they were dark enough and also pleased because he knew he had taken them out carefully and noticed how they had been folded so when he put them back even Grammer would not notice they had been used.

There was nothing on the floor in the way and he shoved the drum directly below the skylight. He set the bucket upside down next to the drum and rested a sheet of the dark material and the tape on the drum. He stepped up on the bucket and then climbed cautiously on the drum which wobbled at first, then steadied underneath him. He stood up all the way and found if he stretched his hand to his full reach he could just touch the highest part of the skylight. Good. Terrific. He could attach tape there. He picked up the gauzy material and the tape and began pulling off a section of the tape, keeping it straight so it wouldn't twist and stick to itself.

He stopped. All at once he wondered if it would not be simpler to shield the light and not bother with the windows. He could take a little cardboard box, a shoe box, say, and put it over the flashlight and point the light down so it wouldn't show.

What would he be able to see then? Glimpses. Only glimpses. But that was all he needed. With glimpses he could tell what had gone on and see if there had been any changes in the attic and look into any of the closed-in parts that had been opened. And it wouldn't take him long to see everything, either. Absolutely not. His father always said he had the sharpest eyes in the family.)

"Wardlaw should be here now," Alan said. And without waiting for an answer from Haskell he said to Larry, "Let's quit. We've sopped up all we can."

He collected the soaked towels. An armload of them, drenched, the different colors, including the patterned ones, turned darkly similar from the black, soot-stained water.

"You better stand out of the way," he said to Haskell, "I'm going to carry these into the bathroom."

When he had, Alan ran clean water over his hands and dried them against his face and neck and did not touch the towels on the racks because the towels were soot-stained, too. He wiped the face of his watch on his trousers and looked at it. "Doesn't the fire warden show up when he says he will?" he asked Haskell.

"Phone and ask him," Haskell said. "It should be easier than calling him from St. Louis."

"Not from there," Alan said, nodding at the damaged phone by the bed. He started out of the room and toward the stairway.

"The phone in the study won't help you," Haskell said, his voice rumbling after Alan. "The study's completely gone."

"That's what it sounded like when you called me in Paris," Alan replied.

He remembered, but did not say, that he had called the house immediately before and a phone—that phone in the bedroom, too?—rang fine. It would sound weird to say he called the house. Impossible to say that to Haskell, who would try to use it in some way against him, convert it into special knowledge, or a secret code, for who knew what Haskell had in mind, now, about the fire.

(Yes, he'd made up his mind he'd use only those quick flashes of light. Little pinpricks, that's all. They wouldn't be seen outside. Then he wouldn't have to cover every window and he didn't need to worry about having brought up the drum to stand on or all the gauzy stuff and the tape. He could take that back later. Anyway, his father would call that being thorough. "Ultra-plexed," his father would say, calling all extra effort wise. "Never fail for lack of an inch more rope," his father said. "Never second guess yourself once you start. Think about it later. Learn from your mistakes. But never second guess yourself. You'll lose your confidence."

He began to search the attic for a small cardboard box, feeling his way carefully. A shoe box was what he wanted. He could hold the box upside-down over the flashlight and let a peek of light shoot out in one stab. The shoe boxes were over here, somewhere, under the eaves.

His foot touched an upended board. He froze. They might have torn the floor up and left it that way. He felt cautiously. A board had been left on its edge, or propped against another board. Yes, his hands told him, that was it, the board was propped against others. They were new, brought in by the roofers.

He stepped over the boards and felt his way gingerly to the pile of boxes. His hands searched among several of them and found a shoe box. He turned the box upside down and held the flashlight inside. He would use the lid to make a loose shield. But if he had to hold the box and hold the flashlight, he wouldn't have a free hand. Maybe he could break off one end of a closed box, or use tape to fasten the box to the flashlight? Maybe.

But a bag would be better. Sure, a paper lunch bag would be perfect. He would get one of them from the kitchen and poke a hole in it. Absolutely perfect. But he would try the flashlight under the box first to see how it was going to work and anyway why not do that before he had to have a hand free? All he wanted was a quick look.

Now wait, he told himself. Use your head, as his father would say. Can't waste light. What did he most want to look at? Into the closed-in eaves. Right. Right. He was almost jumping up and down with excitement. What would he see in those few quick stabs of light and with no light whatsoever escaping out the bald windows?

He brushed at the sweat on his forehead without noticing he did it but was aware the flashlight was slipping in his sweaty hand. He rubbed dry both palms, one at a time, on his shorts and held the flashlight tightly under the box. Now, with the box nearly shut, the slit of an opening aimed at the closed-in section of the eaves, he pushed the switch.

The flashlight was dead. Quickly, adept with his hands, he unscrewed it, checked the tightness of the batteries, closed the cap. He put the flashlight back in the box. Still dead. Yet his mother had used it to check his throat when he had flu. He remembered. The batteries should be fine. He took them out and rearranged them. That sometimes helped. He'd seen his father do it. He screwed the flashlight firmly together and put it in the box. Still no light.

Shit.

He sat down on his heels, his lips parted. His hair was beginning to cling damply all over his head and he was breathing shallowly in the stifling space. Were there new batteries? he wondered. There were none the kitchen. He had felt for them automatically when he took out the flashlight. He was sure there were none in the kitchen.

What about his bike light? Did he take it off before he dismantled his bike and leave it in his room? Or at Kyle's where he took the bike apart? The bike light might work. The bike light would be perfect if it worked. It would be better because of the handle. It would be perfect. He hoped the batteries in the bike light were good. Sure they would be. They must be. For the last thing he wanted was to use a match.)

XIII

Wardlaw had been delayed because someone else had a fire. To Alan the explanation was an outrage. The message left for him said that Wardlaw would call before he came. After they were done at the latest fire. Or, if the fire kept him too late, he would stop by in the morning.

"What does he mean 'too late'?" Alan said indignantly, not to the others in the front of the downstairs hall, but into the phone. "How can it be 'too late'? I flew all the way back here from Paris," he said. "France," he added, to make sure he was being understood. "My wife left a meeting in Galveston. Tell Chief Wardlaw no time is 'too late.' We'll wait for him right here, at the house."

"That's ridiculous," Haskell said as Alan replaced the receiver. "We all need sleep. She, especially." He indicated Nessie.

She had been kept by Millie in the front part of the hall by enticing her to help clean up the wallpaper scorched off the wall. Millie had given Nessie a detached curled strip of her own. Nessie was trying to unwind it all the way across the hall toward the dining room. Millie stayed nearby. She herself had slit several rolls free with a carpet knife and was peeling off other loosened ones, but never very far from Nessie.

"No one could sleep here," Haskell continued.

"You and Millie go somewhere else, then," Alan said. "But I want Nessie with us." He briefly, almost surreptitiously, touched a sore eye and glanced toward the far side of that contact, blinking to lessen the irritation. "Go on if you want," he resumed. "We'll wait for Wardlaw. All of us will."

"Us" meant his own, his immediate, nuclear, family. Once he would have made the statement with no uncertainty whatsoever, but months of living separately from her forced him to glance at Cora for agreement.

"One happy family," Haskell said drily. "Wardlaw will be thrilled. No doubt he'll need everyone's help when he tries to find out what started the fire."

"I didn't mean to contradict Grammer, Dad," Larry said. "It's not like she was saying anything wrong to the fire chief, only she forgot me 'n Ky...I mean Kyle and I... use gasoline in our mower, too."

"Oh, for heaven's sakes, Larry," Ana said. She separated from Norris for the first time that evening and came close to her brother. "Why'd you have to say anything, dumbbell? Can't you tell when someone's trying to help you?"

"But everyone knows we use gas for our mowers. If I tried to keep it secret, that would look worse."

"What gas?" Alan asked.

"In the attic. I had to tell about the gas drum being in the attic," Larry said. He was trying to explain to both his father and Ana and his head turned earnestly from one to the other. "They had to know what could be in the fire so they'd know how to put it out. I didn't know about anything then, Dad. So I thought that would be right. Wasn't it?"

Alan gripped his son's shoulder because that was the first part of the boy his hand reached and holding tightly to him said, "What gasoline in the attic?"

"You mean Wardlaw didn't tell you about the gasoline drum during that little chat you had with him from St. Louis?" Haskell asked.

Alan gazed solely at Larry, then shifted his grip when he saw he had taken hold of the boy's sore shoulder. He said, speaking more softly, "Slow down, Larry. Slow down. I just got here, remember? I haven't been to the attic."

"You can't get there without a ladder or rope or something," Larry said. "The attic stairs burnt. The firemen kept saying over and over they couldn't stop the fire and you always said it makes a difference what's burning. So I told them about it. Because when I did, I was sure that was right. I was absolutely sure, then."

(He was absolutely sure he had left his bike light at Kyle's. He did not look through his bedroom because he remembered just where he had left it over there when they made the cart. Jeez, Kyle's wasn't close, and he'd have to sneak back in and then sneak out again. There had to be something else he could use. Only not candles. Nothing with a match. That would be too stupidly dumb. Matches were bad anywhere near gasoline. Of course, you had fires near gas when you went camping and nothing bad happened. He'd done that since he was little, with his mother and father. So he could do it, but it was too dumb inside. Not for inside.

He sat down on the pile of new boards. So now what? Kyle's was way away. Blocks and blocks away. He could maybe light just one match and be really really careful.

The sweat on his body did not bother him, yet he could feel the movement of perspiration on his lower neck and feel his hair sticking against his head. The air smelled of the mothballs from the dark gauzy sheets. Useless sheets. So what are you going to do now? he asked. Chicken, he called himself. Chicken. Chicken. Go on, do something. OK. OK, he'd do something. He'd go back to Kyle's.)

"Yes, certainly that was right," Cora told Larry. "You were trying to help. We realize that." She was reassuring, confident, a parent bolstering a child. She made an effort to catch Alan's eye to enlist his support, as he had hers, earlier, but he had let go of the boy and started towards the stairs.

"Alan," she called.

"I'm going up to the attic," Alan said.

"What Larry said about the stairs is true," Haskell told him. "The stairway's burnt."

"I won't have trouble," Alan answered. "Where's the ladder?"

"It's at Grammer's," Larry said. And because Haskell and Cora and Alan and the two nearer to his own age, Norris and Ana, all turned and faced him, apparently astounded, he had to say something. He added, "I just happen to know."

Haskell laughed.

"It's a good thing someone knows," Alan said. "It's damn useful, Larry, and I need you to help me. You and I can climb up."

"No need to climb. You can use our extension ladder," Haskell said. "Ramón brought it last night."

"Go get it," Alan said to Larry.

"I'll come, too," Norris said. He went out the front hall, circling around Millie and going after Larry. Ana followed them.

"I doubt if you can tell much merely by looking," Haskell said. "Wardlaw told me *he* would need an expert to test for accelerants. And to double check the wiring. He said you can't tell by plain eyesight after this much damage and water."

"Did you look at the attic?"

"I didn't go up, but Wardlaw did tell me the gasoline container hadn't exploded."

"Why not?" Alan asked.

"Must not have had enough direct heat," Haskell replied.

Alan asked him another question and another. They began discussing the problem of the intensity of heat needed under different circumstances to explode varying sizes and strengths of containers holding dissimilar amounts of gasoline. They described to each other the cooling effects of water, the influences, good and bad, of downdrafts on the heat of a fire in a closed space, the resistance to burning of some containers and the volatility, or lack of it, of gasoline and air in a partly empty can. They were absorbed in the comforting interchange of good solid facts.

"There's still a lot we don't know," Alan said.

"True," Haskell said.

Larry and Norris came into the front hall with the extension ladder. Haskell backed away as they carried the ladder between him and Alan.

"You'll have to angle that to get it around the stairs," Haskell said.

"I see that," Alan said, quickly, the soothing effects of the exchange of information beginning to dissipate.

"The banister's already scraped." From Haskell.

"I'm not an incompetent," Alan said. "We'll tip the ladder up. Straight up, if we have to. Let's go," and he moved along the hall to help with the ladder.

"There's no light in the attic, either," Haskell said. "Wardlaw shut off the electricity where there was the most damage—in the study and the attic."

"I'll use our flashlight," Alan said.

Larry opened his mouth, then shut it. He lowered his end of the ladder, saying, "Dad, wait, wait a minute and I'll get that super flashlight from your car. The new one with the handle. You can hook it on the ladder. I'll run get it."

He tore down the front hall, leaping over Nessie.

"Don't bother, Larry," Alan said.

But Larry was already out on the porch and down two steps and jumping the rest of the long flight of stairs to the ground.

"You don't have to run," Alan called after him.

(Shit. Oh shit. How could there be a fire?

He was running out of the Deemers' yard so fast he could not keep from stumbling because his body was far forward over his feet which were being so stupid stupid stupidly slow. He stumbled and caught himself with a hand, using his knuckles, against the ground and pushed up hard and ran three or four staggering steps then regained his balance and was running full tilt again. Faster. Come on, faster. Got to get to the house. He could not take in enough air, leaning forward, flailing his arms as he ran through Armsteads' alley which was beyond Kyle's, cutting across a yard and through bushes and stumbling again on the sidewalk and once more not quite falling. Come on, he told himself. Faster. How could there be a fire? They couldn't be right. Couldn't.

Oh shit. Oh shit. Flames.

Flames and smoke. He held to the base of an enormous cottonwood tree, gasping for air, drenched all over, his mouth and eyes wide.

It was true. The house was on fire. Jeez, all the way up in the attic where the gas drum was. And guys with two hoses, shouting to each other and working with those ladders, waving one around in the air only it wasn't going to reach. Anyone could see it wasn't going to reach. The drum would blow.

All the time he kept watching the firemen and the neighbors outside the house trying to help and then the arrival of another truck and his grandfather, Haskell, standing by the second truck to talk to the men, he was gasping through his open mouth and holding on to the tree, hanging on to it, for his arms and legs would not stop trembling.

Oh shit. Shit. Jeee-zus and shit.

He saw Grammer and Ramón and Ramón had a spade. Both of them had spades. They were going to throw dirt on the fire, he bet. Dirt would stop gasoline fires. No, they were not. They were digging up plants. They were going to save the stupid plants. The cart, he thought. Get the cart. Use the cart to rescue Dad's and Haskell's and Mother's papers and notes and the things they used all the time. Mother had a lot of them. Tons of them. Toss them all out the study window. Dump them extra fast into the cart and get them away. Get the cart and by the time he got back they maybe would have stopped the fire in the attic and he wouldn't have to tell them and he'd have the cart to help, anyway. Run, then, yes, run. Back all that way through Armsteads' and to Kyle's and get the cart and be able to help. Come on, move, stupid, move. Run.)

The flashlight was indeed superb. Not heavy, because there were no batteries. At nearly full strength even though some time had passed since the cord inside had been taken out and the flashlight recharged. And because the handle was curved so well it was easy to use while standing on the crazily balanced ladder. In the flashlight's wide beam Alan could see the gap where the flames had shot straight up and burned away part of the attic roof. He saw a pile of damp blackened remains of lumber the carpenters had intended to use and the damaged attic floor. The gasoline drum stood immediately below the attic sky-light. It was intact. Not far from the steel container he could see carpenters' tools: a drill, saws, a large metal toolbox open on the floor.

Nothing Alan saw made sense. No one place in the attic was the obvious center, the clearly defined starting place from which the fire had spread.

Larry waited below Alan, bracing the large extension ladder the two of them had set up with difficulty in the narrow space allotted for the attic stairs. At the base the ladder was secured against the outside wall of Ana's tiny dressing room, which had been the linen room when the house had been a hospital and later the nursery during the first year of Cora's life. The top of the ladder balanced unsteadily on the kidney-shaped opening the fire had licked out of the small rectangular entrance for the stairs.

"The floor up there doesn't look like much," Larry called. He had climbed on the bottom rung of the ladder to anchor it and could see the underside of the floor over his head.

"It's good enough," Alan said. Half of his body had disappeared into the attic. He slammed his fist on a floor board to test it but made no move to climb further. He moved the light over every part of the attic, looking in all directions.

Larry shifted his weight from one foot to the other, then stopped. His father was climbing higher. The ladder needed to be firmly grounded. His father was climbing on up into the attic.

"See anything?" Larry asked. He could see the flashlight's shifting beam, hear Alan's steps sounding out one at a time, testing.

Cora entered the little nest of space around Larry.

"That's too steep," she said, of the ladder, and put her hand on it. "And it's not resting right."

"Come on up, Larry," Alan called.

"It's too steep," Cora said. "The floor looks burnt."

Alan's face appeared in the misshapen opening above them.

"It's solid enough if you watch where you're walking," he said. "The fire burned right down, or up, an inner wall. Anyway, where would we fall to? A whole floor? Come up, Larry. Cora, you do what he did—stand on the bottom rung of the ladder to keep it steady."

Larry started up the ladder the instant Cora put her foot on it. He climbed faster and more agilely than his father had and the moment his hips were level with the attic floor he grabbed one side of the ladder in both hands and swung himself up and over, vaulting onto the solid part of the attic near the outer wall. Cora had to brace one foot on the floor to force the ladder back down and steady it.

"Be careful up there, Larry," Cora called. "No more cute tricks."

She kept one foot on the ladder.

Alan reached for his son and turned him around toward the center of the attic.

The fire had destroyed the partitions separating one of the small attic rooms so the large central area—open, unpartitioned, stretching cathedral-like up to the skylight—was left even larger.

"Look," Alan said, pulling the boy close to him. The light from his flashlight gleamed on a dark pile near the gasoline drum. "What is that?" Alan asked.

"Grammer's gauzy sheets. You know, the stuff she uses on the plants when they might freeze."

"How do you know what it is?" Alan asked him. The pile was an amorphous shrunken heap.

Alan's hand, which had been at Larry's back, shifted to the boy's face and held it firmly, held it at the emerging high cheekbones, tilted up so Alan could see him clearly. The light from the upturned flashlight caught both of them.

"You brought those up here, didn't you?" Alan asked softly, his voice low, intimate. "I flew back here to help you. Do you understand?" He held the boy tightly so Larry's attempt to pull his head away was useless. Alan simply held the face tighter in his hand. He could feel the boy's teeth under his thumb, the bottom of the cheekbone pressed beneath his index finger. He held him fast, remorselessly.

"You brought the gasoline drum here," Alan continued in the same low bridled voice. Again Larry tried to move but Alan squeezed tighter, his thumb sinking into the teeth and his strong little finger stretching all the way down below the jawbone and into the soft skin of the boy's thin neck.

Larry struck at Alan's wrist but could not budge it. He grabbed with both hands and pulled, tried to gouge his father with his nails, but his nails were so broken off they were no use.

"How did you start the fire?" Alan whispered to him.

"Alan," Cora's voice rose to them. "Did you and Larry find something up there? Haskell's come up. He says Wardlaw phoned. Wardlaw's on his way over. Can you hear me?"

"I hear you," Alan shouted, and to the boy he still gripped as a rock face he might climb, "Do you understand what I said? I left an international conference to help you. Do you realize that?"

Not Larry's face or his hands on Alan's wrist or the choking noise he made but that one eye of his pulled idiotically down and out of line by Alan's strong finger, making the boy look like a simpleton, an imbecile, that eye made Alan let him go. Released, the boy shot back, out of the beam of the flashlight and over something on the floor because Alan heard him fall, giving out a startled expletive.

Alan reached for the boy but could not locate him. He flashed the light around. Larry was several feet from him, crouched by an upended board and a blackened toolbox.

"Did you use those to do it?" Alan whispered. "Did you bring those up here, too?"

Wide-eyed, mouth open, but both eyes level and even, now, Larry shook his head.

"Workers don't leave their tools out," Alan said. "You used them. You got into the wiring."

Larry sidled away from the tools, his face shocked, desperate. "No," he whispered back at his father. "I never did."

"Alan," Cora called him again.

"Right away. In a minute," Alan answered.

"I'm coming up there."

"Don't. Don't do that. We'll be down."

But he knelt beside the boy, not far from the toolbox, in the damage and ruins of the attic. He pulled his son close to him.

"I didn't do anything," the boy said, in that suppressed and intimate reedy whisper. "I didn't even see them. I wasn't here then. I swear. I was at Kyle's when the fire started. I tried to help the firemen 'cause I didn't know until I heard Haskell talking to Grammer afterwards that you had guys torch the place. Haskell said your new lawyer would love it. Haskell said he probably suggested it to you. I didn't know you were going to have anyone start a fire. No one told me. No one tells me anything."

"Are both of you all right?" Cora called.

Alan had not moved. He did not begin to loosen his grip on his son or take a breath until he heard new sounds coming from below: the

THE EMPTY LOT

front door scraped open loudly, heavy booted footfalls, the voices of
several men. And resonating above all of them, Haskell's, breaking out
on the words, "...too much..." before slipping back into the general
blur of sound.

In the glare of the flashlight, Alan saw the finger marks he had left
printed on his son's face, one so deep it showed blood red.

"Listen," Larry said, whispering to him again, as they had whispered before, leaning so close the words struck warm and moist like
pats against Alan's cheek. "Listen, you didn't have to tell me. I know
that, Dad. Really. I just mean I didn't know what I was supposed to
do."

"You thought..." Alan started. He stopped. Began again, "You
think..." then burst forth in a strangled whisper, scared to death to be
overheard, "Damn it, how could you think I'd do that? I'm your father."

"No, no, listen," from Larry, passionately, for the noises were coming nearer, the spoken words clearer. They heard Cora in a different
manner, in an almost gracious way, yet sounding lost, sounding unre-
conciled, saying, "I never realized there was so much in a house to
burn."

"Sure can be a bitch," Wardlaw answering her, his tone official,
steady, consoling. "It's a real bitch when a person's own home goes up.
A person's home is a very tender place, I can tell you. A very tender
place. You back away, now, Mrs. Belknap, and let these fellows get
their lights and gear past you there, ma'am. That's right, step aside.
We're going to be mighty cramped for space in here. Matter of fact,
you best go on down, ma'am. There's nothing you can do anyhow."

Cora tried to protest but her words were drowned in the sound of
footsteps, of men's voices, of boxes and tools being moved to the base
of the ladder.

"No, listen, Dad, listen," Larry was pleading, and he touched his father's face to deflect it from the noises below. "Everyone was supposed
to be out of the house 'n everything only I fucked up...sorry, sorry,
Dad. I mean I messed up. You'll think I'm nothing but a f...a mess-up
every time now."

Alan laid a finger across his son's lips. The ladder at the opening

173

swayed, shifted, was resettled more solidly from below. Alan stood and his son rose with him so both were on their feet. Alan's stance was not the same. The usual lively, springy, athletic quality he had, that sense of a supple, almost sinuous side—cat-like, Alan called it, secretly, or, even panther-like—that held-back reserve of endless power, was gone. He simply stood.

"You up there, Professor?" Wardlaw boomed.

Alan pulled his arm free of Larry's hand. The flashlight beam swung across the roof, the gap in it, the dark receding corners under the eaves, and fixed on the ends of the metal ladder poking up like empty jaws in the attic space.

"I'm glad you finally got here, Wardlaw," Alan said. "Come on up."

"I brought an expert from Layton," Wardlaw said. "We won't need anyone from State now. We got a virtual science lab along with us."

"Excellent," Alan said firmly. "Excellent." He spoke firmly, with determined enthusiasm. "That's exactly what I want. No more speculations." He stepped over the toolbox and toward the opening. "I want you to find out how this happened. My son and I came up to start looking around."

Larry moved close against his father. Even in the attic heat Alan could sense the warmth of his son's body, could almost feel, he thought, the boy's thin sheen of perspiration on his own skin.

"You shouldn't have ought to gone up there, Professor," Wardlaw said, "We're not sure what's safe."

"Who's your expert who can tell us how it started?" Alan asked.

"Enrique Gutierrez," Wardlaw said. "He knows all a person ever needs to know about fires. He's taken a raft of courses in investigatory discovery and assessment over at State. I brought him and another fellow to help out. They drove their van. I can tell you, they've just about got a whole science in that van."

"Excellent," Alan said again. And again firmly. Larry was beside him, watching him, breathing in every word he said, feeling every move. "I told you on the phone, I want to stop all these idiotic rumors. Anyone can make up stories. You get the facts, settle the matter, and put an end to the guessing by everyone."

"You bet, Professor. That's what you'll get. 'Just the facts,' as they say. You all come on down so Gutierrez and I can climb up there. I don't want more'n two on that floor at a time. I'm not sure how much weight the floor can take."

Alan climbed down the ladder and Wardlaw, huge, massive, a vast man in size, stepped back off the bottom rung and to one side so Alan could squeeze into the narrow space remaining. Alan nodded to Wardlaw and met Wardlaw's eyes—small, busy, surrounded like a turtle's by extra circles of skin beneath.

Not stupid, Alan thought. Sly. Peasant cunning personified. *Bauernschlauheit* to the hilt. A weasel in a hippo suit. Hands, head, neck gargantuan. And little active clever eyes. Haskell's buddy? Maybe. Or maybe no one's.

Alan told Larry to climb down. He braced the ladder for his son and, once the boy had come halfway, Alan lifted him off and slid his tense wiry son down his own body to the floor.

"So that's your boy, Professor," Wardlaw said. His quick eyes moving back and forth from Alan to Larry and back to Alan. "Looks like you. A person would know right off he's your son. But hell, you both ought to hie yourselves on outdoors, Professor. You been in this place too long, I can tell you. It's not good for you. Go on outside, now, and get yourselves some fresh clean air."

XIV

Alan did go outside, finally. Wardlaw and the other firemen were immersed in what they were doing and Alan had sent the older children off with Norris to get something to drink. By now, his contacts were killing him, one especially. He went outside to his car to remove the lenses. He took out both of them and was letting his eyes rest, half shut, when Cora came toward him. She was carrying mugs of coffee.

"Where's Haskell?" Alan asked before she reached him. "What's he up to now?" He put his glasses on.

"Haskell's nowhere near Wardlaw. He's out in the side yard talking to old man Mayhew. Here," she extended a mug.

Alan took it.

"Where'd you leave Nessie?" he asked her.

"Sleeping, at last," Cora said. "She didn't want to but she got so worn out she gave up resisting and let us put her to bed. Millie and I made a makeshift bed for her on the back porch. The air's not too bad there." She blew a few times on her coffee. "We weren't sure she'd sleep without her security blanket," she said, "but we got her to accept a soft old half-sheet. We couldn't find anything else downstairs that was clean."

"I hope Haskell won't tell her you and I started the fire."

"She's sleeping. My mother's cleaning the kitchen right next to her and I told her to call me if Nessie wakes."

Alan set his mug on top of the car and took off his glasses. "What's the rest of the downstairs like?" he asked her.

"God-awful. But once you get over the shock and start cleaning, like Millie, it's not that bad. One of the firemen told me a good deal of the damage is only smoke. Clothes and so on. They could be cleaned. Some of the walls could be washed, too, if we decide to do that." She paused. "The study's ruined though. I was lucky. I've been working most of the month at Dawson. And I keep my duplicates there."

Alan blinked several times and touched his eyelids gently. He did not meet Cora's gaze. He had not thought, before, at all, about Cora's work.

He straightened his glasses. "I see they're still in the attic. I don't care how long they take if they can shut up Haskell."

Cora had been studying him, the way he looked. The way he leaned heavily against the car. "You look beat," she said.

"I ought to be dead. Do you have any idea what time it is in Paris?" He looked at his watch. "It's 6:50 in Paris. In the morning. I haven't been to bed. I haven't even seen a bed, except burnt ones."

As if saying it to her made her responsible and made him angrier, he turned away from her, opened the car door and jerked shut the pocket of the suitcase where he stored his contacts. He slid the bag back onto the floor, beside a larger soft bag for athletic equipment. The one he often used for climbing trips.

He closed the door and rested against the car. His body was listless, draped over the low vehicle.

He tested the coffee and put it back on the top of the car. "Still too hot," he said.

"My mother's solution to all problems," Cora answered, "strong hot coffee."

He did not try immediately a second time but left the coffee to cool.

Cora said, "I don't understand what Larry was doing taking the gasoline drum to the attic. That drum's enormous for him. It must have taken him half the night."

"He was playing some kind of imaginary game. Perfectly harmless. Boys his age frequently do that. Especially boys with a sense of adventure. Anyway, Wardlaw said the drum never burned. Larry had nothing to do with the fire. Don't worry about him."

"You're worried about him," she said.

"I'm worried because he believed we set fire to the house. He believed what your father told him. That's a real reason to worry."

"Haskell would never say that to Larry directly. Not in a million years. He was probably only joking to Millie. Or speculating about what happened. You and I speculate all the time."

"Larry believed that about us."

"Come on, he didn't believe it once we explained. He told us he didn't."

She did not share his outrage. Nothing about her showed any sign of being outraged. She was deliberately sipping the hot coffee.

"You don't understand," Alan said, goaded by the lack of reaction. "Your father makes a few random destructive comments and our son immediately thinks you and I set fire to our own house. He thinks we're arsonists."

Cora answered gingerly, not sharply, not pressuring or provoking him, but as if she were only musing idly aloud, "Are you sure Morand had no part of this?"

"Morand? What's Morand got to do with it?"

"He'd know they can't make us restore the house. There's no law saying we have to restore it. He'd get his third."

"Morand's no shyster."

"He was willing to have us lie. He wanted us to say Haskell committed fraud."

"He did not. That was a legal point, not arson. You never understood what he was saying."

Cora glanced away from Alan and back toward the house. The firemen's powerful lights appeared at other windows in the attic. She sipped her coffee again.

"What made you bring up Morand?" Alan asked.

Speaking partly into the mug, with a hint she could not say the words in the open, Cora answered, "I might have wished for a fire like this one, out of the blue and with no one getting hurt, if I had thought of it." She paused, her lips hovering above the edge of the mug. "On the way home, do you know what I thought? I thought—we'll be rich."

"You better not say that around Larry."

"I'm not. I'm saying it to you." She brushed the hair away from her forehead, away from her face. The air surrounding them was hot even this late, and also humid. And along the front sidewalk the air was tinged with the smell of crepe myrtle blossoms forced by the heat and humidity to release their spicy fragrance.

"I didn't learn about the fire the way you did," Cora said. "It was over by that time and the first thing they told me was that the children were safe. I know you were worried about that when you heard. But later, once you knew no one had been hurt, not the children or anyone, when you were flying back or had that time in St. Louis or when you were driving over here, you must have thought Morand might have had something to do with it? You know he gets a third."

"No," he said vehemently. "I never did. I never thought about it." He was earnest, adamant, denying all the more forcefully, all the angrier, because he had thought exactly that on the plane. He had thought precisely, just as Cora said, of Morand's third.

"At least you were aware of the money?"

"I was trying to arrange plane connections. I didn't know what was going on here. I'd called Mike earlier to check on Larry. I told you, your father started in with suspicions about Larry when he first called."

She believed that he had been worried about the children and about what might be happening at home and about what he said her father had told him. She would have been worried in his place. She could understand. But she did not believe that he never, at any point, if only for a second, thought about the money, and she found it sweet and a little touching and at the same time lessening that Alan could not admit he had.

"You do realize we'll make money out of this?" she said.

"We would have made money anyway. It would have taken longer." He glanced at the house. "You'd think they'd be out of the attic by now."

"If you were someone else," Cora asked, "if you were a complete outsider, would you say this fire was an accident?"

"I'm not an expert. I don't know," he began. And then, because he had not answered, he said, "All right, suppose I agree. Suppose I call it arson, if you want. You realize the truth could still be that it was completely accidental, whatever I call it."

"Oh, pretty, Alan. Very pretty." She pushed her hair away and this time held it back and looked up the street.

"Did the kids say when they'd come home?"

"I told Norris to go to the all-night stand on the thruway for cold drinks and come straight back."

"Since they can't go to sleep, they'd have been better off with a hot meal at Dino's."

"I want them here," Alan said. "I don't want Larry away from us long."

"You're making too much out of that," Cora said. "Larry's only twelve. He won't be permanently scarred because he believed for a few hours that you and I might do something outrageous to help the family. He'd want to think we'd do something like that. It would be reassuring."

"Now you're using pretty reasoning. When did you convert to the 'explain it so you feel good' school of pop psychology?"

She looked at him appreciatively, not openly grinning, yet he knew she was acknowledging his quickness. His quickness even though he was bone tired.

She glanced at the house, saying, "Where have they got to now? You don't think they'll find anything, do you?"

"If you mean that someone started a fire, no."

"What makes you so certain it was an accident?"

"Because Wardlaw told me an accident was the most likely answer. Because I saw it did not start in the attic from gasoline or anything Larry might have done, by accident. Because I believe I can have good luck without there having to be a nefarious plot behind it. You won't accept good luck, but if we had all been in the house sleeping when the fire started and barely escaped with our lives, you'd believe it was our bad luck fast enough."

This time she did smile. "You're probably right," she said, "I would."

She finished her coffee and planted her mug next to his on top of his car.

(They ended not with mugs but with small cut crystal glasses that night. It was the first official formal date they had. In the spring. He took her to a dance, a ball, which was absurd. Serious graduate students did not do that sort of thing. And they did not do that sort of thing. He did not have the money nor she the clothes nor that desire. She needed to study. But because it was absurd and they were infected with their feelings and knowing the other felt the same, they went. Alan borrowed money from his older brother to cover the cost of tickets, dinner, rented black tie with red cummerbund and her corsage. Cora phoned home for the dress she had worn as maid-of-honor at Nancy Lou's wedding. Millie altered the dress, sending it in a different, more sophisticated, version. Sinuous and chic, with the apple-cheeked maid-of-honor look quite gone. Her mother, Cora told Alan, could do anything with her hands.

He wanted to ride in a horse-drawn carriage and see the dawn in with champagne.

"I'll drink out of your slipper," he announced.

"You'll ruin the only pair of shoes that match this dress."

"Don't be mundane. Give me that shoe. I'll do this right if I have to chase you round this bench and through the park to drink out of your beautiful not-glass slipper."

"I'm not running. How could I in these?" She extended her shoes with thin high heels, a gurgle of laughter coming out of her.

Alan paused in uncorking the bottle. Her laugh was irresistible to him.

"Laugh again," he said promptly.

"When we decided to cover these shoes with the same material as the dress, my father knew the right place to have it done. He knows all sorts of unexpected things."

"I want to meet him. I'll like him. There goes the cork, not bad. Ready for some?"

"Out of a shoe? You must be off your head."

"I provided glasses for us."

He had. Two tiny antique crystal glasses nestling in the red plush of a scarred leather case.

"Alan, you're amazing. How did you get them here? You didn't bring them with the champagne cooler."

"I stashed them under the bench this morning. I planned we'd end up here."

"You are truly amazing."

"Don't talk. Laugh some more."

"Where did you find these glasses?"

"Secret. I bought them for you. They're yours. The first of many."

"Listen to the way they ping against the champagne bottle. You can tell they're real crystal. Be careful, they're so small you'll spill."

"I won't spill. I wanted to do everything about this evening in a proper and fitting way. Proper enough?"

"Very fitting and proper. Not our usual style, but very very proper."

"My old man's not like yours. He's not knowledgeable about rich things. He's a tough bird. We didn't have a mother to argue for us. He'd never let us wear jeans. They spoke to him too much of all the manual jobs he did. No fake slumming on our part, he said. College for us. He'd already sacrificed enough."

He took the glass from her fingers. Because the glasses were so small he had to refill them often so they could get something close to the amount they would drink from several proper glassfuls of champagne. And each time he filled them the glasses gave out clear light ringing noises, like glass bells.

"You might call this a fake moving up in the world," he said, "but it isn't. My old man wants us both to make something of ourselves. By 'to make something' he means make money. Your father's made money. He's probably relaxed about what you do."

"He expects something. I'm the only child and all. And no brothers. He expects something. I'm not sure what."

"I'm going to make money. And not like Mike's doing, either. I'll make money as a linguist. There are plenty of ways linguists can make money. I want you to know I'm going to be super successful. You aren't taking any risks. You won't be sacrificing, with me."

He had that raw aching seriousness brought on by caring so much about what he was saying and to whom it was being said and when her face, which he thought incredibly lovely, unreasonably lovely, when her face did not remain serious because she burbled out with laughter, he was startled. Yet he watched happily all the time she laughed. He was not hurt. He took her glass and filled it once more and gazed at her with the bemused blissful silly contentment of someone who could not imagine wanting to be anywhere else or to have anything more.

"So it's not my future success that attracts you to me," he said when she could subside.

"I shouldn't have laughed at you, Alan."

"Now you're the one off your head," he said, his light hazel eyes brilliant on her. "You couldn't have done anything more flattering."

"You really are clever, aren't you?"

The glasses could not shape the bubbling of the champagne and it spattered under her nose and on her upper lip as she sipped it and he reached over, with the same bright shining gaze fixed on her, and lightly touched the tiny separate drops across her upper lip and beneath her nose and with the barest pressure wiped them away.

Her glass tilted sideways in her hand.

"Now I've spilt some," she said. She shook her head about it and bent over to flick the liquid away from the stiff sheen of her dress.

"Tell me," Alan asked. "You know, your parents?"

"Yes?"

"Do they have your color hair?")

Cora half sat, half lounged, on the low droopy-nosed hood of Alan's sports car. The air had almost no movement in it and retained much of the day's heat. The trees on both sides of the street were somnolent and drained. Cora pressed the side of her hand against her forehead and her upper lip, to wipe away the heat.

"I tried to phone you," Alan said.

She was surprised.

"From Paris. I didn't remember you were gone. I was trying to call you when Haskell reached me on another line."

"When he called me I was on the beach," Cora said.

"Before six?"

"Yes."

"By yourself? I mean, you were out on the beach by yourself?"

"Until the hotel clerk came for me," Cora told him. "I couldn't sleep."

"They're back," Alan broke in.

Norris' car eased around the corner and pulled up at the curb before the house, some distance away from them.

Alan waved. "I see Larry," he said. "I think he's waving to us." He began to wave back. "See him?"

"Wardlaw's moving their lights down to the second floor," Cora told him.

"Are you sure Nessie's still asleep?"

"You know Nessie. If they wake her, she'll get out of bed, drag her blanket substitute to Grammer and demand strongly that Grammer do something. Nessie's never shy about getting what she thinks are her rights."

Alan braced an elbow on the top of the car and touched one sore eye behind his glasses, shutting it briefly. He stayed supported by the car, his head resting on his hand.

"Why did you call?" Cora asked.

"I forgot you were in Galveston."

"You said that."

He was watching as the lights probed one room after another inside the house. A beam shot out a window in their direction, poured past a tree, struck the corner of the Mayhews' house and splattered in a round pool on the grass of the next lawn.

"My paper was a flop," Alan told her.

He spoke evenly, his voice bleached of feeling, the words carefully spaced, as if they had somehow been taken out, squeezed free of all connection they might have to him and set back in a single perfect line.

"You're joking," Cora said. "Your big paper?" She slid off the car and stood directly in front of him, trying to get him to look at her. "That one?"

"Yes."

"I don't believe you."

"It did." He faced her and added, "It flopped. Flat. Kaput. Fiasco." He spoke passionately, now, in explosions of pain.

"But how?" Cora said, and shook her head, impatient, fretful, fighting a wild desire to break out in a grin. "How could it happen?"

"There were flaws in the model. That makes the conclusion questionable. Not all of it, not much of it, but enough. My colleagues had a field day. DuBost joined in. Even though he'd been impressed by the idea when he saw an early draft."

"I know. I know he was. That's incredible, Alan."

"He forgot he ever liked anything in it. Basically, it's right. I can fix what's wrong. I have to get some time, that's all. And it is a contribution, no matter what DuBost says. Or what anyone else says."

Again smothering, murdering, that illicit urge to smile, Cora said, "Everyone's touchy about any criticism. You're probably exaggerating."

"I am not exaggerating. DuBost didn't say one good word. He never said anything about phoning me about it from France. The best he said was that it was an 'intriguing aperitif.' 'Aperitif'! And what it truly needed—*ce qui est indispensable*—he said, was for it to be 'executed with exactitude.' Exactitude. Damn his French. He knows how good the idea is. It's a brilliant idea."

He had been staring straight at her, boring into her. When he finished he shifted his gaze away from her and to the house behind and beyond her.

"What about the others?" she asked him. "They must have said something. What about Jamie Rayker?"

"Jamie was decent. He always is." He stood up, away from the car, and took a long breath, as if he were drinking from a tall glass. "Jamie can't stop himself being decent, no matter what kind of dirty fun everyone else is up to. Is relishing, in fact."

He took hold of the car through the open window and pulled on it, pulled so hard the muscles in his arm swelled under his skin. The mugs on top of the car quivered, made quick irregular little rattling sounds. He let go and struck his fist against the bottom of the window, not hard, symbolically only, and grimaced with his teeth bared, symbolically, too.

"What happened after that?" Cora asked him. "What did you do next?"

"Nothing."

"What did you say?"

"Nothing, nothing. What could I say? There's nothing to say. All you have is that dead silence you get after a disaster. You just stand there getting your papers together and putting them all back in your briefcase and what could you say? There's no point talking about it now, either."

Yet he could not quit talking about it. "I had to go with everyone else and hear the other papers afterwards," he said. "There were dozens of papers. Dozens of them. Everyone was going to hear them."

He was not quite looking at her any more. Not looking very much at anything. She could see very clearly the side of his face and temple and the fine high cheekbone defined by the streetlight. The other part of his face was in shadow.

"What else happened?" she asked.

He was quiet so long it seemed he had not heard. "Alan," she prompted, "what else happened?"

"Nothing," he said. Yet starting slowly, compelled, the sentences forced their way out, "There was a furor over this kid. A real furor. Everyone was talking about him. Laposteneau. He gave a fantastic paper. Really wide-ranging, profound. He's super smart."

"Do you know him?"

Alan shook his head. "He's DuBost's latest find."

"A student of DuBost's and you'd never heard of him?"

"DuBost found him in some nowhere university north of Paris." He gave a sharp bark-like laugh. "Not a nowhere university any longer. Laposteneau's put it on the map."

"DuBost loves doing that sort of thing," Cora said. Her easy undramatic tone was soothing, changing what had happened into a familiar event. "DuBost relishes producing new admiring protégés who are full of promise."

"This kid's not a question of promise. His paper was a masterpiece."

"DuBost must have enjoyed the reaction. Was his new devotee suitably deferential? What did he call DuBost, *'maître'* or *'monsieur le professeur'*?"

"You've got to understand, Cora, Laposteneau is the real thing. He's absolutely first-rate. I'm going to bring him to the States. I'll get him a fellowship or a visiting professorship in a good department. I phoned Crimmins from St. Louis to get started on it."

"You did? When you were in St. Louis?"

"Yeah."

"While you were waiting for the plane here?" Obviously while he waited for his plane. The plane to bring him back here.

"You would do that," she said, and as earlier she had fought grinning, she struggled to resist the swell of tears, to steady her wobbly voice. "You would," she repeated. "You're so steadfast about helping that way. Most of your colleagues wouldn't. They'd be too busy, or too wrapped up in their own work. Or too jealous. You never fail at that."

"Laposteneau should have grants when he's young. He should have the time when he can do top work," Alan said, bleakly. Bleakly.

"Alan, don't you realize what happened? You concentrate on the linguistics and don't pay any attention to anything else. You didn't notice why you're done in. DuBost attacked you because he wanted his current favorite to get the attention. Your paper was too important to give it a fair hearing. If DuBost let that happen, his protégé wouldn't win all the acclaim he got."

"But Laposteneau's good. First-rate."

"Sure, but his wouldn't have been the only important paper at the meeting."

"Do you think so?"

"I know it. Look, the fact that DuBost phoned you in the first place shows what he thought of your idea. Think about it, that was way back, before you were scheduled on the same program with his latest discovery."

She had Alan's attention. She could sense the pull of it, feel him taking in every word. She was aware, too, of the quiet between them, and the air of expectancy, heightened by the random noises from the house and the repeated cello sounds of a frog croaking in the yard.

"DuBost had to distract them from you," she said. "It's obvious, Alan. Come on, you've known DuBost for years. You know his temperament. Since he started getting older he's vainer than ever. The prima donna of linguistics. So your paper had a few errors. You said they were minor. DuBost knows that. He's too smart not to. He used those little errors as a way to squelch the reaction you should have had. Don't you see?"

"Maybe. Maybe that is what happened."

"Of course it is. That was the only way DuBost could be sure he'd have the whole limelight for his new favorite. The only way. It's the obvious explanation, Alan. Obvious."

She ended with a ring of certainty, convincing, caught up herself and moved by her persuasiveness. She was good at this. They had told her so in Galveston. She stopped reluctantly and Alan, held by what she said, waited, full of attention for what she might say next.

"You know Galveston?" she began, her manner altered, a hint of shyness, wanting to speak and yet being uncertain.

"Yes," Alan said.

"They offered me a vice-presidency," she blurted out. She half laughed and brushed, foolishly, at her hair, realizing it was not fair, it was the wrong time to have told him.

"At Dawson?"

"Where else?"

"Vice-president of what?"

"Of what I've been doing the last two years."

"Administration and fund raising and so on?"

"As a matter of fact, one of the trustees suggested a combination position exactly like that. Especially for me."

"Did Cable Poinsett suggest it?"

"No, Alan. Cable's a UT regent. Anyway, I may not get the job. They'd have to create the position and arrange for money." A prolonged creak came from the house and then a snap. They swerved toward the sound. A pried up board, perhaps, had flipped back or else broken. Some of the firemen's lights had been moved to the first floor, illuminating the windows like tanks in an aquarium.

"I thought your place had no money," Alan said, returning to her.

"It's called Dawson, not a 'place.' They're beginning to get ahead with the funding. That's what I've been doing."

"They should give you the job," Alan said. "They'd be fools not to. They should give you any position you want, including the presidency. They're lucky to have anyone like you connected with them at all. You're light years too good for them."

She had not expected what he said and she did not know how to respond. The pleasure of telling him was gone. She was disconcerted by what he said, and alarmed, and without having any idea why she found herself saying, actually proclaiming, "I'll take that job if it's offered to me. I'll have to travel but I can make arrangements for traveling. I want to be a vice-president."

She was standing a little in front and to one side of him, and she leaned forward and tipped her head so the hot heavy hair fell free. She lifted the collar of her dress and flipped it back and forth to fan in air.

"You aren't going out with Poinsett are you?" he asked. She stopped moving the dress but stayed bent forward.

"I'm not seeing anyone," Alan said. "Not now. That was nothing before, anyway. I never went out with her until after you and I separated."

Cora straightened. Her hair and the collar of her dress settled back against her.

"You're not serious about anyone," Alan continued. "Not in Galveston or anywhere." He was not asking her. He was making statements, yet with a heartbeat of time after each, in case. "You and I should get back together. I don't mean because of this," he nodded toward the house, "not the house or the money, but for us. I mean for good."

The front door of Norris' car flew open and Ana got out. She pointed to the front porch of the house. The firemen's lights were being turned off. Wardlaw and one of the firemen could be seen near the front door.

Alan called out, but not too loudly because it was so late, "Larry, stay with us," for the boy had started walking toward the backyard.

They waited for him to change direction and cover the distance to them and while he did Alan said to her, softly, hurrying, "We're good together. You see that, don't you?"

"Sometimes."

"I knew you did. I couldn't be imagining it. We can make 'sometimes' all the time. Most of the time, anyway." He glanced at Larry, who approached slowly, scraping the tip of his sneaker in the groove between the wet grass and the concrete sidewalk.

"You stick with us now," Alan called to the boy. "Stay with your mother and me."

Then to Cora, earnestly, "It will be better for the children. They need us together. Larry especially. We were wrong, Cora. I'm willing to admit it. We were wrong about the children."

"The children," Cora said, a plaintive loop of sound sent out with no trace of jubilation.

XV

Before they entered the house they saw Gutierrez. He was coming down the hall towards them carrying a round black pot in both hands. Haskell and Wardlaw followed him. He beamed when he saw Alan and the others on the porch and beamed more when Alan opened the screen door. For Gutierrez had none of the usual long-faced solemn manner of firemen, especially Anglo firemen, at the scene of a fire. He was delighted as a puppy with what he had found, and as they filed into the house, Ana and Norris entering last, he displayed the pot by holding it higher and grinned so broadly his lips pulled back like rubber bands stretched tight against his shiny white teeth.

"That's Grammer's smudge pot," Larry burst out.

Haskell and Wardlaw stared at him. Gutierrez did, too, until Larry added, defensively, "She keeps them in the shed." In the silence that followed he would have taken a step back from them but Alan rested his hand on the boy's shoulder, keeping him where he was.

"Grammer doesn't need them for freezes anymore," he continued. "She's got greenhouses. She keeps them to be flares for Ramón's truck."

"Eees esmart boy," Gutierrez said.

"Well now, Sonny," Wardlaw said, "you know one pot looks pretty much like another. And pots can get themselves moved around, too."

Alan's fingers tightened on his son's shoulder, to quiet him, yet Larry could sense his father's excitement, too, through the rock-hard grip.

"You got a very observant boy there," Wardlaw said to Alan. Alan leaned forward, his body lightly backing that of his son, and asked, "Where did you find it?"

"Dare," Gutierrez said, pointing with his chin over his shoulder, toward the rear of the house, toward the far end of the hall and to the study. "Eees estart dare," he said with the pride of knowing he had made an important discovery and of being sure he was right.

"Matter of fact," Wardlaw said, "that pot's why there was so much smoke. It was jammed back under a shelf in your office. That's the picture perfect place for this fire to start. Just like they teach you. Right there at the bottom of the V shape every fire is dying to make."

"It started with that?" Cora asked, incredulously.

"Could have. Could well have," Wardlaw said. "That's something Gutierrez'll check out for us." Wardlaw stood before them, monumentally large and genial, in no apparent hurry, his little turtle eyes moving rapidly from one to the other. He reached out to pat Gutierrez, covering half the upper side of the smaller fireman's back, and asked if Gutierrez needed anything else. Gutierrez told him no and holding the pot conspicuously before him, in his brown hands smeared with damp black soot, he started down the hall, weaving between Alan and Larry and Cora on one side and Ana and her Norris on the other.

The second fireman, the one who had driven over with Gutierrez, came from behind Wardlaw. He carried several square-ended flashlights and a metal box of tools. He followed Gutierrez on out of the house and toward the van.

"What is he going to check?" Cora asked.

"He'll see what the wick and soot can tell him," Wardlaw said mildly. "He'll scrape soot off first, and test it. Then he'll test the scraped wick separately." He was content to explain carefully and he seemed perfectly willing to continue at this slow easy pace, giving them all the time they wanted. And watching them.

"Test for what?" Cora asked him. She was irritated that she was made to ask. Haskell and Alan knew or pretended they would not question Wardlaw.

But it was Haskell who answered her. "Matt thinks Gutierrez may be able to find out from testing the wick and the soot on it that the scorching first started from outside. That the pot began burning because of an outside fire."

"Or else not," Wardlaw added, mildly and amiably.

Haskell gave his sweet smile. "Yes, certainly, or else not. Or, indeed, Gutierrez may not be sure enough of what he finds to tell us anything, that is not definitely."

"Don't let his English fool you," Wardlaw said. "Gutierrez is whiplash smart. Whiplash smart. He's taken courses," Wardlaw added. "He knew right where to look 'cause he's taken courses. He found that pot under a shelf, next to an old rolled-up rug. I can tell you, if there's a thing to be found, Gutierrez'll find it. And he'll find out if the wick got set alight first. He's got chemical tests he can do and a microscope. He's got a microscope so good it'd show you..." and his eyes taking in the presence of Ana and Cora, he detoured around what he was going to say and ended, "...show you the fleas on a flea."

"No doubt he could," Haskell said, "but no matter how quick the boy was to state his opinion, that still wouldn't tell us where the pot came from."

"It must be one of Grammer's smudge pots," Larry said.

"Oh, come on," Cora said, exasperated with all of them, impatient with the burgeoning swirl of suspicion and ill-will among them. "We're being idiotic," she said. "Grammer'd never use a smudge pot in the house."

The instant she said the words Cora knew the opposite was possible. Millie could have done exactly that. Or had Ramón do it.

"Where is Grammer?" she asked.

"Your mother is upstairs," Haskell said, the words implying in an upstairs bathroom, which he would not say, openly, in front of others.

"My mother," Cora began firmly, intending to make a final statement defending Millie, but stopped. She was too aware, awkwardly aware, that she had in fact no idea what Millie might have done. Or caused Ramón to do. The fire would obviously solve the problem she and Alan had. She'd said that to Alan. Better yet, simply ample smoke, by itself, would have been enough, since there were no laws requiring the restoration of historic houses. It's possible Millie knew that. Millie could have had Ramón drive her into town anytime she wanted. Ramón would help.

It was the sort of thing Millie would do, too, go around them and their foolish quarreling. Free them of the restrictions placed on the house and which Haskell claimed he could not alter, even if he wanted.

Cut the Gordian knot to the core. In fact, smoke them out. And without saying a word to them about it, without a word to Haskell, especially not to Haskell, because she disagreed with Haskell. Haskell understood this. Haskell had understood it before she did. She could tell by his face. That was why he looked so different. He looked older. Old. His face worn and sagging, as though the force of gravity had increased unbelievably the way it does on those mad carnival rides, with a bullet-shaped capsule at either end to whip violently up and over and up and over again so hard the skin and muscles and flesh, even the pouches underneath the eyes, like Haskell's, are pulled desperately away from the unyielding bone.

Cora moved around both men and Larry to stand next to Wardlaw. "Chief Wardlaw," she said, "wouldn't you like to sit down? You must have been standing for hours. We have lots of coffee in the kitchen."

Wardlaw's small eyes blinked. He rubbed his giant hands up and down against his thighs, preparing in case she handed him an exquisite fine cup and saucer. He shook his head, a movement so large it would have rattled cups in their saucers had there been any near. "I best not," he said. "Thank you, anyway, Ma'am. I best wait 'til Gutierrez is done. He and the other fireman drove themselves over here to do this. I best wait until all of us get finished."

"On the phone you told my husband you thought the fire was caused by an accident," Cora said. "You told him that it was likely something went wrong in the air conditioner, but you'd probably never know for certain."

"It sure did look that way," Wardlaw answered, as easy and mild as ever, not reacting to any argument or provocation in Cora's words. "I thought that myself but Mr. Bosk here," another massive movement of his head, dipping down toward Haskell, "Haskell, that is, pointed out to me a historical place, a designated historical place, like this one, had ought to be given more attention than your ordinary run-of-the-mill fire."

"Did he now?" Alan said, with renewed and high-spirited alertness. "I bet finding that pot was a surprise?"

"Well," Wardlaw began, speaking slowly, "Mr. Bosk... Haskell...when we showed him the pot, he explained that a pot like that could have been misplaced or left behind in all the general clutter here lately. He said the house pretty much never got straightened up anyway."

"Did he now?" Alan said again.

"We were untidy," Cora began. "We never had enough time."

Alan jostled Larry, to keep him from saying anything at all, but he noticed Wardlaw caught even this small act. *Was* he Haskell's man? His own?

"What's more," Cora was saying, "we'd all used the study. There were always so many different things in there—my husband's, my own, books and files left behind by my father. We never had cleared out the study properly."

"Or," Wardlaw said, still slow-paced and benign, still seeming to be good-natured but watching each of them, "or that pot might have been taken inside and set burning ahead. I mean before anything else in the house burned."

"Any number of people could have done that," Haskell claimed. His voice expanded and was rich with authority and filled the acrid smelling hall.

A repeated hissing from the front door interrupted them. It was Gutierrez going, "Pssst. Pssst. Pssst." Once he caught Wardlaw's attention, he beckoned to him. Wardlaw angled and edged himself around and between the others to get to the door. He spoke to Gutierrez through the screen and then stepped outside with the smaller fireman.

Haskell muttered furiously to Alan, "Since you left the house empty all last week, anyone could have come into it for any reason. Vandals could have."

"Vandals? Vandals in Riles? What's that, your latest made-up story?"

"Vandals are possible," Haskell said. "Or kids might have come. Youngsters who've learned from observation that they can take things out of here and sell them."

Alan placed both hands on his son's shoulders. "By God, it's time you lost," he said to Haskell. "It's time you learned to lose without trying to bring down everyone else with you."

"Hush," Cora said.

"What are you so afraid Wardlaw will find?" Alan asked, ignoring Cora, focused only on Haskell.

"Stop it," Cora said. The children are here, she meant. And Norris, who is not even a member of the family. And Wardlaw is not that far away, is not off the porch.

But Alan and Haskell were like scorpions. Like two scorpions, once having started maneuvering ceaselessly around each other, edgy and yet undistractable, trembling from caution and fear and the knowledge of what could happen, each feeling anxiously for the higher ground with deadly arched tail raised and quivering above the body, and no longer any ability at all to stop.

"You may be right," Haskell said smoothly. Like Alan he paid no attention to Cora. "It may not be vandals at all. Vandals aren't frantically trying to raise money so their sons can go to special schools."

"Shit," Larry shouted. "Shit, shit, shit."

Alan put his hand over Larry's mouth.

"Shit," Larry began again, jerking his head free. "It's lies and shit."

"Keep still," Alan warned. He bent down, his face on the same plane as the boy's, and succinctly, emphasizing each word, said, "Do you hear me? You keep still."

"Why tell him to keep still?" Ana cried. She was rigid with embarrassment, wrenched out of her mature, sophisticated young woman stance and changed back to a petulant, swollen-faced young girl. "He's the one who's telling the truth. The rest of you...the rest is...." but she could not use Larry's four letter expletive before her parents. "The rest is lies," she said.

Haskell snorted with contempt. "What marvelous histrionics!" he said. "Look what you've done. You woke Nessie. She had to come looking for us, and in her bare feet."

He marched to the half-step stairway and bent down, not far because he had short legs, to pick up Nessie, lifting her and the narrow worn sheet with her. "Here now, Nessie, darling," he said, "I'll hold you."

"You were supposed to call me," Cora said to Nessie.

"You probably couldn't hear her over the ruckus in here," Haskell said. "Could she, Nessie?"

Wardlaw came back into the house and rejoined them as Haskell spoke. Wardlaw's manner was unchanged, comfortable, unhurried, no information being given away. He shifted himself cautiously in among them, finding his way until he reached the open space on the other side of the stairs.

Haskell wanted to keep hold of Nessie but she would have none of it. She wormed her way down, the old half-sheet falling with her as she did. In clear tones she announced she needed to go upstairs to the bathroom. Now. She'd tried the one downstairs and it was too dark. And it smelled yuck.

"I'll take her," Ana said. She had altered once again. She was gracious, charming, very motherly, her face and body angled delicately for Norris's benefit. "Anyway, Grammer's probably scrubbing the bathroom to death the way she does. Or rinsing the towels. I'll take Ness."

She gathered Nessie in her arms. Something in the eagerness with which Ana had offered, the speed, made Larry think there was some other reason. To get away from here, maybe. Or to get upstairs herself and go into her room and look it over. To get her treasure box, with the letters or pictures or whatever. Something.

Nessie was willing enough to go with her sister and once in Ana's arms and mounting the shallow stairs, she announced, "Larry said 'shit,' Ana. Larry said 'shit' six times."

"Sister," Wardlaw called up to Ana, "you pay attention where you walk around up there. We didn't have time to rope off the unsafe places. Stay away from the south side of the house towards the back."

"I'll go tell her," Norris said, relieved to follow Ana and relieved to discard that foolish benign unnoticing expression he tried to maintain while her family fought in front of him. He ran up the stairs.

"Helpful fellow," Wardlaw commented. "I know his father. Boy's outright bowled over by that daughter of yours." Wardlaw pulled out his handkerchief, blew his nose at length and peered at the results in the handkerchief. "Fires," he said and shook his head somberly. "Blacken the lungs." He scrunched the handkerchief in on itself until it made a wad and shoved it into his pocket.

"Y'all expect Mrs. Bosk to be down soon?" he asked. And then, amiably, mildly, "You know, Haskell, we might want to do a few more of these tests later on, maybe."

With a grunt Haskell reached for the sheet Nessie had dropped at his feet and began to fold it. "Mrs. Bosk is undoubtedly busy with her youngest granddaughter," he said. He balanced the folded sheet across the handrail of the stairs.

"Just so I get to talk to her some, when she's finished," Wardlaw said. "Maybe ask a few questions and that sort of thing. Give me a shout, when she's all done upstairs. I think I best mosey along outside now. Check in with Gutierrez." He added, slyly, "Leave y'all alone for a bit, too. Give you some time to yourselves." He tousled Larry's hair in a friendly way as he loomed past, he himself had many children, and he crowded the rest of them back as he eased his bulk between them. He walked ponderously down the hall and out of the house toward the van.

"When we had a fire in a storage room at Dawson," Cora said, "no one could tell anything because they'd flooded the room with water. They can't find out what Wardlaw says with tests."

"They might turn up signs of accelerants, if any were used," Haskell explained. "But tests are mostly indicators. They're used to tell you where to look. Without solid evidence tests never stand up in court."

"We can't let this get into court," Cora said. "We can't let that happen, Haskell." Her face, already warm and damp along her forehead and upper lip, had taken on a full swollen look, as Ana's had.

"Too bad you urged Wardlaw to investigate," Alan said to Haskell. He made an effort not to sound pleased yet Cora glanced at him, anyway. He went on quickly, "Still, I don't see any reason to worry. Wardlaw won't want to cause trouble for an important family. I have the feeling he's giving us time to decide how to approach him. Isn't that the way you arrange these things, Haskell? Always on a first-name basis? Nothing crass?"

Cora frowned at him and just barely perceptibly shook her head at him. She said to Larry, "Go tell Grammer and Ana what Chief Wardlaw said about the risky places upstairs. Tell them to stay away from the back of the house on the porch side. You know, facing the May-hews."

"Ana already heard him," Larry said.

"Your grandmother didn't," Cora said.

"Norris'll tell them," Larry said stubbornly. He leaned against his father.

"He might not tell Grammer. Anyway, I want you to take Nessie's sheet to Grammer. Grammer will need something to dry Nessie's feet. The towels upstairs are sopping."

"Not all of them. I left the little ones in the cabinet."

"Go on, Larry. Take the sheet up. *Now.*"

Larry tilted his face up toward Alan, but Alan smoothed the hair Wardlaw had tousled and gave the boy a light push.

"Do what your mother said," Alan told him. "We'll be right here."

But Cora had already started toward the back of the house, to the living room, where they could not be overheard. Haskell and Alan went after her.

The living room had been little damaged except for smoke stains and the one burnt section of wall between the living room and the hall. There the fire had shot up, or down, scorching the wallpaper on both sides and in places consuming parts of the wall itself. Above the burnt wall was Nessie's room. In Nessie's room the fire had burned so savagely that in some places the floor had been demolished, leaving small open spaces, gaps visible between a network of clinging boards twined together like delicate-looking black lace work.

As he passed under the damaged ceiling, Haskell removed a piece of plaster from the antique love seat and brushed plaster dust and soot from the cherry rim.

"We could call Bunky," Cora said, standing not far from the love seat. She glanced at her watch and grimaced. "Too late. We'll have to call him first thing in the morning. The bank isn't going to lose money so Bunky won't demand an investigation. We can tell Wardlaw that. What's more, the bank wouldn't be happy wasting expensive lawyers' time on this. And if the fire department wants more lab tests with experts, especially outside experts, that will be an extra expense for the city."

"You've learned a good deal about business at Dawson," Haskell said.

Cora was surprised enough to break into her line of thought and pay attention to her father. He was not being derogatory. And he was not smiling. He looked simply old. And worn. And immersed in thinking.

"What about the insurance company?" she asked him.

"They won't ask detailed questions unless they're faced with enormous claims, like a demand for complete restoration. If you ask only enough to cover basic repairs, they'll be happy to settle. Old Cy Phelan won't question the claim. He knows us. I'll talk to him myself. And I'll call Bunky."

"I knew you'd arrange everything," Alan said to Haskell.

Haskell spun toward him in outrage, moving so sharply his ample reddish cheeks vibrated when he stopped. "What if your Morand caused this?" he boomed out. "We'll be clearing him."

Before Alan could reply, Haskell crossed the space between them and stood directly before him. Haskell was not as tall as Alan but looked straight at him, confidently, with the force of a man long used to power over men. "Of course I know all about you and Morand. You should have expected I would know. Are you one hundred percent sure Morand isn't involved? He'll get his percent. How would you like a public inquiry into *that*?"

"Morand is not involved. The trouble with you, Haskell, is you'll try anything at all to keep from losing. Even something ridiculous. Think about it a minute, who the hell would deliberately use a smudge pot in the house? The smudge pot's the issue, Haskell."

With an edge of desperation, Haskell said, "I agree we can't let this be pursued any further. You realize that all of us, including Larry, must agree a smudge pot could have been forgotten in the study? And if Larry doesn't think so, he at least has to keep quiet."

"He will. I'll talk to him," Cora said.

"I don't like that," Alan said.

Cora held up her hand for quiet. She tilted her head, listening. There had been noise overhead, possibly footsteps, but no one came down the stairs. Cora went to the doorway into the hall and called Larry's name. When he did not answer, she tried Ana.

A single unintelligible response was her answer. Were they helping Grammer? Cora called up. Were they doing what they were told? No one replied but Cora heard water running upstairs, at some distance, from the far side of the house.

"Millie probably has them all cleaning, just like Ana said," Cora told them, coming back into the room. "We won't have any trouble explaining to Larry."

"I don't like his saying anything he doesn't believe," Alan said. "He's had enough trouble already from stories that weren't true."

"This is not untrue. It could have been an accident," Cora told him.

"If we thought it was an accident we wouldn't be standing here talking," Alan said.

"But it could have been," she insisted. "You told me when we were outside that you believed it was an accident. Good luck, you called it. A smudge pot could have been left behind in that study and forgotten. Why not? A rug was. We never used the rug. We never even unrolled it. If Mother asks us…if anyone asks me, I'll say of course the fire happened by accident, no matter how it started at the very beginning. No one meant to cause a fire. Smoke, maybe, yes. *Maybe* Millie might have thought of smoke. Or Ramón might have. There are no laws requiring restoration. Enough smoke, all by itself, would invalidate any restrictions on the house. Millie might have known that. Ramón might have, too. Either one of them could have believed that, without ever thinking of anything else and without planning or expecting anything more to happen. No matter how it started in the first place, even if it wasn't electrical failure or an unknown cause they can't explain, it was never meant to end like this. Never."

Both Alan and Haskell paid solemn attention to her, gazing steadily at her while she spoke, gazing almost nostalgically at her, as if she were describing a landscape they knew well, as well as she, and they did not need to ask any questions because the mention from her of even a few small details brought it all back before them with perfect clarity.

A sprinkling of small wet soot clumps filtered down near them and they heard a creaking noise in the ceiling.

"Daddy, I see you through the floor." Nessie's voice from overhead. Surprised, pleased, openhearted. "I see you in a hole."

XVI

An end of that slender sheet Nessie had been using to hold onto while she went to sleep dangled above their heads from a gap in the twelve-foot-high ceiling.

"The floor's got potholes," Nessie said. One of her bare feet flipped past the open space to settle on the sheet. "My foot made the sheet get wet," she said.

She squatted and they saw her pointed face framed in the burnt opening. Her eyes were shining impish slits as she laughed down at them. "All your mouths popped open," she said to their upturned faces.

"Stay where you are," Alan told her. "Hold on to that joist—to that beam by your foot."

"Where's Grammer?" Cora demanded. The words sounding raw from her stretched-back throat.

"She thinks I'm with Ana."

"Where's Ana?"

"She thinks I'm with Grammer. Larry's with Grammer." She paused to rub her nose angrily, attacking the smell with her fist. "My room's yuck," she said.

She raised her head out of their sight, but the section of sheet, weighted by her foot, stayed hanging above them.

"She won't fall far, even if the floor gives way," Alan said to Cora. Cora had pressed against him, holding his arm so she could lean close and stare straight up into the space where the sheet dangled. "I can catch her with no trouble," Alan assured her. "It's no worse than jumping out of a tree."

They heard an abrupt gasp along with a crack in one of the laths, then a hard grunt as Nessie's legs and bare feet plomped down above them. One leg emerged on each side of the fire-gnawed joist.

"I fell," Nessie announced uncertainly. "My leg's stuck." Her right foot had crashed through weakened boards, pulling the other foot and an additional amount of sheet down into the larger hole burnt by the fire. Through the wider opening they again saw her small triangular face. This time her eyes were round and wide.

"You're not that far above us, Nessie," Alan told her. "Don't be scared." He tipped his head back all the way to look right up at her. "You've been in trees that high. When we put up the swing." And to Cora, reassuringly, "I'll catch her easy. Nothing to it." To Nessie, "Want me to catch you like I did then?"

"No."

"It'll be easy, sweetheart," Alan said, infusing cheerfulness and reassurance into his voice. "Poor kid," he said softly to Cora, "she thinks she's much higher than she is." And optimistically, to Nessie, "It's like jumping off the diving board."

"No."

"You've jumped before, Ness," Cora said. "Hundreds of times. For fun, so Daddy could catch you."

"Pull your right leg out," Alan told her, "and slide it over where the left one is, by your sheet. Then drop down feet first."

"No."

"Ness, sweetie," Cora said, "you are hopeless. You shouldn't have sneaked away from Grammer and Ana. You know you're not supposed to. If you won't jump to Daddy, you'll have to crawl back to the hall where the floor's all solid. Then tell Grammer where you are."

"The floor falls," Nessie said.

"Come on, sweetie, try," Cora said. "I don't see any potholes between you and the wall. You can crawl over there."

"No," Haskell exploded. His voice resounded loudly around them, a roll of drums. "Don't do that," he said to Nessie. He had stepped back to examine the area surrounding her from a different angle. "Stay away from that wall," he ordered. Lowering his head, he explained to Cora and Alan, "The wires are loose."

"Christ," Alan said, "and the floor's wet. They must have sealed off the wires?"

"I can't tell." Haskell was staring hard into the opened area, trying to see around the sheet and Nessie's dangling narrow cucumber-shaped leg.

"If Wardlaw didn't disconnect the wires, he must have capped them?" Alan said.

"It's not that easy. Insulation can be destroyed inside so the conduit is dangerous to touch."

"Why the hell did Wardlaw leave the power on?"

"He wasn't finished." Haskell said. He lowered his head so he could face Alan directly, "I told you no one was supposed to go inside the house."

"Along with all the shit you told me," Alan said, but he had moved next to Haskell and he, too, squinted into the room above, the lights in the living room below glinting off the lenses of his glasses. "Where?" he asked. "What wires?"

"Farther back. Towards the other corner. A forty-degree angle. There," Haskell said, pointing, making clear to Alan the line of vision.

"Christ, there are wires."

"Should I be scared?" Nessie called.

"No, sweetheart. Just be good," Alan said. He moved forward to be right under her so she would see him when she looked down, but he said in an urgent undertone to Haskell, "They must have done something to make the wires safe?"

"Can't you tell?" Cora asked.

"Can you, Haskell?" Alan asked. "I'm right here, Nessie. See me, sweetheart? I see you." And to Haskell, "Can you tell if they're capped? They're bound to be capped. No one would leave them uncapped."

"I can't be sure from here. I can't even be sure if there's still insulation on them."

"How the hell could Millie let her get in there?"

"Ana was the one who took her upstairs," Haskell answered.

"Call Grammer, Ness," Cora said.

"No."

"Be a good girl. Call Grammer. Loud."

"She'n Larry are running water in the bathroom. She thinks I'm with Ana." A pause, and then, brightly, "I got a hobbyhorse, Daddy. See?"

She flung forward and back and forward again on the joist but froze when the support creaked beneath her.

"Sit still," Alan said. "Don't move. Don't touch anything." To the others, hurrying, "I'll shut off the power." He started toward the door to the hall.

"You can't go through the back hall," Haskell said. "Ramón boarded up the back because the doorway was burnt open. You have to go all the way around and through the dining room to the kitchen."

"Right."

"It's the fourth switch on the right."

"No, I'll turn off all of them," Alan said.

"Don't turn off the lights, Daddy," Nessie called quickly. "I'll jump down."

Alan came back and stood below her.

"Tell her not to touch the floor near the wall," Haskell said. "The water could act as a conductor if those wires are live. I'll turn off the switch."

"You don't have to," Alan said. "I need to see her to catch her. She'll jump down to me, now. Come on, sweetheart. You've already got your leg part way up. You're a super girl. You can do it."

Nessie had begun to extricate her trapped leg but as she did she tipped in the opposite direction on her narrow unpadded hobbyhorse and whimpered. Her leg slid back down in the same opening, separate from the other leg and the sheet.

"It's too wobbly," she complained. "I'll crawl away."

"Don't crawl on that floor," Alan yelled at her. "You'll get hurt. Put both feet in the big hole. Look at me, Nessie. You can jump to me when you do that. It'll be fun. Like the time we put up the long swing in the yard. Remember? We climbed into the tree and I went way up high with the rope so you kids would have an extra-long swing and when I climbed back on the ground you kids jumped down to me. Remember?"

"Larry jumped out of the tree."

Oh, Christ, yes. She had been too young. No more than a baby. It was Larry, a younger Larry, two or three years ago, who had swung down into his arms from the tree.

"You must have jumped out of some trees. You aren't far up, Nessie. I can almost touch your foot when I jump. See? I almost touched you that time. You can drop down easy."

"She's too scared to move," Cora said. "She's petrified."

"I'll turn off the electricity," Haskell said.

"I'll get it faster," Alan said. "You help Cora." And he started out of the room at a rush, calling up to Nessie, "I'm coming right away, Nessie. You'll be fine. Just stay where you are."

He charged around the couch and bumped into Cora, saying, "Get under her. Break her fall if the boards go," and raced past her and the long high table.

For while he had been talking to Nessie about putting the swing in the tree that summer, Cora had cleared the high table behind the couch. Snatched off the lamp, not throwing it, that would have startled Nessie, but setting it quickly on the floor, removing the books, ornaments, the opened illustrated book of medieval paintings, the magazines. And at last beginning to push the table around the couch to the place where it would be straight under Nessie's feet.

"I'm here, Ness," Cora said to her. "I'm right here." She muttered, "Help me," to Haskell, who stood with his back swayed far back and his eyes on Nessie and that space toward the wall and the wires beyond her.

"Father, help me," Cora repeated. "I'm stuck."

The heavy table had bunched up the rug and lodged firmly against it.

Cora's father's cheeks cushioned out fully as he bowed his head to lift one end of the table, his stomach pressed hard against the edge, tugging to move the weight up and over the rug. "This won't help," he said, but he lifted all the same.

"It's to stand on. I need it to stand on. I won't look so far away to her."

Alan had clasped the door of the living room as he ran out, held the

door frame by his finger tips and swung himself so hard into the hall
he was going full tilt toward the stairway where he caught the bottom
newel post, knowing he could use his momentum in another spin and
maintain that speed, increase it, straight through to the dining room.

"It's jammed on the rug," Haskell said. "It won't move."

"You lift and I'll push. Come on. Come *on*. Damn it." For her hand
had slipped loose. She dried it quickly on her dress and regripped the
table. "Throw the rug back. Hurry."

But the tip of Alan's foot caught on the extended edge of the first
stair—regular glasses no good for peripheral vision, misjudged, should
have known, should have remembered and made allowances for that—
so he pitched forward, hit the stairway wall with a palm to catch
himself, pushed desperately to save his balance, pushed harder, righted
himself and saw Millie in the hall above him, at the top of the stairs.
She must have come out from the bathroom. Something in her hand.
Fresh pink and white...towel? And saw him as he caught himself.
Timeless. Timeless. Millie staring back at him. Her sturdy body, round
round face. Mouth. Her open mouth. She knew. Something terrible.
Saw it in his face and the horror showed in her. So—steady, you're
steady now, Belknap, keep going, only faster, faster, and he lunged
into the dining room.

Cora watched Nessie's feet, saw one of them being lifted away from
her. She snatched a chair and set it by the table, climbed on the chair,
then climbed up on the table, kicking off her shoes.

"You're sure you don't want your shoes?" Haskell asked.

"I'm sure."

"You won't slip?"

"I don't have on stockings. I'll be steadier."

Alan tore through the dining room, using the strength of his fingers
and an arm to toss a heavy two-armed dining room chair out of his
way and brush aside a simple straight one, yet he could not go fast
enough—too tired, can't get more speed, no, this fast enough, mustn't
fall, better than another fall, too tired Christ just too tired—and he
grasped the opening of the service pantry, was through it in two strides
and into the kitchen, and starting across—calm down, should have
done this right off, first thing, not waited for her to...Christ, no, never

second guess, lose confidence, never second guess, do best can, deep breath, deep breath, circuit breakers far corner utility closet, Cora catch her if she, doesn't have to have light, only one floor, hit main switch, fastest way, Christ, cut it all off, can't hurt she gets scared, Cora catch her, Christ, Christ, cut all power....

It made no difference that it had been such a long day and kept going on and on and he was worn out and had not slept and was therefore slowed. He was not even close. Before he was near the circuit breakers or even the utility closet—though in his thoughts he was ahead, was unhooking the catch of that metal door, seeing the top, the central switch, the main one, in bright red—but before he was actually very far into the kitchen or had in fact got all the way across the sag in the worn floor, the charred and damaged joist creaked beneath Nessie and she tugged out her caught leg with renewed urgency and teetered with that one leg pressed tight against her, the board creaking loudly through another long anguished protest.

"I'll catch you, Ness," Cora said to her. "You'll be all right. I promise. Put both feet down together in the big hole with the sheet. Then push yourself off. Just like you do at the swimming pool, sweetie, and I'll catch you. I'm closer to you. You won't be hurt. Look. See how close my hands are to you, Ness? See?"

Nessie gazed down and saw her mother's hands stretched up, her mother standing upright on a table, the table which before always went behind the couch, her mother's face closer below and glistening with sweat, her mother's face upturned there between raised arms and her mother's hair all falling back and away.

The joist moaned. Nessie clutched an edge of the floor determinedly and slid her freed foot down alongside the other one, beside the sheet. The beam sighed with the change of weight, sighed urgently, urging her, and she eased forward and sensed she was slipping down, was starting to fall free, and as she did she irresistibly reached out behind for something to hold on to.

Her scream was shrill and high and the dazzling blue-white light crackled at the same time, exactly, merging with the long unbroken crying out from immediately below her as the lights blazed into blackness everywhere on that circuit.

~~~

DEAR DAD,

I'M GLAD I STAYED THE EXTRA DAY. DRIVING UP
TO THE FOREST PRESERVE AND WALKING AROUND
THERE WITH YOU WAS FABULOUS. I'VE STILL GOT
THE PINE CONE YOU PICKED UP FOR ME, EVEN
FROM YOUR WALKER!

WHEN I GOT BACK THE PAINTERS WERE READY
TO START PAINTING AND WALLPAPERING THE
HOUSE. THE COLORS INSIDE WILL BE BRIGHTER.
THERE'S STILL SOME TALK THAT DEVELOPERS MAY
BUY THE PLACE—SOMEDAY. BUT CORA WAS RIGHT,
THEY'RE GOING TO DEVELOP IN LAYTON FIRST. ALL
THE SAME, THE OLD PLACE WILL BE PUT INTO
GOOD SHAPE. IT WILL BE A LOT MORE MODERN
AND EASIER TO TAKE CARE OF. HASKELL HAS BEEN
OVERSEEING THE REPAIRS. HE'S THERE, ON THE
SPOT, AND HE KNOWS ABOUT BUILDING. SOMEONE
WILL BUY IT.

LISTEN, DON'T WORRY ABOUT US, OK? WE'LL
MANAGE. ASK MIKE. HE AND GAIL HAVE BEEN

DOWN TWICE SINCE THE FUNERAL. HE'LL TELL YOU WE'RE DOING FINE.

LARRY LIKES HIS NEW SCHOOL OK. ANA HAS STARTED WORKING MOST DAYS AFTER SCHOOL WITH CORA'S MOTHER. I SEE THE KIDS EVERY WEEK-END. I USUALLY SEE CORA THEN, TOO.

WHAT YOU SAID IS TRUE, DAD. CORA IS A LITTLE THINNER. BUT THAT PICTURE EXAGGERATES IT. I THINK IT'S THE ANGLE. SHE'S BEEN DOING ALL THIS TRAVELING, TOO, AND EXTRA WORK FOR DAWSON SINCE SHE WAS MADE A VICE-PRESIDENT.

SHE'S ALSO BEEN SORTING OUT THE LAST THINGS IN THE HOUSE. IT'S A HUGE JOB. HASKELL HAD WHAT WAS LEFT AFTER THE FIRE BOXED UP AND SET ASIDE SO THE WORKMEN HAD A CLEAR PATH.

NOW WE HAVE TO DECIDE WHAT REMNANTS TO KEEP. CORA'S BEEN GOING THROUGH EACH BOX. SHE DOUBLE CHECKS EVERYTHING INSIDE, EVEN WHAT WAS BURNT. SHE'S ONLY GOT TWO BOXES LEFT.

I HELP HER WHEN I'M THERE. LAST NIGHT WE TURNED UP ONE OF MY OLD HIGH SCHOOL YEAR

BOOKS. IT WAS LESS STAINED THAN SOME OF OUR
RECENT FAMILY ALBUMS. I'LL PACK IT TO BRING
WITH ME NEXT TIME I COME. I'D LIKE TO BRING
ANA AND LARRY. AND CORA, TOO, IF SHE CAN GET
AWAY. MAYBE NEXT MONTH. OR MORE LIKELY,
THE MONTH AFTER—WHEN SCHOOL IS OUT FOR
THE HOLIDAYS.

I'VE BEEN GETTING BACK TO MY OWN WORK.
I'VE DONE EIGHTEEN PAGES OF A NEW PAPER. IT'S
NOT BAD. I'M GOING TO KEEP THIS ONE SHORT.

SO THAT'S EVERYTHING, DAD. THANKS AGAIN.
IT WAS A GREAT VISIT.

LOVE,

ALAN

Mary Gray Hughes is the author of two short story collections, *The Thousand Springs* and *The Calling*. Her fiction has been published and anthologized in publications such as *The Atlantic, Esquire, Antioch Review,* and *Redbook, Editors Choice,* and *Best American Short Stories*. Her poetry has appeared in numerous reviews including *Tri-Quarterly, Southern Review, Confrontation* and *Descant*.

She grew up in south Texas, received her BA from Barnard and an M. Litt. from Oxford University. Hughes has earned a Phi Beta Kappa key, Fulbright Fellowship, NEA fellowship in Creative Writing, and has served as Illinois Writer-in-Residence. She currently lives in Evanston, Illinois.